W9-CNX-624

TAG MAN

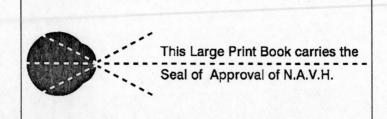

This Large Print Book carries the
Seal of Approval of N.A.V.H.

A JOE GUNTHER NOVEL

TAG MAN

ARCHER MAYOR

THORNDIKE PRESS
A part of Gale, Cengage Learning

GALE
CENGAGE Learning·

Detroit • New York • San Francisco • New Haven, Conn • Waterville, Maine • London

GALE
CENGAGE Learning

LIBRARY OF CONGRESS CATALOGING-IN-PUBLICATION DATA

Mayor, Archer.
    Tag man : a Joe Gunther novel / by Archer Mayor.
        p. cm. — (Thorndike Press large print crime scene)
    ISBN-13: 978-1-4104-4334-2 (hardcover)
    ISBN-10: 1-4104-4334-5 (hardcover)
    1. Gunther, Joe (Fictitious character)—Fiction. 2. Police—Vermont—Fiction. 3. Burglars—Fiction. 4. Murderers—Fiction. 5. Brattleboro (Vt.)—Fiction. 6. Large type books. I. Title.
PS3563.A965T34 2011b
813'.54—dc22   2011034293

Published in 2011 by arrangement with St. Martin's Press, LLC.

Printed in Mexico
1 2 3 4 5 6 7 15 14 13 12 11

To Dominic —
a belated welcome and heartfelt thanks
for the light you bring with you

ACKNOWLEDGMENTS

As I have often stressed in earlier acknowledgments, I rely upon, and am grateful to, many others in the writing of these books. They share their experiences, give me some wonderfully creative ideas, and give me the benefit of their editorial expertise. It is all greatly appreciated.

My deepest thanks, therefore, to:
  Shelby Hearon
  Paco Aumand
  Sally Mattson
  Nancy Aichele
  Castle Freeman
  Gary Boutin
  John Martin
  Chic Paustian
  Julie Lavorgna
  Ray Walker
  Margot Zalkind
  Muriel Farrington

CHAPTER ONE

He sat in the center of the love seat, in the darkened bedroom, settled against the soft pillows behind him. His hands, clad in thin cotton gloves, were folded in his lap; his feet, wrapped in blue surgical booties, stretched out beneath the neatened coffee table before him. High above, dangling from the post-and-beam cathedral ceiling, an ornate Hunter fan barely stirred the air, setting the mood for the sleeping house.

The man was in his realm; the king of his castle.

The standard audible vital signs of any home added to the tranquility — the furnace's occasional rumbling two floors below, the rhythmic heartbeat of the grandfather clock on the first floor, the deep and regular breathing from the two people in the big bed across the room. In a place this vast and expensive, he half wondered if he couldn't hear the very walls chiming in, carrying within them the wiring and fiber optics of Internet connections, TV cable, high-tech security, fancy phone systems, dimmer switches for mood lighting, a camera hookup to all the building's entrances — a veritable nervous system.

The house was a palace, certainly by Vermont standards. Standards that were escalating with the steady influx of wealthy outsiders — dreaded "flatlanders" to the locals — especially following 9/11. But he wasn't among the complainers. The newcomers offered him that much more to explore.

He rose without a sound, drifted across the carpeted floor to the bedside, and gazed down upon its occupants. A man and woman, he in his sixties, she younger, beginning their struggle with the aging process, he less successfully than she. Her outline under the sheet showed an athletic body, with enough of her bare back revealed to confirm it — along with the added detail that she either slept in the nude or at least wore no top. Her husband was the more traditional lump — too much alcohol and snack food. An earlier tour of the workout room had revealed her presence to the exclusion of his.

They slept far apart on the king-size mattress, their respective night tables cluttered with telltale belongings — glasses to replace contacts; nasal strips to control snoring; ointment for sun spots; under-eye cream to stem bags and blotching. On her side there was a small bottle of K-Y lubricant, to ease her through those rare amorous moments when her husband journeyed across the bed's extended acreage.

The lump was named Lloyd, which their uninvited guest found amusing. Her name was Lisbeth, shortened to Liz only in the notes from husband to wife that he'd perused earlier in her office nook off the kitchen. Everyone else appeared to call her by her full name. Lloyd, of course, had an office to himself — large and pretentious. That had been worth exploring, from the easily defeated computer password to the contents of a small cardboard box attached to the back of a foreshortened desk drawer. The man wondered if Lisbeth knew anything about that — separate bank accounts and financial records, all in Lloyd's name only, not to mention a few letters from, as the quainter novels used to put it, "a woman not his wife," named Susan Rainier. He'd been unable to resist doing a little tampering there, to guarantee that Lloyd would know without doubt that he'd had a visitor.

Pure ego, of course. He knew that. A little male-to-male competition. Childish, in fact, and thus all the more irresistible. He'd stolen one of the letters, a whole packet of incomprehensible financial papers — at least to him — and generally rearranged the rest of it, just to drive Lloyd crazy.

He did sympathize on one level, if only one. It had to be hard to set such high expectations and then struggle to meet them daily, even if the aim was selfish, artificial, duplicitous, and — for all he knew — illegal.

The man moved to the bedroom door and stood looking out. An interior balcony extended to both sides of him, overlooking a gargantuan living room. Far opposite, a wall of windows surveyed immaculately groomed fields, now glowing like dull silver in the warm, early-summer moonlight.

He considered the conclusions he'd reached about these two. Huge overhead, staggering bills, social expectations from all corners, embarrassing secrets. An impressive burden of toil, cost, supply, and demand based on nothing more important than the choice between cashmere and lamb's wool. But he wasn't condemning. After all, he spent considerable time researching how and when to break into places like this —

without leaving any trace of his methods. Wasn't what drove him as important to him as Lisbeth's eye cream was to her, or Lloyd's secret stash to him?

Each of us just struggles to keep in balance, he thought blandly, as banal and unsatisfying as that seemed. In his case, he saw himself as a night stalker, a collector of information useful either as a means of support or as pure intelligence about his fellow human beings. He had homework to do, and this was how he did it. To others, he'd be a slightly eccentric burglar.

He leaned forward and placed his hands on the railing, absorbing the feeling of superiority and control. They wouldn't understand how he *enjoyed* the knowledge such moments provided. That was *his* need. He left these clandestine encounters richer for the perceptions he gained.

He and his daughter, Sally, had once chatted about which super power they'd most enjoy having. She'd said flight, not surprisingly; he'd chosen the ability to transmigrate walls. Like a ghost. All-seeing but invisible. The closest she might get to reality was through a pilot's license and a plane, many years and much cash later. He was all squared away.

He heard a rustling behind him and

quickly stepped out of sight, then glanced around the corner to confirm it was only a little tossing and turning.

Still, he'd been here for a few hours, wandering throughout the house, poking into closets, drawers, and, of course, the fridge. No point overstaying his purloined welcome.

He reentered the bedroom and returned to the sleeping couple, standing on the woman's side, close enough that if he bent over, he could kiss her naked shoulder blade. Yielding to temptation, he did at least bow, not to kiss but to feel the heat of her in his nostrils. She smelled good.

Finally conceding that the time had come, he extracted a one-inch square piece of yellow paper and stuck it carefully to the woman's small bottle of lubricant.

TAG! it said in bold letters, inscribed with a broad felt pen. Maybe he didn't want to reveal his method of entry, but he liked their knowing he'd been here.

He gave them a last smile before fading away toward the bedroom door and the world beyond.

CHAPTER TWO

Willy Kunkle pounded on the door of the Brattleboro PD's detective bureau, located across the municipal building's central hallway from the dispatch center, patrol room, and chief's office. Nowadays, he worked for the Vermont Bureau of Investigation, just upstairs. But he'd worked here once — for years, in fact — and it still pissed him off that he'd had to surrender his passkey — enough to guarantee that each time he came by to visit, he knocked as if wielding a sledgehammer.

The flimsy wooden door swung open without revealing anyone, its empty frame substituting for the underwhelming greeting of the cop already retreating inside. "Hey, Willy. What's up?"

Willy entered and pulled the door to, addressing the man's back.

"What's *up?*" Willy parroted sarcastically. "Ronny-boy, you are a serious disappointment. The people you pretend to serve and protect are exposed to peril, crying for help, their homes invaded and violated, and you ask, 'What's *up*'? I thought you *cared*."

Without looking back, Ron Klesczewski, the unit's chief of detectives, laconically held up a middle finger before rounding the corner into his small office.

Willy laughed and followed him in. Klesczewski settled behind his desk and pointed to his guest chair as an invitation. "You want coffee?" he asked.

Willy sat. "Not yours."

Ron hadn't expected him to accept. "Wild guess: You heard about last night."

" 'The Tag Man strikes again,' " Willy intoned dramatically, drawing his one good hand across the air as if Braille-reading the headline that decorated that morning's *Brattleboro Reformer*. "Kind of hard to miss."

Ron leaned back in his chair and clasped his hands across his thin stomach. Both desk and chair — indeed, the whole office — had once belonged to Joe Gunther when he'd headed this bureau and Ron and Willy had worked as his detectives. That seemed a long time ago.

"Sad but true," Ron admitted. "How's the baby?"

Willy waved that off. He and Sammie

16

Martens, although still unmarried, had just had an infant daughter. Sam had worked once here, too, and now shared the workload upstairs with Willy, Joe, and a third investigator named Lester Spinney, all of whom made up the entirety of the regional VBI office.

"Keeping me up all night," he answered gruffly, although not, Ron thought, with the usual biting edge.

Ron smiled. "You're home at night? *There's* a change."

Willy scowled. A complicated man, he could be at once dismissive and caring. He was a crippled, ex-drunk military sniper who was also a judgmental neatnik with little patience, yet capable of staying on surveillance for days at a time or conversing with idiots most sane men would shoot to shut up. Ron didn't know it, but years earlier, Joe had snuck up on Willy at a stakeout and discovered him pencil sketching with an artist's talent — an ability the latter had sworn Joe to keep secret.

As if to prove his perpetual contradictions, the normally thin-skinned Willy now ignored Ron's jab, and simply inquired, "Who do you think the Tag Man is?"

Ron shook his head slightly. "Dunno. The only hot clue we ever got led us straight back here."

Willy's eyebrows rose questioningly.

"The first Post-it he ever left," Ron explained. "Or at least the first reported to us. It had a thumbprint on it — crystal clear. Belonged to one of the women in Dispatch. We figure she stuck the note on some form and slid it under the glass, like a bookmark — who for, nobody knows."

Willy was laughing softly. "So he has a sense of humor."

Ron nodded. "We never found a print afterward."

"How's he break in?"

"Don't know. He's done this six times — or we've heard about six Post-its left behind — and every time, we can't tell how he got inside. He likes fancy homes, locked doors, security systems — the harder, the better — but he's never tripped up."

"And he never steals anything," Willy commented, recalling the news coverage he'd read.

Klesczewski equivocated. "Actually, we held that back. Technically, he does. He always eats something out of the fridge."

Willy laughed outright. "You're shitting me."

Ron smiled despite his frustration. "Good stuff, too, and he doesn't just grab and nosh. He spreads caviar on crackers, maybe pours a little champagne if it's there."

"These're all rich people, right?" Willy asked.

"Very."

Willy absorbed that thoughtfully, adding finally, "And that's all he does? Eat and brag? Nothing else? No vandalism? No jerking off on women's underwear? Doesn't seem worth the effort."

Ron shrugged in response, but his brain began considering the same incongruity.

Willy shoved himself out of the chair with his right hand; the other arm, withered by a bullet years before, was anchored to his side by having its hand buried deep in his pants pocket.

"I think he's doing something more, and you guys're too dumb to notice it," he declared, heading for the door. "Good thing we only do major crimes upstairs, or I'd make you look bad. You owe me if I'm right," he added before disappearing to go to work.

Klesczewski didn't take offense. While Patrol had done a good job with the initial response, taking photos, notes, and statements that he'd considered adequate five minutes ago, now he was thinking, like Willy, that a personal visit was in order.

■ ■ ■ ■

Lloyd and Lisbeth Jordan lived on Brattleboro's northern edge, just shy of the Dummerston town line. It was as close to a suburb as Brattleboro got — a wealthy development that had become over time more like a neighborhood than an entrepreneur's ambition. Even in such purely capitalist matters, Brattleboro had exerted its quirky socialist influence, softening the hard edge of a real estate venture until it looked merely like a gathering of old hippies, all of whom had just happened to get lucky on Wall Street.

Ron Klesczewski knew the underlying truth, of course, for while a few of the houses did look modest enough, he'd been reliably told that almost all of them exceeded the half-million-dollar mark. Certainly the most garish newcomers had tossed self-effacement aside, and gaudily overindulged in columns, fountains, tennis courts, and pools, eroding the gentility that had once charmed and sedated the older residents.

The Jordan spread was such an example, slapped on a raised denuded slope at the terminus of a paved dead-end road like a

Disney castle on a soundstage. All the surrounding trees had been removed and replaced with acres of manicured, putting-green perfection, allowing for a panoramic view of the West River Valley, true, but inviting the winter's galelike winds to wrap the building in an annual icy embrace. Ron didn't even want to imagine the heating bills for forty-five-hundred square feet, all housing a single couple.

Not a concern now, of course, in the early summer warmth. The winter just past had been mild, leading most amateur meteorologists to predict a final, late-season snowstorm. But by now, even men as prone to caution as Ron were conceding that spring might be here to stay despite the old-timer's description of Vermont weather as "nine months of winter and three months of damn poor sledding."

Ron drove up the curved, crushed-stone driveway, past a couple of incomprehensibly abstract lawn sculptures fifteen feet tall, and alongside a dry-laid rock wall, the cost of which probably rivaled his mortgage. He stopped opposite a semicircle of granite steps leading up to a colonnaded marble porch and a pair of solid wood double doors that would have thrilled Mussolini.

As he swung out of his car, one half of

those doors opened to reveal a stocky man dressed in Docksides, no socks, white slacks, a boldly striped blue shirt, and, of course, a red ascot tucked under his florid chin.

"Damn," Ron murmured to himself. "No yachtsman's cap?"

He slammed his car door and raised a hand in greeting, beginning the long climb to where the regal homeowner stood, legs apart and hands on hips, framed by the yawning entrance.

"Morning. You Lloyd Jordan?"

The man in the outfit responded indirectly. "You the cop who called?"

Ron was getting closer by now. "Lieutenant Ron Klesczewski. I head up the detective unit." It wasn't his standard greeting, but he figured a little pennant waving of his own couldn't hurt.

" 'Bout time," was the predictable response. The handshake Jordan gave him was soft, moist, and meant to be perfunctory. It worked. Ron pretended to reach for a note pad and wiped his hand against the seat of his trousers.

"You weren't here when the initial responders came by?" he asked innocently. "Right after your 911 call?"

Jordan scowled and stepped back into the

doorway, allowing Ron access if not actually asking him in. "Flatfoots. Barely knew to scrape their shoes."

Ron didn't tell him that he almost hadn't dropped by, given the thoroughness of their work. He did say, "I'm actually here as a courtesy, Mr. Jordan. There's little more I can add to what they did."

Lloyd Jordan's eyes widened. "You're joking. You here to give me a bumper sticker, then? A sorry-for-your-loss pat on the head? What the fuck do I pay these goddamned taxes for if all I get is a bunch of Keystone Kops bumping into each other?"

Ron pretended to consult the contents of his pad. "I understand your irritation. What did you lose, by the way? Nothing was noted in the report."

Lloyd's pink face darkened and his eyes narrowed, although he didn't immediately respond. From his years of interviewing secretive people, Ron sensed he'd hit a button.

"Nothing," came the answer from a woman's voice back in the house.

Ron stepped inside, his eyes adjusting from the midday sun. He was in a two-story amphitheater — more lobby than entranceway — cool and dark, with a sweeping staircase before him and a palace-suitable chandelier overhead. The owner of the voice was on the fifth step of the staircase, heading down in bare feet, dressed in jeans and a T-shirt. She was as country-casual as her husband was Greenwich-chic.

"We were just shaken, is all," she added, crossing over to him and giving him a cool, firm handshake. "Lisbeth Jordan. Glad to meet you. Thanks for coming."

"My pleasure," Ron answered her, meaning it. "Ron Klesczewski."

"We don't know what might've been taken," her husband broke in. "A place this size . . ."

"Some food," she said, looking coolly at her husband. "Unless he took something of yours I don't know about."

"Crap," he said angrily. "I checked my office, top to bottom. Doesn't even look like he entered it. Nothing was touched. Probably bypassed it entirely."

Ron thought that an interesting layering of denial. He turned to Mrs. Jordan. "The uniformed officers mentioned the food. What was it, exactly?"

She smiled slightly and turned on her bare heel. "I'll show you."

Both men followed her through a side door, down the length of a lavishly decorated dining room, and through a set of

24

swinging doors into a restaurant-style kitchen. She led them to one of two steel-door fridges and pulled it open, exposing enough to feed a platoon of gourmands.

"You can't really tell because of all the junk in here, but a jar of pickled herring was opened, and a small bottle of champagne. Both were put back where they belong, which is why I didn't notice them at first." She pointed to a counter beyond the butcher-block table in the room's center. "We got distracted by the milk and cake."

Ron saw the three-dimensional version of one of the crime scene photos he'd already studied, of a dirty glass and a small plate with the remains of some chocolate cake on its surface.

"The cake was left over from a party two nights ago," Lisbeth Jordan explained without prompting. "It looks like he had a single slice."

"Son of a bitch," her husband growled. "Fucking eating our shit like he owned the place. I would love some time with this creep."

"The eating is part of this man's signature," Ron explained, addressing mostly Mrs. Jordan, whom he considered the more rational of the two, simultaneously wondering what a background check on Lloyd might reveal. There seemed to be a lot of sweatshirt attitude under the yachting clothes. "We are asking all the victims to please keep that under their hats. We like to withhold something from public knowledge, in case we get an impostor claiming to be the crook. Happens sometimes with people needing attention."

Lisbeth was nodding. "I've heard of that. Sure, we'll play along."

Lloyd was pacing the length of the kitchen. "Jesus, Liz, this isn't one of your stupid cop shows. These guys have no clue what they're doing. Holding back information isn't going to get them or us diddly."

Lisbeth smiled and gazed at Ron purposefully — he immediately sensed that she hated the name Liz. "We'll keep quiet about the food. I promise."

Lloyd stopped in midstride and demanded, "Why're you here anyhow? You haven't done anything too impressive so far."

"Honey?" his wife inquired. "Didn't you say you had to call Frank this morning? I can show Mr. Klesczewski the rest of the house."

A telling silence followed the transparent ploy, but apparently they were both well used to reciting their lines. Lloyd obediently

26

took his cue, nodded curtly, and headed for the door, announcing, "I'll be in my office."

Lisbeth made no apology after his departure, except to gesture a little wearily as she offered, "Would you like that tour?"

In many ways, despite its grandiosity, the house ended up lacking character, reminding Ron of a woman's face veiled with too much makeup, or of Lloyd Jordan himself, with his white pants and ascot. Each room's supposed treasures were displayed with the rhythmic dullness of the fancy photos in a high-society magazine. Extravagant, certainly, but reflective only of the bored interior designer who'd coordinated with the builder to stage it all properly — a builder, Ron suspected, who had in turn been working from an out-of-the-box starter castle kit. In fact, in the end, aside from a few photographs, vestiges of Lloyd and Lisbeth themselves were rarely visible. When it came time for them to leave this house, Ron fantasized their doing so in the smallest of moving vans, allowing the next inhabitants simply to fill the empty closets in order to call the place home.

Throughout the tour, Lisbeth answered questions relating to their friends and their general habits, their comings and goings.

Some of these inquiries had already been addressed by Ron's predecessors, others were stimulated by the conversation. The lifestyle that emerged struck Ron as foreign and unenviable.

The last stop was the master bedroom, the most personalized spot in the whole house. The enormous bed was still unmade, its center tellingly undisturbed while both edges revealed where each had swept back the covers to get up that morning. Ron pictured that middle swath as a domestic DMZ, providing privacy as much as extra room for playful wrestling. He was happier with the far more intimate double bed he shared with his wife.

Keeping to business, however, he stepped up to Lisbeth's side of the mattress and looked down at the night table.

"The Post-it was stuck here somewhere?" he asked.

She sidled up to him and quietly removed the small bottle of lubricant. "Yes. I didn't even notice it until I sat on the edge of the bed to put on my jeans, after my workout and my shower."

She reached out and flipped the blanket over the exposed bottom sheet, as if covering herself. "Sorry," she said softly. "The maid doesn't come till tomorrow. She had a crisis in the family."

Ron glanced at his ever-ready note pad. "That's Grace Duquoin? She have a key?"

Lisbeth looked up at him, surprised. "Yes. Well, of course."

"You told the others only Nick Penney had access." Lloyd had described Penney as his "estate manager" to the uniformed team, a euphemism for a subgroup of locals who moonlighted as property caretakers when homeowners were out of town, which among this set was often for months at a time.

She nodded. "I'm sorry. You're right. I forgot about Grace. She's almost like family, she's here so often." She looked around. "It's such a big place."

For the first time, Ron wondered how long she'd been married to Lloyd, and under what circumstances. He wandered over to a dresser beside the love seat under the broad window. Scattered messily across its surface were cuff links, two expensive watches, a wallet . . . all belonging to Lloyd. Two framed photographs showed a couple of children.

Already knowing the answer, he cast a glance her way and pointed at the photos. "Nice-looking kids. Yours?"

Her expression didn't change. "Lloyd's

grandchildren. I'm his second wife. We don't have any children. We don't even see those two very often," she added.

He nodded and moved to an open closet door. The light was on inside, revealing an area the size of a small bedroom, lined with racks, shelves, and hanger space, all stuffed with belongings. It seemed that neither Lloyd nor Lisbeth was overly neat. Thank God for Grace, Ron thought, and the money to keep her.

"That's a little embarrassing," she said from behind him.

He turned. "The mess?"

She was faintly taken aback. "No. I meant the sheer mass of it all. I never actually thought I was that much into clothes. Lloyd keeps pushing me to buy more."

He saw her dilemma, if without much sympathy. "It can be a balancing act, all right," he said vaguely. "But nothing was disturbed in here, that you know of." He was thinking of Willy's disgusting suggestion of at least one of the Tag Man's possible interests.

"No," she told him. "I checked."

He resisted looking for her underwear drawer and instead moved back to the master bedroom. As he stood there, taking it in as a whole once more, his eyes fell to the coffee table before the love seat. Given the room's general disorder, the coffee table's surface was perfection — from magazines to a small tasteful vase to an antique art deco ashtray — every item neatly placed and squared away. It looked as if a highly efficient maid had applied her talents to this one spot only.

He pointed to the far wall's doorway. "Bathroom?" he asked.

She smiled ruefully. "If you thought the closet was messy . . ." She nodded in its direction before adding, "Plus, we've both used it since your men came. They did take photographs. Even fingerprinted the toilet toggle thing."

He knew that. They'd outdone themselves, spending excess time here, no doubt enjoying the combination of low-level crime and high-end environment — a rarity for any of them.

He addressed her embarrassment. "That they did. No need for me to intrude any more, Mrs. Jordan. I'll get out of your hair right after I have a final chat with Mr. Jordan." To indicate his intention to do the latter alone, he thrust out his hand for another pleasant shake, adding, "I can't say your husband is wrong to be pessimistic. We don't have much to go on, even though this guy has hit so many places. On the other hand, that may be how we get him in the long run — it doesn't look like he knows how to stop, meaning he'll screw up sooner than later."

She frowned at that. "All he ever took was food?"

"That's all we've been told, from people just like you."

"And he never came back to the same place twice?"

He saw her concern. "Again," he stressed, "not that we know of. He seems to like the novelty of a new place every time. That being said, you might want to change your locks and maybe have your security looked at."

She nodded seriously. "I'll do that. You remember where Lloyd's office is?"

Ron laughed. "Barely, but yeah. I'll find it on my own. Thanks for your help and I am sorry we met under these circumstances."

He took his leave, alone for the first time. As he traveled the balcony, the staircase, the rooms and hallways on the ground floor, heading to the office, he tried imagining the Tag Man doing the same thing hours earlier. For Ron was confident that he'd taken thorough stock of the entire house, not just its fridge. Whoever he was and whatever his motives, Tag Man was a collector of sorts. Ron was sure of it.

He just wasn't sure of anything else.

The door to the office was closed, but rather than knock, Ron simply turned the knob and entered. Lloyd Jordan was sitting at his oversized desk, his hands in his lap, his features speaking of worse news than he was admitting.

He raised his eyes as Ron entered, neither surprised nor angered by the latter's presumptuousness. "You still here?" he asked tonelessly.

Ron closed the door behind him. "So what *did* you lose?" he asked quietly.

Jordan glared at him. "Nothing. I told you."

"Your body language says otherwise." Ron closed the distance between them and made himself comfortable in a leather guest chair.

"You a shrink, too?"

Ron took a calculated guess. "Enough to know you're missing something you're worried'll come back to bite you in the ass."

Jordan let slip a regretful half smile, and for that split second, Ron thought he'd get what he was after — and what by now he was convinced existed.

But the other man wouldn't play. He straightened slightly in his seat and said,

"Well, that's for me to know and for you to find out, along with the bastard who broke into my home. Just stick to that and I'll worry about whatever I may have misplaced here."

Ron could recognize a stone wall when he saw it, but it was early yet. He'd have time to dig up Jordan's little secret.

He rose and looked down at the hodge-podge covering the desktop — not unlike the clutter crowning the dresser upstairs. Except for a small trio of objects located high and center, where most business managers usually keep their nameplates. There, an antique clock, a pen holder, and an expensive Brookstone weather-instrument cluster all stood neatly ranked, side by side, as if on parade. The striking orderliness of it reminded him of the bedroom coffee-table array earlier.

"Nice toys," Ron said blandly.

Jordan dropped his gaze to the collection, then instinctively reached out and moved the pen holder out of place, putting it closer by. "Too much crap," he grumbled, adding, "Are we done? Can I get back to work now?"

"Absolutely," Ron conceded, not bothering to extend a hand, walking to the door instead. "We'll be in touch."

He didn't look back to see the expression he already knew would be there.

CHAPTER THREE

Sammie Martens sat in a rocking chair by the window, her baby daughter asleep in her arms. The window was open, the air soft and soothing. She was feeling more settled than she had in a lifetime.

She knew the consensus among her friends and colleagues — that she was ill-suited to motherhood, too driven, and her job too unpredictable, not to mention too violent. And, naturally, the never-ending complaint: that her choice of partner in Willy Kunkle proved that she was emotionally self-destructive.

But she didn't care. What she had snuggled up against her breast disposed of it all, reducing all protest to a murmur.

Besides, she wasn't a complete idiot. She'd been among the first to recognize Willy as a loose cannon and a fierce moral force — she and Joe Gunther, of course. In fact, it had been Joe's steadfast acceptance of Willy's careening eccentricity that had helped her to see past the stinging smokescreen of Willy's public persona.

And she and little Emma were now the beneficiaries of that effort. It didn't mean that Willy had lightened up much. He could still be jarringly blunt and dismissive with people. But he and Sam had developed their own language there, none of which applied to Emma, with whom he was as soft and gentle as he wasn't with everyone else.

She heard a car coming up the street and glanced out the window to see a familiar vehicle pull into the driveway. The three of them now lived on the edge of Brattleboro, at the bottom of a cul-de-sac in a quiet, barely noticed neighborhood. The house had originally been Willy's alone, chosen to address his suspicious nature. It was screened from the houses on either side, had a full view of all approaches, and was unobtrusively wired with alarms and cameras. It was also peaceful, quiet, modest, tidy, and attractive — without a doubt the most embracing home Sam had ever known.

She watched fondly as Joe Gunther slowly climbed out of the car, preparing to drop by as had become his almost weekly habit. Herself the product of a neglectful and chaotic childhood, Sam viewed this man

37

unabashedly as a father figure. When they'd first met, she a young woman out of military service and new to police work, her affection had been more romantic, if unrequited, but it had quickly found its proper place, and had strengthened there ever since.

In her eyes, this was a remarkable man heading deliberately up her walkway, his shoulders slightly bowed and his brow somber. Thoughtful, deliberate, steady, and loyal, he was no life of the party. He didn't tell stories, didn't participate in practical jokes, wasn't good at idle banter, and usually stood alone at social functions with his back against the wall and a Coke in his hand. But he was the proverbial rock — the man you needed when you were having doubts, and the one to have at your back in a fight.

He was also a man in trouble. Several months ago, Lyn Silva, with whom he'd been in love, had been killed in an assassination attempt aimed at Gail Zigman, Joe's previous long-term companion. But the shooter hadn't known about the recent change in Joe's love life. In fact, it wouldn't have mattered — Joe would have been devastated in any case. But the irony of this misdirected bullet hitting precisely the right target only added to the pain.

Sam regretted that her own unanticipated motherhood had come to bring her joy just as her mentor had been brought so low.

"Hey, stranger," she called out softly through the window as he drew near, heading for the front door.

He stopped and looked up, scrutinizing the house before he saw her against the sun's glare off the white clapboards. His face was creased with a sudden smile, sad but genuine.

"Hey yourself, little mother. You two enjoying the sunshine?"

Sam laughed quietly. "One of us is. Emma's in La-la Land. Come on in. The door's unlocked."

The older man chuckled. "That's got to mean Willy's not around."

She joined him. "And don't you tell him, either."

"No loose lips, Sam. Count on me."

Joe continued on in. Sam heard him enter the house, carefully closing the door behind him to at least pay tribute to Willy's sense of security.

Moments later, he stepped into her living room, crossed over, and kissed her and the baby's forehead before settling into an armchair opposite the rocker.

"How're you two doing?" he asked.

"Fine," she answered, adding, "You look tired."

He nodded without comment.

"Feeling any better?"

"Not really," he answered. "It shifts around inside my head too much, like a dog looking for a place to lie down. I keep thinking 'what if?' What if I'd done this or that? What if I'd said one thing or the other? Or not? If Lyn had crashed in a plane visiting friends in Omaha, I would have been heartbroken, but I wouldn't be feeling so guilty. I know that sounds self-centered," he added as Sam held up her hand to stop him, embarrassed by such vulnerability in someone usually so stolid.

"Still," he said, "I feel totally responsible."

She'd known him to make mistakes in the past, and to suitably atone for them. But this ran outside any behavior she'd witnessed before in him. It was uncharted territory and, given her current calm and serenity, a little frightening.

"You know none of that's true," she tried.

He didn't argue. "I know. But just because it's irrational doesn't make it less real."

That didn't give her much room, and she wasn't skillful at this kind of conversation anyhow. That was Joe's strength, sadly. He was the one they trusted to see clearly into

40

a troubled psyche.

Fortunately, he seemed to realize that now, and changed the subject to get her off the hook.

"I know people have been giving you grief, Sam," he said. "But I think motherhood suits you to a tee."

Despite her misgivings, she smiled broadly and hugged her baby slightly, making Emma stir in her dreams. "I've never been happier."

"Willy looks good, too," he suggested.

She laughed at the thought. "Only you would notice that," she told him. "You're right, though. He hates to admit it, but this has given him something I don't think he knew was missing. I understand the scuttlebutt, though. Giving Willy a baby must look like giving a lamb to a hyena."

Joe wrinkled his nose. "Lovely thought."

She kept smiling. "You know it's true."

"I do," he agreed. After a moment, he said, "I'm sorry about the timing of my own mess, by the way, what with Emma arriving on the scene. I know it's putting a strain on the unit, too."

She saw where he was heading. "It's okay," she countered. "Things are quiet — down to a dull roar, anyhow. Willy and Les aren't complaining, and I'll be back in a few weeks, maybe sooner. I have child care for her all lined up already."

"Still," he persisted. "I left you high and dry, ducking out the way I did."

She was already shaking her head. "Since the day we met, Joe, the only time off you've ever taken was when you were in some hospital, usually half dead. Give yourself a break. We're fine; I'm fine. Take advantage."

She was ill at ease, wishing she could find the eloquence to match her feelings. But she apparently had done well enough. Joe nodded as if in confirmation, stood, and kissed them both again.

"I will," he said. "Thanks, sweetheart."

He squeezed her shoulder and left as he'd come, deliberately and deep in thought.

Willy Kunkle removed the pen from his pocket and used it to tap sharply against the glass door of an Argentine restaurant named Bariloche. It was late, and Brattleboro's Elliot Street was empty enough that a single cat felt free to stroll down the middle of the road a hundred yards away, looking around like a tourist taking in landmarks.

To gauge from the surrounding architecture, this moment could have been a hundred years earlier. Brattleboro was a poster child for the archetypal New England, Industrial Revolution museum piece — all red bricks and stone moldings with bas-relief titles like the Union Block, or Amedeo de Angelis. In fact, if anything, the few parked cars looked out of place in the gloom, rather than the buildings that seemed as cemented in place as the pyramids themselves.

A shadow moved in the dimly lighted restaurant, and a narrow form in a trim white apron and T-shirt approached the door like a specter, pale and silent.

The lock was thrown, and the door opened to reveal a clean-shaven, short-haired, nondescript man who smiled as he recognized Willy — not the latter's usual reception.

"Mr. Kunkle," he said, stepping back to let Willy inside.

"Dan," Willy countered, not bothering to shake hands, knowing the other's dislike of the form. It also didn't surprise him that, although Dan Kravitz had been working in the restaurant's kitchen for a full shift — a restaurant with open grills and a reputation for preparing juicy steaks — Dan's white clothing looked as fresh as if it had come from the washing machine.

Kravitz was an intelligence source of Willy's — a denizen of the town's unnoticed lower levels, among the bums, fences, prostitutes, drug dealers, runaways, and others as invisible to society as the lamp-posts and parking meters lining the streets.

But Dan Kravitz was also something else, something Willy hadn't known for the first ten years of their acquaintance. During that time, as cop and CI, respectively — or confidential informant — neither had put enormous effort into getting to know the other. Willy had found Dan to be reliable when consulted, and Dan had told Willy of certain illegalities only when they'd sur-passed his own standard of outrage. This strictly business relationship had been ad-ditionally constrained by Dan's almost exclusively monosyllabic speaking style, which had naturally led Willy to write him off as simpleminded.

A prejudice shattered just last year.

That was when a major case had occurred involving several of Dan's friends, with whom he and his daughter had been living. When Willy had asked for his impressions at the time, Dan's response had left him speechless. The insight, thoughtfulness, and careful, elegant phrasing — seemingly straight out of nowhere — had revealed a man of education, culture, and experience, steeped in the vagaries of the human spirit and refined in psychological analysis. His advice and guidance, in a single conversation, had been of enormous help. Willy had found the entire event comparable to a dog suddenly speaking English.

He had been both caught off guard and thoroughly impressed, not that he hadn't immediately given Dan hell for engaging in such duplicity.

He recalled Kravitz's response. "We're alike in some ways," he'd told him. "People think you're a crippled asshole who acts like a Nazi, while they think I'm a retarded bum with good manners who knows how to shower. They're wrong, but they buy what we're selling."

That comment alone had shot Dan Kravitz to the top of Willy's estimation, if not just for his blunt clear-sightedness. More quirkily, Willy also liked the man for his perpetual cleanliness, a trait they happened to share.

Willy's neatness didn't match Dan's. But, like Dan, he kept his need for order internalized, not holding others to his own standards. It allowed him to travel amid disorder and filth albeit uncomfortably, which may have influenced each man's personality quirks. In Dan, spotless in the confines of a messy, commercial kitchen, Willy therefore saw a kindred soul.

"To what do I owe the pleasure?" Dan asked.

Kunkle snorted at the phrasing. "For ten years, all you gave me was yups and nopes. I still can't get used to you sounding like Richard Frigging Burton."

"Who is both British and dead," Dan responded, also smiling.

"You talk like this to anyone else?" Willy asked.

"My daughter," Dan conceded, tapping his right temple, "myself, and sometimes people I don't expect to meet again."

Dan's daughter, Sally, who was now about seventeen, was a precocious, pretty, very smart girl who, because of Dan's marginal income, attended a prestigious boarding school in nearby Massachusetts on a full scholarship. Now that he was a father himself, Willy wasn't sure if he wanted Emma to turn out quite so intelligent, or if he'd be scared of her should she do so. He sure as hell knew that he didn't have Dan's brains.

As if reading that very thought, the latter said, "I hear that congratulations are in order. How are mother and daughter do-ing?"

Normally, such questions were hot but-

46

tons for Willy. His privacy was paramount to him. But this was a man on whom he depended and who'd played him like a pro — clearly someone who could keep his mouth shut. He overcame instinct to answer levelly, "They're fine. I've given up sleep altogether."

Dan laughed softly. "I remember those days."

Willy studied him. There had never been mention of a companion or wife in Dan's life. He'd been questioned over the years by police, for one reason or another, but never to the point where they'd probed deeply into his affairs. On that basis, he remained an official enigma — a man who'd simply appeared one day, complete with child, as if dropped from another planet.

"How is the young inheritor?" Willy asked, taking a gentle return jab at Dan's own privacy.

But the other man didn't mind. Instead, his face softened. "Amazing, in a word. Despite being worlds apart from her classmates in origin and background, she's more than holding her own. She seems custommade for the place."

"She boarding?" Willy asked, although already losing interest.

"Yes, but she comes home often."

"Where's home these days?"

"Oh, here and there. You know."

What Willy knew was that he'd crossed the subliminal line between them.

He took it as a cue to proceed. "We alone?" he inquired, looking past his host into the half-lit restaurant beyond.

"Yes. The boss trusts me to close up," Dan said vaguely, making Willy consider that they might well be standing in what Dan was calling home at the moment. The man moved compulsively around town, sometimes living alone, other times sharing a bed with some woman, often equipped with children of her own. He was a friend of many and a guest of quite a few.

Willy let it pass, his curiosity trumped by his need to keep an ally.

"You hear about the Tag Man?" he asked.

Dan removed a chair from a nearby tabletop and placed it on the floor for Willy's use, setting another just like it directly opposite. They looked like two lingering shadows of the many diners who'd crowded the place earlier, when it had been full of light and noise. Now, in the pauses between them, they could hear the refrigerator cycling on and off under the bar against the far wall.

"I'd have to be fresh off the bus not to

have heard of him," Dan conceded, adding, "I don't know who he is, though."

"No rumors?" Willy pressed.

"What would there be?" Dan challenged him. "The guy doesn't do anything. The papers say he breaks in and leaves a note. It's not like he's fencing jewelry or stealing underwear . . ." He studied Willy more closely before adding, "Unless you people are holding something back. What *is* he doing, Mr. Kunkle? You work for a major-crimes unit nowadays."

Willy shook his head. "I'm just being nosy. This has nothing to do with me. It's a local case."

"So why the interest?"

Initially, Willy considered a routine denial — a cop's instinct to slam the door on all questions. But he liked this enigmatic man, with his preference for the night and his interest in human nature. He appeared to have a code, a guiding principle that kept him level. With Willy's past of violence, alcoholism, and relational chaos — of which his crippled arm was but the most obvious symbol — he needed to stay open to someone like Kravitz.

"Because I can't make sense of it," Willy admitted.

"It or him?"

Willy hesitated. "Both, I guess," he said. "Why do you ask it like that?"

Kravitz considered his answer carefully. "They are distinct entities. The man — assuming it is a man — and his actions. We know a human being is breaking in and leaving notes. What we don't know is what else he might be doing. So the 'it' part of the equation is a little elusive, if you get my point, kind of like a discussion about something that isn't there."

Willy stared at him. "I liked it better when all you did was grunt."

Dan laughed. "No, you didn't. I was just a snitch then. Now I'm a fellow soul. You have to care about me."

"The fuck I do."

"What are you doing here, then?"

Willy frowned. He hated this kind of exchange. He preferred things straightforward. And to leave the mental gymnastics to Joe. "I'm trying to find out what you know about the Tag Man, which is looking like shit."

Dan nodded thoughtfully. "I can't tell you about him, Mr. Kunkle, but if I were you, I'd lay bets that he's up to more than leaving messages like Kilroy."

"Like what?"

The answer was a shrug.

"Money?" Willy pursued.

Dan's eyebrows rose. "I hadn't heard that. Is that what you're holding back?"

"Jesus," Willy growled. "This is getting me nowhere. Tag Man is probably you, just to dick me around."

Dan laughed. "Why bother? I seem to be doing that anyhow."

"Seriously," Willy asked, trying to justify the visit in some way. "Is there money being lifted? Is that what you're hearing?"

Dan considered his companion philosophically. "That does raise an interesting question," he mused. "What if this fellow is stealing something from all these people, but no one is reporting it? You'd have to wonder what that could be."

Willy just watched him.

"Something to consider," Dan continued. "How seriously are the police interviewing the victims?"

Willy realized it was a genuine question. "They have a decent enough guy on it," he blurted, trusting that the compliment would never get back to Ron. But in fact, he wondered about Kravitz's point. Back when he was working this very turf, he would have given little time to a crime with no real consequence — go through the motions, say all the right things, file reports with the brass. But that would be about it. He knew Kleszewski was more of a grind for procedure, and that he'd give even the stupidest case a thorough once-over, but nowadays he had an entire squad to run. Was he in fact digging that deeply?

As if to run the point home, Dan asked, "Is he really applying a microscope?"

Willy decided to grant Ron the benefit of the doubt. "That's his style."

Dan sat back, his body language dismissing the whole topic as a trifle. "Just a thought — to bring as much depth to the 'it' as to the 'who,' that we were discussing a minute ago."

Willy nodded and stood up. "I'll fly it by the locals. You tell me if you hear anything, okay?"

Dan joined him and escorted him back to the front door, unlocking it to let him out. "Of course, Mr. Kunkle. You've piqued my interest. I'll ask around."

Dan stood by the restaurant window and watched Willy walk down the sidewalk, cross the street, and vanish from sight. He sighed and pulled back into the darkened dining room, enjoying the solitude and quiet of a place designed for everything but.

He was interested in the interplay of opposites, which explained his attraction to Kunkle. If ever there was someone at odds with himself, Willy fit the bill. Dan sincerely hoped that the baby girl he and Sam had just brought into the world would only and forever be a reflection of Willy's good side.

He suspected so, but he'd had enough education at the hands of people more emotionally stable than Willy to know it could play out one way or the other. He imagined that for Willy's child, it would boil down to luck — and whatever weight Sammie Martens might bring to bear.

But he'd been blessed with his Sally, and he wasn't vain enough to think that she'd wound up so well through any effort of his.

He stopped in the middle of the floor and looked around, double-checking his final tidying up. Satisfied, he switched off the last light, leaving only the one over the bar, and climbed the narrow staircase behind the door off the tiny stage at the back wall. It was a tight fit, even for him, and very steep, which he enjoyed for how it made him feel like a gopher heading into his hole.

Above, the stairs opened up into a single large room with a tall ceiling and a row of windows overlooking the Harmony parking lot behind the restaurant.

The room was painted with ghostly tendrils of light streaming in from the surrounding town. As always, Dan hesitated at the top step to take it in. It wasn't rentable space, because of the restricted access and lack of a fire escape, but the owner let him stay here in exchange for Dan's caretaking the place at night. It was one of Dan's better finds, too — spacious, sparse, easy to clean, and with an alcove for Sally when she came to visit.

He crossed to the table he'd set up as a desk near one of the windows and sat down in a straight-backed chair, barely making a sound, as was his wont. He liked to pass through life unnoticed, even while taking note of all its workings.

Prompted by his conversation with Willy, he reached into a canvas bag he used solely to transport his stolen prizes — eventually fated to end up in a cabinet, safe and sound in folders, and indexed according to their homeowners' last name — and extracted the wad of papers he'd removed from the Jordan residence.

He'd known the police were withholding evidence. That was standard practice. But he'd thought it amounted to his trademark of eating from every fridge. He'd assumed that whatever items he'd collected — pictures, letters, documents — had either not

been missed or were deemed too embarrassing to have been reported lost in the
first place.

Like Lloyd Jordan's hidden love letter
from Susan Rainier.

But Dan had stolen more than that. He
hadn't liked Lloyd, both for betraying his
wife and from what he'd interpreted of the
man's personality. That's why he'd grabbed
a few of the hidden financial papers as well.

It wasn't his habit to carefully read the
documents he stole, in a contrary conces-
sion to people's privacy. It usually didn't
seem that important after the thrill of breaking in.

But maybe this time deserved an exception.

CHAPTER FOUR

Dr. Eberhard Dziobek removed his glasses and placed them on the arm of his upholstered chair. Opposite him, Joe Gunther sat — slouched, tired, and morose — staring at some spot on the ancient oriental rug between them. They were in the therapist's office at the Retreat, Brattleboro's mental health facility, where Dziobek had been treating alcohol- and drug-dependent patients for decades. Dependence wasn't Joe's problem, of course. He was simply in mourning. But Eberhard liked him, and had offered to be a sounding board. Gunther had given enough of his time and talent to others to deserve a small kindness in return.

"In your rational mind, of course, you know that you shouldn't be blaming yourself," he suggested in his carefully phrased English.

Joe allowed for a thin smile. "Yeah. I saw that movie too. 'It's not your fault; it's not your fault.' That's when the poor bastard breaks down, bursts into tears, and is instantly cured. Not a dry eye in the house."

"You don't believe me?" Dziobek's voice was soft and gently modulated, his German accent almost a parody.

"I believe it on paper, but I'm not sure I give a damn. She's dead, and she wouldn't be if I hadn't indirectly put her in harm's way."

"How did you do that?"

"You ever hear of a black cloud?" Joe asked him.

Dziobek shook his head.

"The cruder expression is shit magnet. I laughed when I first heard it, a thousand years ago when I was a rookie. It's someone who, every time he comes on shift, attracts all the antiaircraft fire within a fifty-mile radius. If he's in EMS, the ambulance rolls nonstop; a firefighter, half the town burns down; a cop, every bad call comes in during his shift; and on down the line."

"And you are one of those?"

"I never complained," Joe went on. "In those days, you didn't want to be standing around, doing nothing. The job calls for type A personalities, and what better than to be running flat out when you're on?" He added, "But it's a young man's game."

Dziobek waited silently for him to reach his point.

Joe was still staring at the floor. "It's also not really supposed to be dangerous. I mean, cops talk about the threat of violence all the time. It's part of the mystique. TV shows dramatize it; movies deal with nothing else. But this is Vermont. We roll around the floor with a drunk or a pissed-off husband now and then, but the death toll among cops up here involves some screwup more often than machine-gun fire. One of us drowns during a rescue operation, or gets hit by a car by accident. It stands to reason, right? There just aren't that many people up here."

His eyebrows rose and he finally looked at his companion. Dziobek smiled and nodded. "Right. Of course."

"But not me," Joe said, beginning to get to his point. "Over the years, I've been knifed, shot at, nearly frozen, and pounded half to death too many times to count, and several people have died or come close just by standing nearby."

"Like Lyn?" Eberhard asked, knowing that she'd been half a state away from Joe when her killer had opened up on Gail. The therapist couldn't overlook the small detail that, according to Joe's black-cloud theory,

58

it was Gail who should have been sitting here, feeling guilty.

"Tell me what happened," he said instead.

"How much do you know?" Joe asked.

The older man shrugged. "Not very much. I do not read the papers as I should, and I do not own a television. Silly, I know. I will tell you a confidence: When I go home at night, after my daughter Hannah has gone to bed, my wife and I prefer to read novels in complete silence. Maybe some quiet music."

"You listen to people all day," Joe sympathized.

Dziobek's face brightened. "Oh, and I enjoy it, too. I just appreciate the contrast every evening." He waggled his fingers briefly in the air. "In any case, to answer your question, I do know a few things. I know that Governor Zigman was then running for office and that the gunman had been aiming for her, thinking she was still your girlfriend. I also know that while she and you had been a couple for many years, the young lady who died was in fact your new companion. Is that essentially correct?"

Joe's expression was rueful. "In clinical terms, yes. Nice detached way to describe a train wreck."

Dziobek shifted in his seat, took up his

glasses again, and vaguely pointed them at Joe in emphasis. "Now, I'm not asking this to disagree with you. I am simply seeking an explanation. How does any of that make you at fault?"

Joe sighed. "Look, Eberhard, I know it's foolish. I've gone over this a bunch on my own. It's not that I put them both at risk directly. It's less concrete than that. It's not blame; it's more like I feel accountable for what happened. And not for some action I did or didn't take, but for what I do and how I do it. That's why I mentioned the black-cloud thing. The shooter who killed Lyn was no different than the guy who rigged Gail's condo with incendiaries a few years ago, or blew up Dennis DeFlorio with a car bomb — they were both after me. And they're not the only ones. The real irony to all this is that Gail essentially left me because of exactly that. She didn't like the risks I took every time I went to work — that's true — but she also didn't like how the shrapnel kept coming her way."

"She was once raped, was she not?" Dziobek asked.

Joe stopped abruptly. Everything he'd just said had come out in a rush.

"Yes," he said deliberately. "That wasn't my fault either, but you can see how it made her a basket case forever after. She had to get away from me to lighten that load."

"Of course," Dziobek agreed.

"And then some crazy son of a bitch goes after her anyhow," Joe said without emphasis.

"And your role in Lyn being there?" Dziobek asked.

Joe passed his hand over his face, rubbing his eyes in the process. Eberhard imagined that Joe hadn't had a decent night's sleep in months. He felt deeply for Gunther's dilemma. As a leader of police officers for so many years, first locally and now for the VBI, Joe had in fact become a father figure to many. At any given time, he *was* responsible for dozens of people, having directly or otherwise dictated where they should be and what they should be doing. If he okayed an operation and things went wrong and injuries resulted, he did own a part of the burden. That was the fate of father figures — they were acknowledged and admired for their status, but they carried the weight of all who so revered them. It was no surprise to Dziobek that traditionally, senior officers in such high-pressure jobs tended to burn out in under ten years. The fact that Gunther had been operating at that level for so much longer made him a statistical anomaly, and perhaps a meltdown waiting to happen.

"That's complicated," Joe said in response to Eberhard's question. "I had used her as a sounding board for the case I was on then. I do that a lot — did it with Gail, too, in the old days, and with the people on my squad. It helps to hear your own ideas out loud."

Dziobek smiled a little indulgently. "I understand."

Joe got the point. "Right, you know that. That was stupid. Anyhow, I got her involved. And she came up with a winner idea I won't bore you with now, but it was good. In and of itself, that was fine, but later, after everything happened, I began thinking that it drew her in more than it should have."

He spread his hands wide. "The woman owned and ran her own business, for crying out loud. It wasn't like she had the time or the need to help me out. But I think the Gail factor played on her mind — that Gail and I had been together so long; that she was so high-profile, running for office; that she'd been a good listener. I think Lyn maybe felt a little insecure, and that without intending it, I made it worse."

He stopped to take a breath before resuming. "Anyhow, that's why she went up to

Montpelier to see Gail — because of me. And that's why that sorry prick took his shot — regardless of who he hit — because of me. You can say it wasn't my fault all you want, and maybe you're right. But what I just said holds true, too. All these people did what they did because of me."

"People always act because of something or someone, Joe," Dziobek counseled. "It doesn't mean that person is responsible for what happens. It's just not that clear cut."

Silence followed as each man considered what Joe had just said. Eberhard reflected on what he knew of this unusual man — a combat veteran; married only once, long ago, to a woman taken by breast cancer; highly regarded by colleagues, and yet only vaguely known to the public, in large part because of his instinctive self-effacement. Not a man easily given to self-pity or depression, and yet suffering from both at the moment.

Joe, for his part, seemed to have recognized the confusion he'd sown. He rose from the old leather chair that had comfortably engulfed him and crossed to the window overlooking the lakelike confluence of the West and Connecticut rivers on the edge of the Retreat campus — a peaceful place that welcomed ice-skaters in the winter and kayakers now.

Joe addressed the window. "I'm sorry, Eberhard. I know you're doing me a favor here, and I'm wasting your time trying to get the words right." He turned to smile at the other man. "Three guesses how many times I've spoken to a shrink."

Eberhard returned the good will. "It is my profession, but we are meeting as friends, Joe. I am happy to try to help."

Joe returned to the view. "I've made this sound like it's all about me. Like these women were moths around a candle flame. That's crap, of course. It's not what I meant. I'm feeling sorry for myself — I'll give you that. I miss Lyn, and I still feel guilty that the love I have for my job drove Gail away. But what I was saying a minute ago misses the point."

He retreated from the window and resumed his seat. The office was what he'd always imagined Sherlock Holmes's might have looked like — overstuffed with old furniture and mementos of an interesting life. He remembered that the same thought had struck him when he'd first met Dziobek here in consultation about a case.

"I made it too personal," he went on. "What I said just now. There's something else pulling at me — bigger — like an

64

undertow. The way this whole thing worked out has made me wonder what the hell I'm trying to prove out there." He waved an arm to include the world in general. "When good people put their heads together and work to solve a problem," he asked, "shouldn't the results be rewarding?"

"It would be nice," Dziobek said cautiously.

Joe almost didn't let him get the words out before continuing. "And the joke is that this time, we actually solved the problem. We got the bad guy, figured out what his motive was. We put this thing to bed, just like we were supposed to."

"Well . . ."

Joe held up a finger. "Right. Not exactly. We had collateral damage, big time. Again."

He paused to make his point. "It's not so much self-pity, Eberhard. For the first time in my life, I'm feeling tired — down to my bones. That some peckerhead with an obsession for his mother should cause so much harm and loss, just so he can be replaced by another peckerhead I haven't even heard of yet, who'll do Christ knows what to somebody else. That's really gotten into my head."

He leaned back, his voice quieter. "I dropped by to see one of my officers this morning. She just had a baby girl. It was a happy accident — not planned but wonderful news for everyone involved. And what kept running through my head was, 'Oh Jesus, now *you* have someone to lose and break your heart, because you're a hard worker and diligent and you take risks because you believe in right over wrong, and all that is going to expose you like it does few other people.' "

Joe lapsed into silence at last, and pressed his fingertips against his temples, his elbows resting on the arms of the old chair.

Dziobek studied him for a moment before commenting, "Joe, for someone who has never spoken to a psychologist before, you've started out very well. If you feel that there might be some comfort in it, I would like to see if I can help. It will take time, though, and more sessions like this."

Joe looked up tiredly. "As things have worked out, time I got."

Dan Kravitz stood for a moment inside the doorway, absorbing the satisfaction and excitement he experienced every time he breached a home's defenses. The silence he worked to maintain — from the whisper of his bootie-covered shoes to the minute clicks from his lockpicks and electronic gadgetry, to the rhythm of his own breathing — each was seen as a single part of each outing's overall orchestration.

Not that he'd ever reached perfection, of course. Which was precisely the point. The enjoyment was in the struggle, not in the achievement. Once hearing mountain climbers comment on how the summit view was secondary to the ascent, he'd instantly empathized. Dan was a man who happily lost himself in process.

He did have to admit that this time, however, reality had proven less daunting than he'd anticipated. The house was large, ancient, situated in the heart of crowded Brattleboro, and had been placarded with signs from a reputable alarm company — one from which he'd expected a true challenge. But it had turned out to be largely bogus. The old lady who lived here alone, Gloria Wrinn, was either forgetful or had been catering to her nephew's nagging by installing security but not turning it on, since Dan had found the system unplugged.

He suspected the latter explanation, since his research into the Wrinn family dynamics revealed that Gloria's sole living relative, her nephew, Larry, seemed more interested in the house's contents than in its resident. Larry was financially strapped, an idiot with the little money he had, and a jerk to Gloria whenever they were seen in public. To Dan's mind, this helped explain the dormant alarm system, the fact that the old lady lived alone, and that she had as little to do with Larry as possible — notwithstanding the politesse instilled by her age and upbringing.

Dan instinctively liked the house, and immediately sympathized with Larry's interest in its holdings. There were antiques, art works, collectibles, and precious items crowding every room Dan silently visited. But to him, the interest was less in its cash value than in the sense of a life lived surrounded by objects collected carefully and with love. Gloria Wrinn, he knew, widowed early in life, had spent most of her middle years traveling, learning, meeting bright people, and generally enriching herself with both experiences and artifacts. Dan imagined that every item he was enjoying in the darkened house's twilight, from gargantuan pieces of furniture to miniature sculptures gracing a side table, held a special meaning or a fond memory for Gloria, a woman he was beginning to like greatly, the further he trespassed into her home.

He proceeded as usual, according to pattern, first scoping out the house as a whole

— its exits, levels, layout, and eccentricities. Did it have guests he hadn't accounted for? Backup alarms he might have missed in his research? What about creaky floors, precariously placed objects, sticky doors, or affectionate and/or outspoken cats? He'd once met a large dog he'd known nothing about, which had thankfully turned out to be old and uninterested.

None of these was necessarily a deal killer, according to Dan's self-made rules of engagement. But they did crank up the game a few notches.

This first sweep of any house was always a survey only, often simply identifying which rooms were where. After committing the place to memory, Dan repeated his journey a second time, methodically, absorbing the personality of home and owner. This is where the fascination began to grow, and the anthropologist in him replaced the pure technician.

Paying proper homage to the homeowner, though, he did start this next stage by entering Gloria's bedroom, not just to informally introduce himself but — being no fool — to check on the possibility of guns near the bed, and to estimate the quality of her sleep. Insomniacs had a scary way of yielding to hunger, thirst, or the need for a pee right in the middle of his visits. He'd been there before, and preferred to avoid repeats.

Despite startling him with her posture — sitting up in bed — she looked like someone who happily and regularly clocked out for the whole night. Her breathing was deep, slow, and peaceful, and her blanket and pillows were unwrinkled by restless tossing. He glanced around the bedroom then, connecting her belongings to his expanding impression of her. As he'd expected, her bedroom contained her most prized keepsakes, some of which made him smile with their humor and iconoclasm.

Dan left her and carried on, choosing this time not to disturb a thing. It was his prerogative to eat from the fridge or leave a note by the bed, and while he did steal several grapes while passing through the dining room, he didn't want Larry to say later "I told you so" to his aunt and chastise her about the alarm. To Dan's way of thinking, he and Gloria were united against the real creep of the story.

That didn't mean he didn't drop by the kitchen, however. He had his own needs. Things had to be done in order and in proper sequence. And it was while he was taking inventory there that he opened a door he'd taken for a closet on his first go-around.

It wasn't much — narrow and half hidden by a hanging apron. It might have led to a pantry. But he should have remembered that the house's exterior projected a little beyond the kitchen wall, and was equipped with windows. There were no windows along this side of the kitchen. He turned the knob and stealthily pushed, his vigilance back in high gear.

Beyond the door was a narrow hallway running parallel to the kitchen wall, and lined with the missing windows. At its end was a stairway leading down.

Dan frowned. Cellars usually weren't on his itinerary, frequently being dirt-floored, dank, and uninteresting. But this one, from the top, appeared more domesticated somehow, which led him to think that in a house this age, the stairs might lead to the old servants' quarters.

Intrigued, he used the dim moonlight to guide him to the top step, where he extracted the small narrow-beam flashlight he carried among his other equipment. Shielding it inside the cup of his hand, he quickly played it downstairs to see what lay below. He saw a second door at the bottom, firmly shut.

Now completely captured, he took to the

stairs, one carefully tested tread at a time, until he was standing by the door. He tried the handle, half expecting it to be locked or stuck, and felt it easily and soundlessly give way, albeit to reveal an odor unlike anything he'd encountered upstairs.

He hesitated in the pitch black, his nostrils flared and his instincts on guard. This wasn't mildew or rot or the cloying smell of a neglected cellar. This was human. In Dan's peregrinations throughout the town's trailers, flophouses, and shacks, he'd developed a familiarity with the hygienically challenged.

And to put a finer point on it, he was sure that this particular pungency belonged to a male.

He pushed the door wider, waiting for the inevitable creak that would reveal his presence, and then froze when it didn't come. This was his least favorite situation — utter darkness in an unknown place with someone potentially lying in wait.

Huddling near the jamb, so that he could pull back toward the stairs if necessary, Dan squinted and flashed his light once into the room, like a strobe, creating a near-photographic image on his memory while reducing the risk of being hit by any random shot.

He saw a fifteen-foot-square room, cluttered, messy, windowless — and most important, uninhabited.

He stepped fully into the room and hit the flashlight again, this time leaving it on. For a second, he feared he'd just made the error of a lifetime, for he thought he'd seen a man sitting slumped in a chair in the far corner. But it turned out to be a heap of clothes.

Still, the first impression of this being a man's lair held true. Looking around more carefully, his ears tuned and his body tensed for flight, Dan saw the disorganized, telltale signs of a male living alone, complete with a pair of boxers dangling off the end of a bedpost.

From the looks of it, the furniture came from upstairs, if perhaps on its way to the dump. But Gloria's rejects were high grade, so whoever lived here was still faring better than the average renter.

But was that who this was? After confirming the absence of windows, Dan turned on the overhead light. He didn't have much time. He wasn't fond of lingering in the best of circumstances, and now he was faced with a true wild card — a missing man he knew nothing about who might appear at any moment.

He worked methodically and at speed, cataloging the room from the right and traveling counterclockwise. He didn't have a huge amount to go through — a dresser, a bed, a desk with one drawer, an armchair, and two reading lights. A rug on the floor, two calendars, and a postcard pinned to the wall sum totaled the decorations. There were tabloid newspapers and celebrity magazines strewn about, a few paperbacks, the usual sampling of pornography, and of course the clothes, mostly dirty. For Dan especially, this was onerous labor. He preferred to hover, like a ghost, and so relied on his gloves and his concentration to protect him against the filth all around. As charmed as he'd been by the contents of the house above, he was now horrified by the overwhelming sense that he was foraging through less a home than a cave.

But home it was, to one Paul Hauser, according to a tiny and neglected stash of paperwork, who'd signed a lease with Gloria Wrinn to work on and maintain the property in exchange for the use, rent-free, of a single room in the basement.

Dan suspected this was all a reflection of not just Gloria's good heart and compassion, but yet another example of her needling Larry.

However, to pay Larry his due, Dan thought the nephew might have had a point this time. Just as Gloria had won Dan over through her collections, so Paul Hauser's assortment of knives, torture porn, and discarded fast food containers repelled him now.

And yet, by the end of his search, all he'd really uncovered were the mundane contents of a human hovel, suitably located under ground.

Until he noticed the tiniest of imperfections on the floor.

One attribute of Dan's obsessive-compulsive disorder was his awareness of three-dimensional patterns. He had the spatial sensitivity of an eagle studying the ground below, noticing the slightest abnormalities. And he saw one now, in the minute misalignment of a single floorboard.

He dropped to his knees, removed a slim prybar blade that he carried in one of his jumpsuit pockets, and eased it into the hairline gap between one board and its neighbor. Slowly and with extreme care, he lifted the wood free, and the two planks to either side, and peered into the black void below.

Given what he'd seen so far, he wasn't prepared to reach blindly in and paw

75

around, so he used his flashlight to reveal a large black suitcase, its handle invitingly glinting.

Knowing that he was running out of time, Dan grabbed hold and pulled the heavy case out into the open, surprised by its weight and half dreading the urge that was forcing him onward.

He flipped back both catches, thinking of Pandora, and edged his fingertips under the suitcase lid.

It opened without a sound.

The odor struck him first — sweet and light in this stale-smelling place. A shock he wasn't expecting. And the contents explained it, for the first thing he brushed with his gloved fingertips was a soft and delicate woman's scarf — decorative and light.

Puzzled and apprehensive, he gently explored further, uncovering other pieces of women's clothing — none of it underwear, all of it seemingly talismanic in nature, as if carrying a message. Finally, supporting this implication, he found six photo albums at the bottom of the case, lying neatly arranged, side by side.

Dan gingerly lifted out the center one and opened it. Each page held a single photo, not taken with any expertise or high-end equipment, but each carefully placed in the middle of the page. They were location shots to begin with, some taken during daylight, and showed a trail in the woods and a clearing with a picnic table. The table was stained with something dark.

He kept turning pages. The stain predictably explained itself. Shot after shot, all taken at night, showed a young woman lying nude on the table, stabbed repeatedly, her blood having seeped out to cover the wooden slats and the ground beneath. The photos were taken from all angles, some from a distance, others excruciatingly close up.

Stunned and dizzy, Dan reached the last page to find a long hank of hair, the same color as the dead girl's, carefully taped in place.

He closed the album, sat back on his heels, and tried to breathe away the nausea clutching at his throat, all the more conscious of the stifling air around him.

He wiped his forehead on his sleeve, and quickly opened another album at random, to a middle page, where he found a similar picture of another girl, in a different setting, her eyes wide and glassy, reflecting the sparkle of the camera's flash. He slapped the book closed, opened a third one in the same quick fashion, with the same result, before he dropped everything back into the suitcase in a near panic and slammed it shut, closing only one of the clasps in his rush.

He hurried from the room and stumbled upstairs blindly, craving the outdoors, having forgotten about Gloria entirely and his earlier plan to check out her fridge. The sense of playfulness that acted as powerfully on him as his other obsessions had been seared to oblivion.

Outside, in the cool night air, shaded from all eyes by a thick, overgrown hedge, he stood with his hands on his knees, gasping and fighting for the control he so cherished.

He had killed the light in Paul Hauser's room, and locked the door behind him as he'd left the house. His self-preservation instincts hadn't ceased to function entirely.

But he was definitely off-balance — shocked, sickened, dismayed, and confused — and paid little attention to his environs as he finally straightened, took one last gulp of air, and set off distractedly for home.

He took no note of the man who'd been coming up the walkway, had seen him first, and who now stood in the shadows, watching carefully and silently as Dan walked by, unaware.

Chapter Five

Ron Klesczewski looked up from his desk at the knock on his door. The Brattleboro police chief, Tony Brandt, who'd held the job for so long people assumed he'd welcomed the town's first settlers, stood leaning against the doorjamb, smiling enigmatically. Fond of tweed jackets with elbow pads, and once addicted to a pipe with which he used to fog his office, he appeared more the college dean than a cop — tall, slightly stooped, and professorial — but this only allowed him to better manage both his department and the ever-changing string of half-baked politicians who'd populated the board of selectmen during his biblically long tenure.

"Morning, Chief," Ron said, rising and offering his guest a chair.

Brandt's smile widened. "You're the only one who's ever done that, Ron, including when Joe ran this squad."

"What?" Ron asked.

"Stand up when I come in. It's very old-school."

Ron looked around doubtfully. "I'm sorry . . ."

His boss immediately sat down to better put his colleague at ease. "No, no. Don't apologize. It was just an observation. You were brought up that way, right? Respect for your elders and members of the fair sex? You open doors for your wife, I bet."

Ron hesitantly regained his own seat. "Sure," he admitted, wondering where this was going.

But Brandt just said, "Wonderful. Don't change. Maybe it'll spread, although I doubt it."

Ron nodded. "Want some coffee?" he asked.

"No. My stomach doesn't need any help right now."

Ron was slightly alarmed. "What's wrong? You all right?"

Brandt dismissed the concern. "Oh God, yes. I just came from a meeting with Nicholas." He pronounced the name by drawing out the middle syllable to three times its length. Nicholas Jones, the town manager who hated to be called Nick, was generally despised by the cops. Jones's first reaction to every fiscal inquiry by the board was to suggest trimming the PD's budget. It had become so commonplace that even the *Brattleboro Reformer* had commented on it in an editorial.

Ron relaxed slightly. "Squeezing you for cash again?"

"Actually," Tony countered, "not this time. He was busting my chops about the Tag Man."

Ron's shoulders slumped. "My favorite subject."

"I take it we're no closer to identifying him than when he first hit?"

"This didn't have anything to do with Lloyd Jordan, did it?" Ron asked instead.

"The latest victim? Not that I know of. Why?"

Ron explained, "Just a weird feeling when I went over there to interview him and his wife. She was fine — very helpful — but he was hinky as hell. Made me wonder what had really happened."

"You think they know who this guy is?" Brandt's interest grew.

Ron hesitated. He hadn't thought of that. "Either that," he conceded, "or Lloyd Jordan got something lifted he's not talking about."

Tony Brandt frowned thoughtfully.

"Willy dropped by a couple of days ago," Ron admitted. "He thinks Tag Man's doing something we're not being told — maybe to all his victims."

The chief's eyebrows rose. "Oh?"

"Nothing solid. He just wondered why someone would go to all the effort of busting into high-security places, complete with sleeping homeowners, to put a sticky note by their bedside. He said it a little more crudely than that, but that was the gist of it."

"I bet," Tony responded. Willy Kunkle had once worked for him, longer than he might have, only because of Joe's protection. Brandt did not miss the man, or having to rationalize his methods to the town leaders.

"And you think he may have something, based on Jordan's reaction?"

"Partially. I also think we interviewed the prior victims solely in that light, without thinking about what they might be hiding. I mean, we saw the Post-its, the left-out food, noticed the similarities. It became like tracking a graffiti vandal."

"Without taking note of which walls were being painted, and why," Tony finished the simile.

"Right."

Brandt nodded slowly. "Right. Interesting.

Would the implication be that the Tag Man's up to a lot more than we think? Like blackmail?"

"Because he knows who he's targeting and what they're hiding?" Ron continued. "Could be."

"Makes more sense than if he's just randomly hitting them and hoping to get lucky," Tony suggested.

Ron was happy to move on from his earlier embarrassment. "Maybe, unless we're missing a crucial possibility. What if he's doing this more than we know, and only leaving notes now and then, with a specific goal in mind?"

Brandt was amused. "Telling us which ones are crooks? Jesus. Like we have our own demented version of Batman?"

They shared a small laugh, but only over Brandt's choice of words. Neither one of them dismissed the idea out of hand.

"So what do you want to do?" Tony asked.

"What I am doing," Ron told him, "is checking out Lloyd Jordan, but I don't think it'll hurt to run all the victims through the system, just to see if anything pops up."

Brandt rose to his feet, content for the moment. "Good. That'll be one expense I don't think Nicholas'll bitch about. Keep me informed."

■ ■ ■ ■

"Dad? Are you okay?"

Kravitz turned away from his apartment window overlooking the restaurant's front entrance. His daughter, Sally, had caught a ride from school to visit friends and see him. She wasn't spending the night. This had been a spontaneous opportunity, and normally was something Dan would have loved. In his universe of privacy and patterns and compulsively maintained order, Sally was the free agent — the one human being who could do what she wanted, however she wanted to do it, without consequence from him.

"I'm sorry, sweetheart. A little distracted. When are you headed back? You have time for something to eat?"

She crossed the tidy, austerely spare room and gave him a hug, not something he tolerated from anyone else. She looked up lovingly into his face. "I can do you one better. Remember Andy Weissman? He manages Swifty's now. I asked him to have some lunch delivered. My treat. Well . . . actually, Andy's treat. Should be here in about ten minutes."

He kissed her cheek. "You are too much."

He let her handle the details of greeting her friend at Bariloche's closed door a little later, while he set up the apartment's board-on-bricks arrangement that served as a dining table, setting out paper plates and cups and napkins in his peculiarly precise way.

When she returned, she bore a salad, two sandwiches, and a couple of soft drinks, all ordered with an eye to his various phobias. Not that she worried overmuch — she knew the slack he allowed her. But she was a considerate child, and loved her father deeply.

Which caused her to revisit her earlier concern as she saw him picking at his food.

"What's up, Dad?"

"Just something I saw," he tried reassuring her. "You know how I wander around."

"Something or someone?"

He allowed for a half smile. "Someone."

She took another bite of sandwich, depositing a blob of mayonnaise on her lower lip in the process. Normally, he couldn't have borne watching it — not on someone else. But on her, it just looked sweet.

He explained, "I ran into a guy with some odd habits. A little creepy, actually. It just put me off."

"You think he's dangerous?"

He considered the question seriously, both

out of respect to her and from pure habit. Dan was a man given to the literal truth, and not much prone to protective social niceties.

"He may be." He stared at his plate for a moment, thinking back, trying to override his emotions with a rational answer. It didn't come easily. His mind was usually in a tug-of-war with itself, his intellect struggling with his compulsions. This recent memory was no help.

He finally gave up and smiled. "It doesn't matter. It was just a chance encounter. I'm not likely to see him again."

"Sounds like a good thing," she said with her mouth full. "I'd stay as far away as I could."

He couldn't argue with that, but after he'd escorted her to where she was grabbing a return ride to school, he yielded to the urge to give the subject the attention it deserved.

He did not retire to the monastic apartment and his perch by the window, however. Instead, he walked across Brattleboro from where he'd left Sally, using back streets and alleyways he knew like the rooms of a family home, until he reached Arch Street — narrow, poorly paved, and largely ignored by the general populace. This dropped off from Main Street down a steep embankment and led to the railroad tracks that ran between the picturesque Connecticut River and the backs of the commercial buildings that fronted Main. As with so many New England industrial-era towns, Brattleboro had shunned the river — at the time, considered no more than a power source and a delivery route for merchandise.

Now, however, aside from a couple of trains every day, this strip was quiet, empty, and sylvan — assuming one's gaze overshot the nearby tracks, trash, and urban grime in favor of the view.

Kravitz walked alongside the curving rail bed, enjoying the early summer weather, the broad river, and the mountain looming over the opposite shore. But he was also watchful, checking for any movement either on foot or at any of the windows scattered across the redbrick walls above, like the holes of a gigantic colander.

Satisfied, he faded into a recess at the foot of a nearby building, worked the lock of a small, battered door, and vanished from sight.

Once inside, he negotiated the dark hallways with the aid of a flashlight before coming to another door, this one equipped with a combination lock, a deadbolt, and an alarm system. There, he knelt down to make sure the slim strip of Scotch tape he'd left spanning the door and the jamb was still intact, and let himself in.

Beyond was an immaculately maintained, white-walled, windowless room, not unlike a surgery, but outfitted with electronics, reference materials, a desk, and a bed. This was his combination operations center/ meditation room, the inner sanctum where he both studied the security systems he needed to defeat and — as now — where he retreated to wrestle with the confusions that too often assailed him from outside.

No one knew of this place, including Sally. Even the landlord and Dan had never met in person. Nor did the landlord know Dan's actual identity. It was as secure as the places he invaded should have been.

He crossed to the office chair he used when planning his operations, before a semicircle of computers and reference books — a place of comfort and control, with his world at his fingertips — and returned to both the conversation he'd barely broached with his daughter and the far more substantive experience of the night before.

On the face of it, his choice was simple. He should report what he'd found to the police — specifically, his sparring partner, Willy.

But his was not a simple worldview, and his daughter's advice to simply stay away notwithstanding, he instinctively knew that he'd have to take a more complicated run at a solution. The way he kept his balance in a tumultuous universe was not to run away or delegate a solution, but to supply his own. Even if it amounted to using a sand pail against the incoming tide, it remained a display of effort, and since he was the only audience he wished to persuade, it was sometimes all he needed to maintain equilibrium.

The question here, though, was what to do. Excluding the authorities was well and good, but he wasn't the man to replace them. Nor did he have or want anyone to act on his behalf. It wasn't the police he was avoiding, after all, but the whole concept of any outside help.

His first impulse was to do more research. Given his fondness for studying other people's lives, what more tempting subject — mysterious, horrifying, perhaps even threatening — than Paul Hauser?

Also, Hauser posed an unexpected problem. For the same reasons that he proved interesting, he'd also become a hurdle. Just as Dan could not leave any mess untended — if only tidying it up in the smallest way — so did the specter of Paul Hauser represent a show-stopping example of disorder: Dan couldn't continue as the Tag Man until straightening this out. Last, digging into and exposing Paul Hauser stood to be truly worthy. Dan didn't know the significance of the pictures he'd seen, but he doubted that they were staged. And if he was right, and could identify them and link them to Hauser somehow, would that not be the ultimate justification for Dan's own behavior?

Joe was sitting in his wood shop at home — midweek, midafternoon — an alien situation for him. This room, tacked onto the back of his small house, was filled with the enormous, ancient, cast iron woodworking tools his late father had used to help keep the family farm running, and routinely served as Joe's sanity restorer — where he went ostensibly to make things like bird houses and small boxes, but in fact to repair himself by proxy.

However, that was usually after hours, and he hadn't actually touched a tool, anyhow. He was just sitting there, staring into space, when the phone rang.

Out of habit, he'd brought the cordless

phone in and laid it on the bench beside him — perpetually aware of how dependent so many people had become on having him within reach.

"Hello?"

"Hey," said Gail.

Joe smiled sadly at the phone. "Hey yourself, Governor. So bored already that you're calling old pals?"

She laughed outright into his ear. "Holy shit, Joe. If I'd only known, I never would have run for this job."

He doubted that. Much as he loved this woman — if now only as a best friend — he'd never been blind to her unbridled ambition. As lofty as being governor sounded to most, Gail was most likely already pondering something higher up the food chain — a few months into her first term.

"They running you ragged?"

"What did you used to say?" she asked. "It's like being nibbled to death by ducks?"

He smiled at the phone. "Yeah, according to George Bernard Shaw, I think."

"Well, it's nonstop," she said. "From people telling me I suck as a governor and have a lousy fashion sense, to toadies blowing me kisses, I'm feeling like a human piñata. Christ only knows what half of them are really after. I doubt if *they* do after all the posturing."

"I bet," Joe said politely.

She then asked, "How're you doing? I'm worried about you."

"You got enough on your mind. I'm fine."

"Right. You back at work yet? Must not be if I caught you at home."

"No," he conceded. "Still working out a few kinks. Seeing a shrink."

"Good," she said enthusiastically, as he knew she would. She was younger, more liberal, and more urbane than he. For her, psychologists had the same standing as pharmacists had for his generation — neighborhood experts you consulted almost casually about the most intimate of details.

"How's that working for you?" she asked.

"It takes time," he answered carefully.

"Don't I know it," she said sympathetically, the rape she'd suffered years earlier suddenly rearing up. He was embarrassed that by comparison, his burden seemed a triviality — a broken heart, inevitably to be healed by time.

To give her credit, she sensed this in his silence. "It's a real loss, Joe. Like losing a limb. A part of you died with her. Once again," she added, alluding to his earlier loss of his wife, Ellen.

"Yeah," he acknowledged. "I'm thinking I'll give all that a bit of a rest."

"The job or relationships?" she asked like the lawyer she was.

He hesitated.

"Joe?" she pushed.

"I'm working on that."

"Work on the relationship angle if you want. There's no rush there. But you need to get back to work. I know you, Joe. Does the unit have anything interesting going?"

"This and that," he said vaguely. "I just needed a breather, Gail."

He heard some voices in the background at her end of the phone. "You better go," he counseled. "You don't want to miss out on another tongue-lashing."

She ignored the humorous out. "I do have to go. I'm sorry. I'll call again. But listen to what I'm saying, Joe. I love you. I always will. You need to get busy. Have you seen your mother?" she asked suddenly.

Joe's mother lived in their old house in Thetford, with his brother, who helped care for her, about halfway up the Connecticut River Valley toward Canada.

"Oh, sure. A few times. She sends her love. Solid as a brick."

"No offense, but I wasn't asking after her health. She tells you the truth, and I bet she's saying the same thing I just did."

He could tell she was shifting back into executive role.

"You're not wrong," he told her, about to hang up the phone. "You know your players. Good luck out there."

Ron Klesczewski sat back in his office chair and studied his computer screen. He had spent the last few hours researching Lloyd Jordan — first through local records and files, identifying when he'd moved into the area, how much he paid in property taxes, and how diligent he'd been in meeting his obligations. He'd then expanded his scope to Vermont's criminal and civil databases. From there, it had been on to the famed NCIC — the National Crime Information Center — and last, he'd consulted the mother ship, Google, where, no surprise, he'd found the most ore to mine.

Lloyd Jordan, it appeared, had no criminal record beyond a couple of speeding tickets, but he had generated a lot of chatter among the Boston media and bloggers.

"You look like a bird dog hot on the trail."

Ron twisted in his seat, already smiling at the familiar voice. He rose quickly and shook hands with his old boss and mentor.

"Joe," he said, moving a chair invitingly.

"Take a load off. My God, it's good to see you. How're you doing?"

Joe Gunther settled down and dismissed the question with a wave. "Hanging in there. The family hale and hearty?"

"Terrific. My boy is getting top marks at school and knocking them dead on the ball field, and his mother has just gotten her Realtor's license and is pounding the pavement as we speak."

Joe smiled. "Jeez. Moving right along. I remember when that kid was just a bump in his mom's belly."

Ron laughed, wondering when he'd last seen Joe in these offices, or with enough time on his hands to simply drop by.

"You want some coffee?" he asked, using it as a filler as he considered what to say next. Small talk had never been his strength.

"No," Joe told him. "People are offering me more coffee than I can handle — won't sleep for a week."

Ron started there. "Doing a lot of visiting?"

Joe smiled, but his eyes were watchful. "Like dropping in on people who're trying to work?"

Ron flushed slightly. "Oh, hey. That's not what I meant —"

Joe interrupted him. "Not to worry, Ron.

It doesn't matter. Regardless of what you meant, I am rattling around a bit. I can't get my feet back under me. I'm not used to that."

"Lyn?" Ron asked leadingly.

Joe didn't argue the point. "I miss her. I'm even seeing a shrink." Repeating the words he'd used earlier with Gail didn't make them sound any better. He disliked the idea of psychotherapy, even while he was grateful that it was available. He added, as if to prove something to himself, "It's more than that. Something deeper, I guess. Could be an age thing, or just burnout. I don't know . . ." His voice trailed off.

Ron looked at him, nonplussed, before Joe saved him from further embarrassment by pointing at the screen. "You working on anything interesting?"

Ron gratefully twisted the computer screen toward his guest. "The Tag Man struck again, and I decided to look more carefully at his latest victim. Willy steered me that way. Might have potential."

Joe leaned forward to see better. "Lloyd Jordan? Never heard of him."

"He's a flatlander from Boston," Ron informed him. "Rolling in dough and arrogant as hell. The minute I met him, I thought he was hiding something. He and his wife are recent arrivals, looking like quite the local fund-raisers and do-gooders — or at least she does; I doubt he gives a shit — but it turns out he may have been up to his neck in the mob in the old days."

"No kidding?"

"Nothing he was ever caught at," Ron continued. "But the chatter's convinced he was dirty."

Joe's expression had revived to something more reminiscent of the Joe Gunther Ron knew well.

"The question to ask," Joe suggested, "is how this has anything to do with the Tag Man's visit. Or if it does."

"That's what Willy was thinking," Ron agreed. "What if the Tag Man isn't as harmless as he looks?"

Joe sounded like Tony Brandt. "Meaning he's targeting these houses because their owners won't report what he's really stealing . . . That's interesting."

Ron was heartened by the other man's enthusiasm. "I'd like to hand this one off, to be honest. Could get complicated, if any of this is true, and I don't have the time, the budget, or the manpower, especially now that the detective squad's been reduced to just me and Tyler. This is the thinnest we've been since before your time."

Joe knew of his troubles — the board of selectmen had been cutting back on everyone's funding like never before. Still, he chose to avoid that discussion and stick to the topic at hand. "Beware what you wish for, Ron," he cautioned. "Think of what we just hypothesized: If the Tag Man has that kind of intelligence going for him, and you're right about Jordan being mobbed up, we'll be talking major crimes before you know it. And you haven't even looked into the other victims, right?"

"No," Ron conceded. "Up to now, we just saw them as targets, not as people who had something to hide. This conversation's introduced a whole new ball game."

Joe held up a cautionary finger. "Maybe, maybe not. Don't forget that all we know for sure is that he leaves a Post-it at every scene. The rest is purely hypothetical."

"Speaking of which," Ron added, "the chief thinks blackmail might be an angle, too."

Joe laughed. "That would add an extra layer."

"If true, though," Ron ruminated, "I can't say I'd mind seeing Jordan twist in the wind for a while. For all we know, the Tag Man could be doing us a favor." He considered what Tony Brandt and he had discussed along similar lines. "Maybe he's a masked avenger or something."

"You really don't like Mr. Jordan, do you?"

Ron thought back to his encounter not with Lloyd but his wife, whom he truly didn't envy.

"You're right," he agreed. "I don't. I'd love to bring him down a few pegs. The man's a jerk."

Joe stood up and moved to the door, checking his watch. "Ron," he said on the threshold, Gail's advice still echoing in his head. "I know this may be out of line, but if you need any help — off the books — don't hesitate to ask. I'm officially on medical leave, or vacation, or whatever the hell, but I'm thinking it wouldn't hurt to sink my teeth into something."

Ron rose and shook his hand. "You working for me? You think I'll turn that down? You got a deal."

Joe patted his younger colleague's shoulder. "You may be singing a different tune a week from now, when you find out what a crazy old bastard I've turned into."

Ron opened his mouth to soften the comment, but then decided to pay the man his due. After all, he thought, I have no idea what he's going through — or what it's costing him.

"Let me worry about that, okay?" he said instead. "We'll just start and see where it leads."

CHAPTER SIX

"Was Joe here?"

Willy Kunkle looked up at Sammie's voice. She was standing in the VBI doorway with Emma in her arms. He glanced over at Lester Spinney, who was working at his desk, before answering neutrally, "Nope. Why?"

Lester swiveled in his seat. "Hey, Sam. How's the little monster?"

"Hi, Les. Still not sleeping through the night."

"You gotta give 'em time. It's not like cats and kitty litter."

"Cute," Willy groused. "What about Joe?"

"I saw him going into the detective bureau downstairs, so I figured he'd been here."

"Lester," Willy said gruffly, "why don't you check that out — invite him up for a cup or something?"

Lester's mouth fell half open before he grasped the subtext and rose quickly to his feet. "Sure. Be back in a few."

He slipped by Sam, giving Emma's thin blond hair a quick stroke as he passed. "Hi there, sweetie."

Willy waited for his footsteps to fade before he, too, got up and approached Sam. He kissed his child murmuring, "How're you doing, little daughter?"

Sammie smiled while shaking her head. "You couldn't do that with Lester in the room?"

Willy was sniffing Emma's hair as if it was a cure for melancholy, which it undoubtedly was. "Don't give me crap," he barely whispered. "I got an image."

"Which applies to your street-bum friends," she countered.

Willy straightened and tousled her hair, which she couldn't protect with her arms full. "Half of them are your snitches, too," he reminded her. "What're you doin' here? Getting restless?"

"A little," she admitted candidly. "I'm not bucking to speed things up, but I am getting curious about how things'll work out when I come back to work."

He looked at her carefully. "What's that mean?"

She shrugged and Emma stirred. "I don't know. I used to pull twenty-four-hour shifts when the shit hit the fan. Now I've got something bigger to think about."

She had thought he would react as he'd trained everyone to expect. Instead, he made a dismissive face and said, "We'll figure that out. You're not alone, you know?"

A slow smile creased her face as he retreated to his desk in the office's windowless corner. "I do know, Willy. Thanks."

They heard footsteps coming down the hallway, announcing Lester's return, complete with company. When he entered, however, it wasn't Joe but Ron who stopped in the doorway, as Lester continued in and immediately asked Sam if he could hold the baby. She handed Emma over willingly. Lester had two of his own, older teenagers by now, and made no apologies for considering himself a dad first and foremost. Several years ago, he had even risked jail time when his son had gotten into a legal bind. Typically, Joe had helped him get out of it.

Lester crossed to his office chair and gently sat down, cradling Emma in his lap. His focus on her excluded everyone else, allowing Sam to give Ron a hug and a kiss on the cheek.

"Hey, stranger. You don't write, you don't call . . ."

"Thank God," Willy cracked.

Ron laughed. "It's not like you guys don't walk by my office every day, coming and going."

"Good point," Sam conceded.

"It's called moving on, Ron," Willy commented. "We spent enough years in that hole."

Ron didn't take offense, taking in the VBI's spartan furnishings. "Right. You guys really moved up."

It was true that the VBI, for all its elitist cachet, had never had the funding to match the image. A typically political animal, created by a past governor, reluctantly supported by successive legislatures, and staffed by often quirky and self-motivated defectors from a dozen other agencies, the Bureau had become the law enforcement community's bastard brother — inside the fold, but awkwardly isolated.

"Tell them what you told me," Lester said, not looking up because he was touching Emma's forehead with his nose.

"You're pregnant," Willy prompted.

They all ignored him.

"Joe's working for me, unofficially," Ron said.

Even Kunkle was impressed. "You're kidding me. On what?"

"The Tag Man case," Ron explained. "He walked in a while ago — I thought just to be sociable. He's kind of at loose ends. On his way out, he volunteered to pitch in."

There was a moment's silence, during which Willy said under his breath, "The old man's really losing it."

"He is not," Sammie reacted, flushing slightly.

This time, Lester did look up. "I think it's the reverse — he wants to get his feet wet again."

No one responded, each momentarily lost in his or her thoughts about what the "boss" might be up to — and how he'd fare in the process.

Leo Metelica favored a .45 caliber model 1911 semiautomatic. It looked like the one seen in all the World War II movies — big, heavy, black, and ominous — but he'd actually made it himself — in a fashion — assembling it from the best components available, custom fitting them in his kitchen-based workshop. It was beautiful to handle, a perfect fit to his hand with its checkered walnut grips, and a hair trigger and night sights that had set him back a chunk of change.

All to good effect, though. Merely poking

the thing into a man's face was usually enough to wrap up whatever argument Leo was making.

He practiced with it endlessly, at the range and in the woods, training himself in a variety of environments, and he stripped it, cleaned it, and reassembled it incessantly. It was the primary tool of his trade, of course, but in moments of self-contemplation, Leo saw himself physically as a part of the gun, and the gun as a reflection of him.

This was a good thing in his eyes. The gun, or the conviction behind it, was what kept Leo employed, and it was the gun that got people to act — keep their mouths shut, pay what they owed, or, on rare occasions, to stop breathing. Leo hadn't actually killed too many people — real life wasn't like fiction, after all, where Sylvester Stallone or Bruce Willis could kill twenty people before strolling away. But he'd used this same gun on three men so far, and it had worked to perfection every time. Quietly, too, because of the silencer he'd also built in his basement. Leo was a handy man, well trained by the navy and by working for his uncle as a kid in a welding shop. Not a great thinker, perhaps — something he'd been told time and again by his betters — but good with tools, and good at getting back at those betters when they least expected it.

He also knew about ballistics and made sure of two things while on the job: He always used frangible ammunition, to ensure that the bullet fragments were many and untraceable, and he always went for a contact head shot, to guarantee the effectiveness of his trademark single lethal shot. He was a decent marksman, but why bother aiming when such bravado was unnecessary?

He slipped the pistol into its holster, stubbed out his cigarette, killed the motel room lights, and opened his curtains to reveal the parking lot beyond.

Brattleboro. Totally hick town. Nothing to do, nothing to see. No strip joints, no X-rated-movie houses, no hookers as far as he could find. Even the bars sucked — filled with too much music, too much designer beer, and too many people all laughing and pretending to have a good time. Leo liked his bars quiet, dark, and cheap — designed for serious drinkers.

He opened the door and stepped into the balmy night air. At least the weather was holding. He walked to the end of the balcony, took the metal staircase down into the parking lot, and crossed over to the anonymous rental car he'd driven up from Massachusetts. Leo didn't own a car. He didn't see the point. Everything he needed was either included in the contract or available over the Internet when he wasn't working. As for the rest, he walked or took a bus. He lived in the kind of neighborhood where his particular appetites could be met within a four-block radius.

He pulled into the Putney Road, as clotted with fast food joints and cheap motels as any commercial strip anywhere, and headed south, back into downtown. Brattleboro had three interstate exits, which had surprised him, given its size. The first had offered one motel and limited amenities; the second, little to nothing except a major feeder road heading east and west; and the third had landed him right at the top of the miracle mile he was now navigating. Perfect for him — a nondescript environment with a quick on-ramp heading out of town.

But for the moment, that escape route could keep. Now, he wanted inside the belly of the beast. That's where the target worked, and where he'd seen him earlier.

He crossed a bridge over the confluence of the Connecticut and West rivers, exchanging the Putney Road's commercial stretch for a long, curving, tree-lined avenue accented by stately Victorian mansions. Not as fancy as some he'd seen in Massachusetts, but holding their own in the useless-hard-to-heat-antiques category.

They were also a good foretaste to the red-brick downtown next in line. He hated towns like this — throwbacks to a time of sweatshops and union busting and market manipulation. He understood New England's vanity about its antiquity and fusty customs and highborn ways. And despised it all. The people he came from had been under the heels of those traditions for more than two hundred years, as servants, slaves, and immigrant factory workers. He was delighted to be one of the few who could speak now and then of his independence with a well-placed bullet.

Fuck 'em all, was his motto.

Not that he was transposing any of that social outrage onto his target. In fact, that poor slob just looked like a working stiff to Leo.

But he still didn't care. The money was good, the target looked easy, and anyone who'd earned a visit from Leo Metelica clearly hadn't been minding his manners, no matter how working-class he might seem.

Metelica was a practical socialist.

He parked his car in the public garage on Elliot Street, near the entrance and aimed toward the exit, as he did every time similar circumstances presented themselves. Also from habit, he took note of the surveillance cameras to make sure none of them had a clear shot of his face as he headed for the street.

It was late. Earlier, he had eaten at the restaurant where Dan Kravitz worked, both to confirm that he had the right target and to study the way the man moved. It didn't amount to research per se, since it didn't truly inform Metelica of Kravitz's habits or preferences, but he saw himself as a cheetah assessing a gazelle from a safe distance — it was a form of zeroing in, and, for Metelica's basic style of operation, it was enough.

His plan was equally unsophisticated. He was going to wait for Kravitz to lock up, as he'd been informed he did every night, follow him to a suitably dark and isolated spot, and kill him.

Or not.

Metelica was no fool. He knew that sometimes things didn't work out according to plan. And if he didn't get an opportunity tonight, then he'd use the time to learn more about Dan's routine and kill him tomorrow night.

He walked down the sidewalk to where he'd noticed a dark alleyway opposite the restaurant, and vanished from the glare of a distant streetlamp to see what developed. He saw the purpose of his visit across from him, working a mop up and down the length of the empty dining room, where the chairs had already been upended and parked atop the tables.

To Metelica's right and left, as far as he could see along the street, there was not a movement.

Twenty minutes later, Kravitz put the finishing touches on his evening's work, killed all but the night-light above the bar, and vanished from view, Metelica presumed to maybe grab a jacket or something else from a closet.

Instead, after a minute, the light on the second floor, directly above the restaurant, came to life, revealing what appeared to be an apartment.

"What the hell?" Leo said quietly.

He stayed where he was, hoping to see something appear in one of the windows. He was soon rewarded with Dan's profile passing by.

"Jesus Christ," he told himself. "The motherfucker lives there."

Metelica faded a step back into the gloom, rethinking his plan. This was something he'd never considered. How the hell was he supposed to ambush a man behind the locked door of a building he never left?

As if to answer that very question, the second-floor light just as abruptly turned off.

His heart quickening, Metelica waited hopefully. A dark shadow appeared from the rear of the restaurant, followed by Dan's outline at the entrance as he opened the door and stepped into the street.

"Gotcha, you son of a bitch," Leo murmured.

In fact, Dan Kravitz had caught sight of his unknown nemesis immediately upon closing the restaurant door.

Once more, Dan's fanatical sensitivity to his surrounding world's makeup — a skill that had failed him outside Gloria Wrinn's house, if for good reason — served now to reveal the just-barely-discernible shape of a man across the street.

Suspicious, he swung right, away from well-lighted Main Street, and headed west down Elliot, toward the gloom of an increasingly residential neighborhood.

But he didn't keep to that course. Instead, as much to torture his tail as to discover his identity, he suddenly crossed the street by the parking garage Metelica had used and took the metal staircase connecting Elliot

Street to Flat Street some thirty feet below. It was an exposed and noisy route, and he knew it would force his pursuer to wait for him to reach the bottom before engaging the top step, for fear of attracting too much attention.

He was right. Only dimly, as he left the ground floor of the garage to cross Flat Street, did he hear the stealthy sounds of someone discreetly giving chase.

Flat Street was aptly named. Running west to east alongside the rock-strewn Whetstone Brook, it was one of the few level pieces of Brattleboro's hilly terrain.

It was toward the Whetstone that Dan now proceeded, and the newly built pedestrian bridge leading to the Brattleboro Food Co-op's parking lot on the other side. Here, he intended to confront his fear and either lend it credibility or prove it to be a figment of his highly tuned paranoia.

As with so many of the town's nooks and crannies, this area was well known to him, along with its current conditions — up to the Dumpster having been placed at an odd angle near the bridge's entrance, and the nearest streetlamp bulb having died the night before. He was counting on his follower's losing sight of him in the shadows, and not seeing him duck behind the large metal bin instead of crossing the bridge.

Dan cautiously peered out to see the man emerge from the garage into the light hanging over the facility's front ramp.

Dan's fears instantly yielded to reality. This man he recognized. He remembered seeing him at the restaurant, sitting near the door, eating an appetizer only and — most important — paying close attention to what Dan was doing.

He hadn't liked it then, so seeing him again struck him with dread. That was the burden for paranoids — there was no joy in being proven right.

Dan quickly looked around, his night vision having kicked in. He found a short piece of two-by-four lumber shoved under the Dumpster and worked it loose to have it ready, all the while listening for his stalker's approaching footsteps over the rush and tumble of the nearby water.

He crouched to lower his profile as the quiet scrape of a shoe indicated the man's proximity, and then slipped in behind him, a mere two feet from his back.

"Don't move. Don't turn around." Dan poked him in the back with the two-by-four.

Metelica froze in place, his hands slightly extended to his sides. Christ, he thought. How the hell did that happen?

"Why're you following me?" Dan asked.

"I don't know who the fuck you are," Leo tried bluffing.

"You were watching me at the restaurant."

Leo scowled. There must have been fifty people in the place. It was jammed.

"I was having a meal, like everybody else. That's what restaurants are for." He began wondering how to make his move. The implication was that Kravitz had a gun on him, or at least a knife.

"You were having the hummus appetizer, and you didn't finish it once you were sure who I was," Dan countered.

"You know what I was *eating?*" Leo blurted, too astonished to be coy.

"I also saw you in the alley a few minutes ago, waiting."

Metelica shook his head slightly. No one had told him this pecker had X-ray vision. What the hell was going on? He hadn't asked why Kravitz was wanted dead. Now he was beginning to understand.

"The people who hired me want to talk with you," he tried, back to calculating his next move. Generally, if a man has a gun, he doesn't care if his target sees him, so that meant a knife — maybe.

"They knew how to get you onto me," Dan said. "That means they know how to use a phone."

"It's not that kind of conversation," Leo went on, suddenly aware that what little he did know of Kravitz's background might be useful. "It involves your daughter."

That was a mistake. Dan instantly hit him with the two-by-four, hard enough to make him stumble onto the bridge.

"You slimy bastard," Dan yelled at him, following the blow with a kick. "You don't go there."

Instincts overriding strategy, Leo used his forward momentum to stagger ahead a couple of feet, pull his large .45 from its holster under his jacket, and twist around to bring Kravitz down any way he could.

But it wasn't to be. Dan moved like a tomcat and sidestepped out of Leo's vision in a blur. The next thing Leo felt was an explosive pain in his right wrist as Dan's club sent the large pistol clattering to the wooden decking. In almost the same move, Dan then swung the two-by-four in a full circle and used it as a battering ram to punch the hit man once, hard, in midchest, sending him reeling backward.

That was the penultimate sensation of Leo Metelica's life. Immediately after, he felt the bridge railing strike the small of his

back, followed by a split second's weightlessness, wrapped in the sound of rushing water.

CHAPTER SEVEN

"That's it? A jumper?"

Ron Klesczewski turned to see Willy Kunkle step onto the bridge and glance at the dead man below, whose broken body was draped face-up over a large boulder, his legs weaving gently back and forth as the water tried to tug him the rest of the way to the Connecticut River downstream.

"Would I bother you for that?" Ron said with a smile.

"Somebody pushed him?" Willy approached until he was standing beside his old colleague, making them both look like spectators admiring a scenic landscape.

It was early morning. The bridge had been cordoned off with yellow crime scene tape. Three uniformed cops were standing around, working on cups of coffee since there was nothing to do with the two passersby who had stopped to watch. The medical examiner had yet to arrive, and the state's attorney had barely been called.

Whoever this was — pasty pale and ghastly — had simply become the reason for a carefully orchestrated process.

"Take a good look," Ron urged. "You won't even have to get wet."

Willy studied the set piece more carefully, squinting slightly to compensate for the twenty-foot distance.

"Far out," he finally said.

Ron glanced at him. "You get to the empty holster?"

"You find a gun?" Willy asked in response.

"Nope. We might. The dive-team guys are getting ready over there." He gestured vaguely toward the co-op parking lot, half of which was blocked by a nearby building. "But it could be in somebody's pocket right now."

Willy pointed without removing his elbow from the railing. "You can see where he crushed the back of his head. See the deformity?"

Ron merely nodded.

"I guess you have a canvass going," Willy suggested.

"Yup." Ron remained gazing at the man below and added, "We're also looking for whatever regulars might have been around here last night — delivery people, late-night workers, and the rest."

Willy straightened with a grunt. "Let's just go down there and yank him out. We don't need any dive team. This is stupid."

Ron had expected no less, but was saved by the appearance of a group from the parking lot. "There they are, *and* the ME." He headed toward them and the embankment leading to the water's edge. "No need to piss off several agencies simultaneously, after all."

"Yeah," Willy growled. "What a thrill."

The procedure was sadly familiar. A member of the dive team waded out into midstream, suited up for safety's sake — minus the flippers and tank — and tethered to the shore by two of his colleagues. Willy predictably snorted with disdain, but Ron was more appreciative of the history behind many of the procedures they increasingly followed. People had been injured or killed because situations just like this one hadn't appeared life-threatening.

The diver never got deeper than his knees. The water was fast but shallow, and no less dangerous for that. He moved slowly, taking photographs with his waterproof camera, then carefully looped a rope around the body and maneuvered it to where his backup team could tow it to shore.

There, the assistant medical examiner took over, examining his subject from head to toe, lifting and opening its clothes without actually removing them. By then Willy had suffered enough by his standards, and all but shoved the poor man aside as he "assisted," in his words, in completing the survey.

Ron observed and took note. Due to the case's appearing to be a homicide, it was going to end up as Willy's anyhow. In the same vein, the medical examiner didn't mind, either, knowing that by protocol, the body would soon head north for autopsy. Plus, his boss in Burlington was okay with local cops going through a decedent's pockets for evidence. It just meant less paperwork for him down the line.

As a result, Ron bided his time before getting close enough to study the body's water-bleached face.

"Head trauma, like we thought?" he asked Willy.

The latter stepped back, expertly peeling off his one latex glove by pinning it under his useless left arm and exerting a single smooth gesture.

"Yeah — totally smashed up. Probably from the fall. Indicates he went backward, though, so he didn't jump. Plus, I found an indentation smack in the middle of his chest — a rectangular bruise, as if something hit him square in the sternum."

He squatted again and almost touched the man's right wrist. "And there's this."

Ron leaned forward. The hand appeared out of alignment somehow.

"Fractured," Willy explained. "Right before he died, so no bruising, really, no swelling. That probably explains the missing gun. He was holding it."

Willy pointed to a square of canvas that he'd laid out on the riverbank. On it were the few items he'd removed from the body.

"The missing gun's a .45, by the way. That's the ammo he was carrying."

Ron's eye widened. "That's quite the cannon."

"There's more," Willy continued. "They're frangible rounds, like what air marshals use. No penetrating power at all. And I found an extra barrel." He held up a short black cylinder, already wrapped in an evidence bag. "Which is even weirder."

Ron looked at him, expecting more. Weapons were not an interest of his. He carried a gun as part of the job, and had even used it to shoot someone, which was, thankfully, unusual for most Vermont cops, but he paid the whole topic little attention. Willy's past as a sniper made him an almost obligatory firearms aficionado, however.

Of course, he was also a pain in the ass, and so didn't allow Ron's silence to serve as a prompt for the next obvious question. Ron sighed and patiently asked, "Why's that, Willy?"

Kunkle gave him a pitying look. "Come on, Ron — ace detective like you? The only reasons you swap out barrels is either you target shoot on an Olympic level, or you don't want anyone matching bullets to your gun — assuming you also police your brass after shooting so they can't match that, either."

"Okay," Ron said to keep him moving, already aware of all this.

"But if you're using frangible ammo, it fragments," Willy pointed out. "There *is* nothing to put under the microscope. Why bother switching barrels, too?"

Ron shrugged, expecting that Willy was heading somewhere. "Belts and suspenders?" he posited. "The guy was super-cautious?"

But Willy had nowhere to go, and returned to gazing at the dead man. "Could be," he admitted. "Damned if I know. First time I ever ran into it."

"Might still come in handy," Ron observed. "Maybe NCIC has a signature listing that includes both ammo and barrel."

"Yeah," Willy conceded. "Good thought."

Ron was caught by surprise. From Willy, such a comment was as bracing as a slap on the back from anyone else.

"What else you find?" he asked.

He should have known better. Willy glared at him. "A birth certificate, a full confession, and a note from his mother. What did you think? I was holding back?"

But Ron remained stolid, pointing to the canvas square. "There's more there. A scrap of paper."

Willy acted as if he hadn't spoken. "Yeah," he said thoughtfully, reaching out and pushing the exposed piece around with his pen. "Might be something." It hadn't been bagged like the barrel, being soaked through and open to disintegration. It would have to be handled more gingerly later.

Ron joined him by the body's side. "Looks like a note."

"Give the man a raise," Willy muttered, manipulating it until it opened just enough. A single word appeared: *Bariloche.*

"Huh," Ron said. "Might be what they call a clue."

"Better," Willy suggested, straightening. "We have a gunman with no gun and specialized ammo, an extra barrel and no ID, and the name of an unusually named restaurant every local's heard about but any outsider would have to write down to remember. If this dude's not an out-of-town hit man, our next lunch together is on me."

Ron nodded in agreement, reflecting that in all the years they'd known each other, they'd never once shared a meal.

Several locks were noisily thrown back before the front door eased open two inches to reveal a slackened chain and the somber face of a clearly suspicious woman.

"Badges can be bought in a catalog. I've heard about it," she said.

Joe was still holding his credentials out, as he had been moments earlier before the door's peephole.

"I understand, Mrs. Hodgkins, and I don't argue with your being cautious. You've been through a lot lately."

"What's that mean?"

He tilted his head back to take in the front of her enormous home. "You were broken into by the Tag Man. He left his calling card. That had to have been frightening."

Frightening?" she exclaimed, yanking the door wider and hitting the chain's limit with a jar. The door bounced free of her hand

and almost shut again.

"Stupid thing," she growled, working the chain free and finally opening the door fully.

"Are you sure?" Joe asked. "I'm happy to wait if you want to call my office and have somebody describe me or something."

She rubbed her forehead in frustration, trying to smile and failing. "No. I mean, I know you're all right — look at you, after all."

Joe smiled faintly.

"I'm sorry," she then said, flushing. "That didn't come out right."

"Sounded right to me."

"Shit." She finally gave up, stepping back to let him in. "Let's move on, okay? Forget I said anything. What is it you want?"

The question was faintly old-fashioned, as was the woman, Joe thought, although in an appreciative way. Merry Hodgkins, he'd learned from his research, was long divorced, a successful businesswoman, and by her own admission pretty paranoid even before the Tag Man had made her a target. The Brattleboro detective he'd consulted who'd followed up on that break-in had described Hodgkins as remarkably straightforward with both her strengths and weaknesses.

Joe stepped inside. She glanced around

126

him as if to check that he hadn't brought along a SWAT team or more thieves, then closed and rebolted the door.

She smiled apologetically at that point. "Sorry," she said. "I was crazy enough before that happened, but he really did it to me. Did you catch him? Is that why you're here?"

"I wish I could say that," he told her. "But we're still looking."

She frowned. "Then what? I don't have anything new to tell you. I changed all the locks, upgraded the alarm, I even switched to another security firm, just to rule out that it had been an inside job."

Joe was nodding. "I know. I do apologize. I've just come onto the case, to help out with a new set of eyes, if you know what I mean. I was hoping I could ask you a couple of questions."

That caught her interest. "Okay," she said slowly. She gestured through a nearby doorway, offering, "Would you like to sit down? Maybe have a refreshment of some sort?"

He passed into a large living room, answering, "I'll pass, thanks, but feel free if you want something yourself."

They were located off Western Avenue, also called Route 9, the main road connecting Brattleboro to points west. Merry's was one of several old mansions that used to house some of the industrial magnates ruling the town a hundred years earlier. It was brick with a slate roof, meticulously tended, and seemed a ridiculous home for a woman alone.

Joe perched on the edge of one of the sofas facing an antique coffee table, and waited for Merry to settle across from him.

"What would you like to know?" she asked.

"What I understand," Joe began, "is that nothing was actually stolen. Is that right?"

"He ate some food I had."

Joe checked his notes from a pad he'd extracted from his pocket. "Pâté? And a jar of caviar?"

"And crackers." She smiled ruefully. "He went for the good stuff — I'll give him that much."

"And he left the remains out, so you'd see what he'd done?"

"Yes." She knitted her eyebrows. "Your people took photographs of all that."

"I know. I saw them," he told her. "What I'm after is more what made him tick."

To her credit, she thought about that carefully before answering, "You want to know why the caviar, instead of attacking me or stealing my TV."

"Exactly. And I'm asking not because I think you knew him, although that's possible, but because I gather you traced his movements after you discovered he'd been in the house."

She studied him for a moment before responding like the executive she'd once been. "And since I'm a recognized security nut and a neat freak to boot, I might have noticed things other people wouldn't?"

Joe didn't argue with her self-assessment. "Call it wishful thinking," he conceded. "I'm looking for a psychological portrait based on his actions. If it's any comfort, you're not the only one I've approached. I'm trying to visit everybody he hit."

She sat back and crossed her legs. "It's not a comfort, but I do understand. What have the others said?"

"If it's okay, I'd like not to say up front."

Onboard with that, she nodded before staring at the carpet in concentration for a moment.

"He didn't violate my private things," she said. "And he didn't touch me that I know of, or do anything unseemly."

"Okay," Joe encouraged her.

"He did go through my papers, in my office," she continued. "I thought that was odd, and pretty alarming. In my business life, it wasn't belongings you worried about so much as confidential information. So that had me going. I alerted my business manager to be extra watchful, and I changed all my accounts. It was a real pain, actually, and cost me a bundle. Passwords, account numbers, all forms of identity. I had everything checked or altered."

"And had he done any damage?" Joe asked.

She shook her head. "No. That was the funny part. Not a dime was stolen, not a figure changed or altered."

She suddenly stared at him with a smile of admiration. "I'll be darned."

"What?"

"I hadn't thought of it until now. Never crossed my mind. Someone breaks into your house, you think of your personal safety, maybe your jewels, secrets, like I said . . . not that the guy might be after just old-fashioned data."

"He stole data?"

She shook her head. "I never would have . . . Do you know what I did? When I was in business?"

"A stockbroker?" Joe answered hesitantly.

"An investment analyst," she answered. "Close enough. It's all a little voodoo, to be honest. But you're right. I played the market, both with my money and other people's." She waved her hand around to indicate their surroundings. "And I did well. I had a knack for it. Between you and me, I made more money than I know what to do with. But it became like a game, and after I officially retired, I stayed at it with just my own funds, for fun. That's what he accessed."

Joe scowled. "What?"

"I could tell from the time stamps on my computer," she explained. "Up to now, I thought I'd done something I couldn't remember doing. Which isn't like me at all. Now, I'm all but positive that your Tag Man got into my personal investments portfolio and basically stole my hottest prospects. He looked over my shoulder, like someone cheating in school. And if he followed it up by buying according to my strategy, then he made some decent money, depending on how much he invested, because most of those prospects panned out handsomely."

Joe stared at her. "Is there any way we could follow up on that? Find out who he is by tracking his purchases?"

By now, she was actually laughing. "No. That's the beauty of it. It's not like it's insider trading. He copied off the smartest kid in class — assuming he bought anything afterward. But why wouldn't he? What would be the point of breaking in otherwise? But no, to answer your question. He could have bought any number of stocks through any number of brokers and gone totally unnoticed. I mean, a thousand years ago, the Hunt brothers from Texas tried to corner the silver market by buying everything in sight, and they got caught because they were stupid and obvious. But if we're talking about somebody so desperate and broke that he has to do this, then he's not a millionaire — he's an incredibly smart, lazy guy trying to make a buck."

She leaned forward, her pleasure at this discovery written across her face. "There's your portrait. This is a smart man you're after, but an unconventional one, and a risk taker. He doesn't opt to do the homework before investing, like the rest of us. He watches for the people who consistently come out on top, and then he picks their brains without asking permission. I'm no shrink, but that's got to narrow your field of suspects considerably."

Joe couldn't argue the point. Unfortunately, he had no list of suspects to consult. This kind of crime was a first for him.

He rose, closed his note pad, and slipped

it back into his pocket. "Thank you, Mrs. Hodgkins. This has been a huge help. Exactly what I was hoping for."

She escorted him back to the front door, saying, "Please, call me Merry, and the appreciation is all mine. You've helped me put a face on this man, or at least some sort of personality. He's less anonymous to me now. More familiar. I can't say that I know him — it's not that — but I recognize the type."

She opened the door and shook his hand. "So I thank you. I hate the idea that someone came in here while I was asleep, and I'm still going a little crazy over the whole security thing, but maybe this'll help with the nightmares. I really appreciate your coming by."

Joe said his final farewells and took his leave, walking across the lawn to his car. He was happy that she'd seen this as an opportunity to feel better, but his life experiences had taught him to view things less optimistically.

He got into the car and put the key into the ignition. But he didn't start up the engine quite yet, choosing to gaze thoughtfully at the large house for a moment longer.

His mind returned to what Ron Klesczewski had told him about the break-in at the

Jordans', with its hints of possible mob involvement and of Lloyd Jordan's being a whole lot cagier than the woman Joe had just left.

He seriously doubted that the Tag Man had restrained himself to merely peeking at Jordan's investment portfolio. But, if not just that, what else?

CHAPTER EIGHT

Dan sat very still in the womb of his secret room, as cut off from the rest of the world as possible, staring at the .45 pistol that lay menacingly in the center of his tidy desk. Thoughts of the snake in Eden crossed his mind.

Two things might have attracted the owner of this gun: Dan had removed some of Lloyd Jordan's confidential papers, and at Gloria Wrinn's he had uncovered the gruesome trove of a man whose activities had been giving him nightmares ever since.

The papers he understood, at least as far as he'd bothered to pursue the matter. The love letter spoke for itself and hadn't been all that revealing; the financial records, of which he'd grabbed but a sampling, had clearly shown transactions going to and fro, but had also been coded, to preserve the names or entities involved. They possibly reflected something illegal, being kept either for blackmail or life insurance, but since he'd left the bulk of them in place, and had stolen what he had as an irritant only, it seemed unlikely that his life would be a reasonable price to pay for their removal. Also, the man with the gun hadn't mentioned them.

He had said that the conversation desired by his clients involved Sally.

Which brought Dan to thinking about Paul Hauser.

He hadn't looked at all of Hauser's albums. Just most of one and single pages of two others. Enough to reveal that they involved the homicidal deaths of women either Sally's age or not much older.

There had been unsolved deaths in upper New England over the years. Now and then, a woman might be found dead in her home, or buried in the woods, or dumped in an urban alleyway, with her killer never caught.

But they were rare, and none that Dan could recall had been as overtly violent as what he'd witnessed in those photographs. Not that he would have known, necessarily. He was not a tabloid fancier, and the local media tended not to go in for gory details. Generally, there was a propriety to rural newspapers and TV news shows that he'd come to appreciate. Politicians cheating on spouses were usually left alone, civic leaders caught in embarrassing legal situations got by with a police-blotter reference. The double-spread coverage of killings so common to big cities was treated up here with a virtual primness, with photographs of the house involved, perhaps, or a high school graduation snap of the victim.

There had been the infamous Connecticut Valley Killer, of years ago. Dan had heard the police theorize that in fact, those murders — six in all — had possibly been the work of two unrelated perpetrators, both of them probably long dead or on death row elsewhere for different crimes. That string of deaths had gripped the area and caused widespread alarm, but they had also stopped in the late 1980s, had presumably not been resumed, and had involved women of a broader age range than what Dan had seen in those pictures.

He kept staring at the gun, as if it might suddenly make a move.

Of course, a killer could change his approach, learn to be more circumspect and not attract so much attention. People across the country simply wandered away nowadays, by the dozens every week, escaping the tentacles of an unhappy life. A few of them — carefully selected — could be culled from the herd and killed, with no one the wiser.

Was that what was going on with Hauser? Had he developed a sense of caution? And had any of this even taken place in New England?

Dan tapped his chin doubtfully. He didn't know, and — most surprising — his memory of what he'd seen in Hauser's apartment had been blurred by his horror.

The same horror and anger as had virtually blacked him out when the gun's owner had mentioned Sally, and made him react like a demented robot.

He closed his eyes for a moment, thinking back. The woman on the picnic table had been young, slim, a brunette, if he recalled correctly.

But he couldn't bring back her face.

Had there been a bloody murder that had taken place in such an area? A picnic table near some woods? He didn't know. The world was awful enough for Dan Kravitz without his recreationally collecting details of lurid killings.

He kept his eyes shut, trying to put the pictures in context, replaying in his mind how he'd noticed the slight imperfection in the flooring, and thus had discovered the cache. How he'd opened the suitcase, and how the albums had rested under a collection of ghoulish souvenirs.

His eyes opened suddenly and he straightened in his chair.

He hadn't completely closed the suitcase. He'd left one of its catches unhooked.

He'd left a trace of his visit to Gloria Wrinn's house after all.

And — he now knew for certain — that error was the connection between the contents of that suitcase and the gun lying before him.

He'd have to go back.

Abijah Reed raised his hand in the back of the somber restaurant so that Joe could pick him out.

"There he is," Joe told the maître d', who was hovering by his side, suspicious of his intentions.

Joe wove through the other diners toward the distant booth. He was in Massachusetts, in the Concord of Emerson and Thoreau — now an upscale combination of tourist attraction and snooty Boston suburb — to meet a man deeply versed in the world of Bostonian finance, both aboveboard and less so.

Abijah Reed had come to Joe's attention twenty years earlier, through a contact whom Joe had befriended at the FBI Academy in Quantico, Virginia, in a prime example of one of the academy's bragging points, which was that it was a great place to network.

Reed had served the FBI as both advisor and informant on occasion and had been introduced to Joe when the latter had needed financial information on a case with ties linking Brattleboro and Boston.

That was all mundane enough, although the two had in fact kept in touch as much out of friendship as from professional need. What had been less clear at the start was the nature of the man himself, whose birth name, for example, turned out not to be Abijah Reed.

He rose as Joe reached the table and extended a hand in greeting.

"What a treat," he said, waving Joe into a chair and sitting back down. "We haven't talked in years, and now, here we are, face-to-face. Absolutely wonderful. Much better than a phone call. I hope you didn't mind the long drive. I tried to accommodate you by suggesting this place. It is a little closer to Vermont than downtown Boston. But I know it's still quite a trek. I'm sorry that I just have too much going on right now to leave my desk for more than a few hours."

Joe was already shaking his head dismissively. "It was nice to get out of town, to be honest, and the drive was beautiful. Please don't apologize. Besides, it's worth it to see you again."

They continued this way for a few minutes more, catching up and exchanging memories of mutual acquaintances and past adventures. Reed had entered the world as Charles Clutterbuck, which Joe considered reason enough for a name change. In fact, it had played little role in the man's story. Charles had experienced an early life as Dickensian as his moniker, being the child of two alcoholic con artists, and while his recounting of those early years was entertaining and lighthearted, Joe knew enough to realize what a toll it must have taken.

Eventually, and probably inevitably, it had all ended poorly, with both parents fading from sight in a haze of legalities, alcoholic stupor, and, finally, death. Charles, at last on his own, had at various times embraced spiritualism, communism, aestheticism, and several other distractions before finally settling on old-fashioned capitalism. The name Abijah came both from the Bible and in honor of some long-dead black freeman who had settled in New England; Reed came from Jack Reed, the complicated, rabble-rousing pro-Communist journalist who wrote *Ten Days That Shook the World.* Looking at the erstwhile Charles Clutterbuck now — dressed like a gentleman of means, complete with a fondness for cigars and expensive restaurants — it was impossible to guess at such a past. Only the name gave a hint of it.

"So," he said at last, after the waiter had drifted off with their orders. "You told me that the man of the hour is Lloyd Jordan. Why him?"

"Research, mostly," Joe admitted. "If anything, he's the latest victim in a rash of B and Es. But there was something about his attitude that got the lead investigator's brain ticking."

Abijah's eyes widened slightly as he finished a sip of his wine. "You're not the lead, after all these years?"

Joe allowed for a half smile. "I've been taking some time off. I'm just lending a hand."

Reed slowly placed his wineglass on the tablecloth, his thoughtfulness reflecting his reputation for scrutiny and care.

"I heard you suffered a loss recently, Joe. I wanted to express my sorrow about that."

Joe nodded. "Yeah. She was a good friend."

"The shooting made headlines, even down here, maybe because we wish people would take more potshots at our own politicians. At the time, I didn't know of your ties to both women involved."

Joe didn't respond. He'd never given it much consideration, but in fact, the attempted assassination of a gubernatorial candidate, and the death of someone in her stead, had of course made national news. He'd been so numb at the time, he'd missed the attending frenzy that had escorted Gail Zigman into the governor's office — although by now, the event had been relegated to history. Only Joe, Lyn's mourning family, including her daughter, Coryn, and the then-incumbent Republican governor, James Reynolds — whose take was that the bullet had killed his career — were left behind with their memories.

Abijah Reed reached out and barely touched the back of Joe's hand. "How are you holding up?"

Joe considered belittling that with the usual polite dismissal and thanks. A person of his high profile in Vermont got such sympathies with painful frequency. But whether it was because Reed's kindly demeanor reminded him slightly of Eberhard Dziobek or simply because they saw each other so rarely, he ventured a little further down a path he generally avoided.

"I was going to quit," he told him. "I've put in the years, and for a backwater cop, I attract a lot of trouble."

Reed was chuckling. "So I understand."

Joe nodded. "Exactly. I thought it might be time to hang it up. I mean, despite the time I give this job, I do have a life."

Abijah sat back and crossed his legs. He glanced out at the quiet groupings across the restaurant, each cluster lost in its own conversation.

"And yet," he finally commented, "here we are."

Joe frowned. The same thought had crossed his mind. Once again, something he'd been thinking of broaching with Dziobek.

"Joe," Abijah said softly. "Perhaps you might consider that you do have a life, and that this is it. There are worse things than helping people out of their misery."

Joe rested his chin on his fist and sighed.

"We all have our regrets," Reed told him. "The people we let go, the places we didn't visit, the jobs we turned down. The richest man in the world wakes up now and then and wonders why he bothers. I know. I'm surrounded by some of the most privileged people this country has to offer, and all they do is piss and moan about their needs and disappointments."

Joe was smiling in turn by now. "Thanks, I think."

Reed held up his hand. "I know, I know. It sucks to realize that your problems are no worse than a headache and the common cold. What I'm suggesting is that your solution is better than most. My associates think that money is how you keep score. You know better."

Joe laughed at last. "Good thing, given what I get paid."

Reed joined him in taking another sip of wine before getting back to business. "And speaking of such people, what would you like to know about the unsavory Mr. Jordan?"

"Just that," Joe responded, grateful to leave the previous topic of conversation. "I want to know what makes him unsavory."

"In a word?" Abijah suggested. "The mob. Or better yet, the Irish mafia. Jordan was a bad boy from a bad neighborhood. But smarter than most by a long shot. As a kid, he was the one who organized things and never got caught. Usually, such people eventually piss off a nervous competitor or one of the little people they stepped on, but

Jordan had that latter category figured out, probably because he remembered what life at the bottom was like."

"So he was an up-and-comer?"

"Early on," Abijah amended. "Although I'm talking about from his teens to his early twenties. He was a punk with a gun and brass knuckles, even if he was bright. The major players used him and his small gang when they wanted something done — a specific job. A store owner needing educating; a rival's family member to be hurt as a warning; maybe a robbery or a break-in or a highjacking to do. Gutter-level stuff that the big boys didn't like but that couldn't be avoided."

"I thought he handled finances," Joe pondered.

The first course arrived, and they chatted of other things as the waiter set everything up, asking if they wanted something already placed on the table, like pepper.

"He *ended up* in finance," Abijah supplied when they were alone again. "But that's only because he turned the tables on his handlers. He made them an offer they were too savvy to turn down, and never looked back. His secret was that he knew how to evolve."

Reed tasted his appetizer and rolled his

eyes in appreciation. Joe had ordered soup, largely to be polite. He usually couldn't stand it when people made a big production over food, he being as happy with Spam as with filet mignon.

"You see," Abijah resumed, still chewing, "little Lloyd had learned early on what to do with the money he made, and to use it as leverage. He was probably the only street punk in the 'hood who owned stock, or knew what the Dow Jones was. And he fed his need through the jobs I described, plus a little blackmail, fraud, or loan-sharking. He was a broad-minded financier."

"Almost sounds as if you like him," Joe said.

Abijah shook his head. "I like some of these jokers. The ones with style. Jordan has brains, but he's also a brute. I actually knew him back when. Not well, but I was aware of what he was doing, and who he was doing it with. Not that I'm truly drawing a comparison, mind you, but think of Mike Tyson — an undeniable champion, but such a sociopath that he drains away any respect he might have due."

"So what happened to him?" Joe asked.

"Lloyd began giving advice to the people who counted. They'd noticed that he was dressing better than they were, and driving a better car. In the end, he got them to approach *him,* which is unusual in that circle, and soon after, he was on the inside, managing their portfolios and feathering his own nest. In that way, you could say that he started like I did and ended up straddling both worlds. Except that where I went legit and now use my knowledge to help law enforcement, Lloyd Jordan stayed friendly with the bad boys and only acted legit as a front."

"Why did he give it up?" Joe asked. "He sounds like the type to stay in the game."

"Things got hairy," Abijah explained simply. "The market took a hit he didn't see coming. His clients proved less forgiving than the average Beacon Hill resident. And his wife turned up dead under iffy circumstances. He had the proverbial ironclad alibi through a girl named Susan Rainier, but the pressure on him became pretty intense. He claimed the wife was killed as revenge against him, but not many of us bought that. Insider knowledge had it that they hadn't been getting along, and that he'd been stepping out for a long time with Susan, chafing at the bit because the wife refused to give him a divorce. I heard he actually got remarried, although not to Susan. Did you meet the new one?"

Joe shook his head. "My colleague did. Said he liked her, despite her being treated like a trophy."

"Well," Abijah commiserated. "If she's lucky, she'll get out of it. This is not a nice man we're discussing."

"Okay," Joe said, bringing them to what had prompted this meeting in the first place. "What we know in Vermont is that somebody broke into the Jordan home, ate some of their food, and left a note that he'd been there."

"You're kidding," Reed interjected. "That's bizarre, and given that it was Jordan, I love it."

"The press has dubbed him the Tag Man because the note always says, 'Tag!' The problem is, we can't tell if he's stealing anything other than a few bites of food, and Jordan's the only victim acting cagey. The others are simply clueless. One of them thinks Tag Man lifted her investment strategy for his own use — or copied it, I mean — but that just tells me he knows how to play the market. Still, it's a coincidence I can't ignore: Jordan's a financier, too. So, what might Tag Man have stolen of a financial nature that Jordan can't or won't reveal?"

"Did I mention blackmail as one of his

many tools?" Reed asked suggestively.

"Go back to what drove Jordan out of town," Joe requested. "You talked about the wife's murder. Presumably, the Boston PD put that under a microscope. What about those clients you said were less than thrilled to be wiped out by the stock market?"

Reed smiled. "Assuming it *was* the market, you mean? A man like Jordan could just as easily claim a loss while he's actually pocketing the profits. Risky but doable for him. To answer your question, though, I heard that a friendly parting was worked out. Now, I should be clear about something here." He placed his elbows on the table and leaned in, dropping his voice for emphasis. "This is not the movies. The people I'm talking about are dangerous, irrational, often hyped up on drugs or stoned on booze. They may have nice cars and expensive clothes and sometimes live in good neighborhoods, but they don't sound like Armand Assante or the head drug runner in *The French Connection* — all polish and tailored suits. These are often psychopaths, which is what gives them their competitive edge. You piss off someone like that, they kill you without sweating the details."

Joe was wondering where this was heading. "Okay," he said.

"I know you know all that. What I'm saying, Joe, is that when it came time for Lloyd to part ways with his clients, he had to be at the top of his game. He had to make sure they wouldn't follow instinct and just kill him for having lost their money."

"So he took out insurance?" Joe ventured.

Abijah straightened, a smile on his face. "Precisely. The blackmailer's instinct served him well. From what I heard — and I did a little homework before we got together — he'd been collecting facts and figures for years. Maybe even tape recordings. But enough evidence to guarantee that his former clients would absolutely go to jail if any harm came to him."

"And they bought that?"

The two of them paused again to let their waiter remove their plates and bring in the main course.

"What choice did they have?" Reed asked after they'd had their first bites. "He had them over a barrel, but keep in mind that he also removed himself from their direct realm of influence. He left town. That's when you inherited him. He had brains enough to recognize that if he got out of sight, it would help in putting him out of mind. That was his gift in all this — his key to survival. He made his apologies, promised to sever all ties, got out of the financial-management racket, *and* he took out insurance, making sure everyone knew what he had and what it would cost them to come after him. Smart, like I said."

"And it worked?"

Reed raised his eyebrows dramatically in midbite before agreeing, "It worked. But you've got to wonder what's going through his head now that your Tag Man came by to visit, especially if — as you suggest — he took something as a souvenir."

He laughed suddenly and asked, "Can you imagine? Not only can a blackmailer be blackmailed, but so can somebody else put the squeeze on the original targets if he managed to get hold of the right incriminating information."

Joe scowled, following the complicated suggestion.

"I love this stuff," Abijah admitted gleefully. "I'm not saying it happened, by the way. But it's all possible. Think of it: Tag Man steals what Jordan was using as insurance. What's that do? If Tag Man was hired by the Boston crooks, then Jordan is dead. Period. If instead, your mystery midnight snacker merely stumbled over the goods by accident, then he's got two options: He can either approach Jordan and sell the stuff back, or he can do the same thing to the original blackmailees. That would be the riskier route, of course, since it would put him in their crosshairs."

"Would you have the pipeline to hear about something like that?" Joe asked.

Reed tilted his head thoughtfully. "Probably for the second scenario. I'd have no way of knowing if Tag Man approached Jordan directly. Of course, if the truth is behind door number one, you'll find Jordan dead in a ditch soon enough. How long ago did this happen?"

Joe told him.

Abijah scratched his chin. "They don't usually sit on this kind of thing for long. Like I said, they're not terrific planners. My instinct tells me that you may be dealing with someone who fell into a really lucrative deal, if a highly risky one. For his sake, I hope you find a 'Tag!' note at another house soon, and not some anonymous corpse, without ever knowing who and what he'd been. That would be a bummer."

"Jesus," Joe murmured. "What a mess." He thought back through the various topics they'd covered, and chose to add to his own complications. "You have names of Jordan's past associates?"

"You mean the most likely targets of any

secret paperwork?" Abijah asked. "Benjamin Underhill comes to mind first. A ruthless man, utterly humorless. He's probably the one Jordan would have to watch the closest. It's safe to say that if Jordan doesn't have something on Underhill, then he doesn't have anything on anyone, and my theory is flat wrong."

"Tell me about the first wife," Joe asked after chewing awhile thoughtfully. "Where was that left?"

"Actually," Abijah conceded, "the medical examiner never even ruled it a homicide. All of us just figured it couldn't be anything but. She fell down a flight of stairs. Simplest thing in the world. Was there anyone else in the house? Nope. Could Jordan account for his whereabouts at the time? Yup. Was the time of death narrowed down to everyone's satisfaction? Yup again. It was ruled an accident and Jordan was off the hook. Next case, please." He pretended to dust his hands off.

"Did the police give it a fair shake, like I was hoping?" Joe asked, exploring Abijah's implication that they had the usual urban caseload weighing them down.

"Yes," he said affably. "It was hard to argue with the evidence. Jordan was rich and mobbed up, which caught their attention. But," and here he smiled broadly, "Jordan was also rich and mobbed up, which meant that he could have arranged whatever he needed and made it look airtight. That's where the smart money put this."

"Meaning," Joe ventured, "since we're talking about blackmail, that somebody might still be around who has what we need to pin a murder charge on him."

Abijah raised his glass. "Correct. Good Lord, Joe. We should do this more often, don't you think?"

Joe lifted his glass and returned the toast, thinking that every few years was fine with him, given all the new homework he'd just picked up.

Still, there was something stirring inside him as a result — the old hunting dog's eagerness to be back on the job.

And that, he did enjoy feeling.

Chapter Nine

Dan crouched in the bushes outside Gloria Wrinn's old mansion, his black clothes making him all but invisible on a moonless night.

His first visit here had been according to his rules — the time, the target, the risk level, and the challenge of the obstacle had all fit his comfort zone. Dan had no interest in being caught, after all. It was his anonymity he wanted to play large in people's imagination. Being the Tag Man appealed to several needs — intellectual; financial, when it caused no loss to the victim, as with Merry Hodgkins; and playful. At his most even-keeled, Dan — as Sally well knew — could be as light-hearted and even mischievous as any impish boy.

In the past, he had picked from a wide selection of targets, giving weight to the security systems opposing him, as well as to what he could learn of each home's inhabitants. For example, the Jordans, being nouveau riche and Lloyd a stuffy know-it-all who bought extravagantly, tipped poorly (as Dan knew from personal experience), and he treated his wife dismissively; Merry Hodgkins, being smart and talented and self-made, if a little paranoid; and Gloria, with her love of travel, her generosity to others, and her simple old-fashioned grandeur. All of them and the others, too, had offered Dan the chance to stand covertly in their midst — a thief in the night — to eat their best food, enjoy their possessions, and absorb their contributions — good and bad — to human nature.

But never before had he been in his present position, having to act at his peril by entering a house a second time, with at least one of its residents both knowing of his existence and wishing him and Sally harm. For a man as committed to the shadows as Dan Kravitz, this was the equivalent of stepping out onto center stage buck naked on opening night.

All because, simply put, it had to be done.

And that wasn't all — he had made a practice of dogged research in the past. Houses and house owners had been subjected to thorough scrutiny, his computer skills put to use, his background in electronics and security systems, his fondness for surveillance. He'd sometimes even gotten short-term jobs that put him close to the people whose privacy he planned to invade. That was one reason he'd worked at Bariloche — to study the Jordans.

But Paul Hauser? Dan had found no mention anywhere, and the more he'd searched, the more he'd felt the pressure of time. The words of the man he'd killed on the bridge — the first person he'd ever harmed in his life — burned like a fuse in his head. "It involves your daughter," he'd said of the reason he'd been stalking Dan.

Whatever that was, whatever it meant, it told Dan that he didn't have time to conduct his usual homework. He needed to take back control, and he needed to do it to save Sally from the evil he'd glimpsed in those albums.

This was now combat. He'd been driven to kill once, if admittedly in self-defense. Now he was ready to do it again, to protect the only human being he'd ever held dear.

But he needed to understand his enemy.

And therein lay his dilemma.

He studied the house as if for the first time, a confusing but appealing mixture of brick, clapboard, and Victorian flourishes, clearly remodeled over the centuries, and resulting in a maintenance nightmare and a visual treat. It utterly lacked any architect's guidance and showed off instead the Yankee penchant for independence, accented with no small measure of humor.

Dan, however, was all business this time, paying no attention to the minutiae he favored and focusing instead on the threat level alone. He watched the windows and doors for light or movement, the bushes near the walls for shapes and shadows that didn't fit. He tried with his will simply to sense the presence of another living soul.

But he picked up on nothing besides his own anxiety.

He'd been out here for an hour already, studying the building from every accessible angle. Considering a final approach, he decided against repeating his previous means of entry, or trusting what he knew of Gloria's lack of interest in security. As before, he assumed all alarm systems to be on and all locks thrown, and even that, for once, someone might actually be watching.

Having thus weighed his new point of entry, he crossed the lawn at a silent run and quietly scaled a tree near the back wall. Once securely positioned on a sturdy branch fifteen feet off the ground — still a good ten feet from the second-floor window he'd selected — he removed a coil of rope from his close-fitting backpack, triggered the spring-loaded grappling hook on its end, and gracefully and successfully sent it looping over the top of a decorative piece of woodwork protruding from under the roof's elaborate edge.

Once the rope was made taut and tested, Dan clipped it to his harness, alongside a second line attached to the tree trunk, and eased himself free of his branch, rappelling horizontally over to the window directly across from him. He arrived without a sound, high above the motion detectors designed to be monitoring the outside perimeter of the wall — that's where he would have fallen prey had he simply used a ladder to reach the same window.

Comfortably tied off, dangling directly before the window, Dan removed several tools from his cargo-pants pockets and quickly extracted a single pane of glass. He reached inside, unlocked the window, and then replaced the pane, applying putty prestained to look old and weathered.

He repacked his tools, cleaned up his handiwork, placing the fragments of old glazing into a small plastic bag, and slipped inside the house. Leaning out the open window, he pulled on the accessory lines he'd laid out, above and across from him, and loosened his two primary ropes, reeling one in and catching the other as it fell toward him. By the end, he'd eliminated all but the tiniest signs of his ever having been there. The entire operation had taken fifteen minutes.

Only then did he shut and lock the window behind him and stand stock-still, listening, inside the house once more.

He knew the layout well by now. His mind, with its obsession for detail, retained memories of spatial relationships and lighting angles as he imagined cartographers' did of cherished maps. A major factor in his choice of which window to assault had been based on his recall of the floor plan and even the actual window's characteristics.

So now, he stood as still as a piece of furniture, in a small sitting room down the hall from Gloria's bedroom, reacquainting himself with the heartbeat of the house.

But whether it was the truth or simply his own heightened anxiety, he didn't like what he was sensing.

Something felt distinctly off-kilter, as if his every movement was being tracked.

He left the room, stopped in the hallway, and tried to peer into the surrounding darkness, wishing he'd invested in a pair of night-vision goggles.

Relying on his memory, he stole down the corridor, avoiding a side table here or a creaky floorboard there, headed for the master bedroom to confirm the home-owner's whereabouts.

At Gloria's slightly ajar door, outlined by the barest glimmer from a night-light at the rear of the room, he placed his hand on the knob and pushed, knowing the hinges to be well oiled and silent.

The scene was what he had expected. This time, he wasn't startled to see the old lady propped up in bed, but he was tense never-theless, more nervous about what he couldn't see than about what was directly before him. He stepped free of the open doorway and placed his back against the wall.

He grimaced, fighting his growing unease. What the hell felt so wrong?

He studied Gloria carefully, or what little he could see of her. Her face was in shadow, her shape under the covers little more than a bulbous lump. A bit of cloth had fallen over the distant night-light and made of her a virtual apparition — the suggestion of a human being.

Chilled by the thought, Dan sidled across the rug, working his way around the foot of the large four-poster to get a better angle on his subject.

What he finally discerned was no face at all. The sleeping Gloria he was expecting had no eyes, no nose, no features at all. Planted atop the pillow, slightly turned away as if in slumber, was the blank orb of a volleyball topped with a wig.

Dan whirled around, convinced that someone had to be standing behind him, having lured him in with this subterfuge.

There was no one there, but he swore that there'd been a flicker of movement, framed in the now open doorway.

He dropped into a crouch behind the hulking bed, peering over its blankets at the door. A moment later, he glanced again at what he'd thought to be Gloria, concentrating on the ramifications of his situation.

One thing was safe to assume: He was now caught in this house like a rodent in a trap. He no longer needed to return to a cellar room for evidence of a monster on the loose. The monster was coming for him.

He considered his options. He was on the second floor of a house whose magisterial dimensions dictated a drop of fifteen feet or more to the ground below. Dan was light and athletic, but such a distance, onto invisible terrain possibly strewn with lethal debris, was too daunting.

That eliminated the easiest course of just leaping out the window.

But he had his ropes, and the leather gloves he'd used earlier. It would be a simple matter to rig a knot and rappel to safety, before Hauser had time to react.

Dan scuttled across to the nearest window, not taking his eyes off the door. He reached up and pushed against the lower half of the window. It was locked. He straightened and felt for the lock. It was nailed in place.

"Damn," he murmured, and as quickly as he could, twisted around, shielded his eyes with his hands, and peered through the glass. As he'd expected by now, the shutters were closed.

He didn't need to establish that they'd probably been screwed down as tightly as bulkhead doors.

He returned to the barricade of the large bed.

Dan was essentially a cat burglar, predisposed to stealth, silence, and deliberation. His opponent would think of him thus, and prepare himself accordingly. He'd shown that much by his construction of this trap — he'd known that Dan would initially check on Gloria's whereabouts.

Salvation, therefore, possibly lay in violating that presumption — Dan might increase his chance of survival by turning on every light he could locate, and running like a maniac for the front door, leaving his nemesis flatfooted in surprise.

But did he dare? It was a long stretch to that door, and one of the few things he rarely cataloged in his memory was the location of light switches. Did he really want to base his entire strategy on correctly guessing which switch lay where? And what if Hauser had already seen to that, and killed most of those lights? He'd certainly been sharp enough to plant a dummy of Gloria in this bed and to seal the windows. He'd had to have anticipated moves that Dan might make if he returned for a second visit.

This man, as twisted as he seemed, clearly could think things through.

So what had he not foreseen?

Dan racked his brain, sensitive to the passing seconds, convinced that Hauser lay in wait, ready to execute the plan that would convince authorities that the now dead Tag Man had been caught and killed in defense of home and hearth. Wherever Gloria really was — and Dan was confident she'd been sent on some bogus journey in order to empty the house — she'd probably return and have only praise for the protector of her worldly goods.

Up, Dan suddenly thought. That would be something Hauser wouldn't have considered — that Dan would head upstairs, even to the roof. In fact, the roof might be preferable. He tried to remember that topmost aspect of the house from his prior visit here. However, along with the location of light switches, it wasn't something to which he gave much attention. Still, there had to have been something . . .

The top floor had the usual collection of small rooms, once reserved for the servants — garrets with dormer windows, and a shared bathroom at the end of the hall. Dan steered his memory back to an outside view of the house — and its flat-topped mansard roof.

He left his spot by the bed and moved quickly to the edge of the door frame, pausing to chart his route.

To his right was the main staircase leading down to the foyer, the living room, and the other formal spaces. Given what Hauser seemed to be planning, that was the direction where the danger would be greatest. Fortunately for Dan, to the left, directly above the kitchen, was a second, narrower staircase to the cramped and largely ignored third floor.

He took a deep breath. This was far from

his operating norm, even when he was situated in a setting of his choosing. The irony would have been comical if he hadn't been so scared.

Fighting his previous urge to run at full tilt, Dan slipped out into the hallway, his shoulder blades against the wall, and strained to pick up on Hauser's presence. Of course, that worked all too well — the menace of the man enveloped him like a fog.

Hoping to quell his rising panic, Dan slid down the hall, toward the back of the house, convinced that at every step, his stalker would suddenly appear from behind some door or passageway. The trade-off of his having chosen a moonless night to break in was that he'd rarely been in such blacked-out surroundings.

Paul Hauser could have been standing right behind him, and he would have been none the wiser.

On the other hand, he rationalized, unless Hauser had the same night-piercing goggles Dan had been wishing for earlier, he was at the same disadvantage as Dan.

Dan reached the end of the hall and was confronted by a closet before him and a door to either side, one leading to the kitchen below, the other upstairs. He groped for and took hold of a small side table decorated with a flower arrangement he remembered from before, and gently dragged it across the rug to where it blocked the entrance to downstairs. It wouldn't prohibit that door from being opened, but it would create a hell of a noise were that to happen.

He then cautiously opened the door opposite.

Just then a faint noise rose up behind him like a chill — the muted brushing of a foot against the carpet.

He dropped to one knee and swung around, staring wide-eyed into the gloom with his hands out before him. His fingertips grazed a man's pant leg just as he felt the breeze of something heavy barely miss the top of his head.

Without thought, he launched himself forward like a linebacker, using his legs for explosive propulsion, and caught his opponent by the waist. There was a thudding outburst of air, a strong smell of human being in Dan's nostrils, followed by a tangle of arms and legs and fists as they both went sprawling to the floor.

Instantly, Dan knew he was up against a far bigger man than he, so he pursued his momentary advantage by pummeling the face beneath him, leaping to his feet, and reaching back to the small, vase-equipped table to bring the whole of it crashing down on the body still struggling before him.

Without pause or thought, he followed that by bolting for his original escape route. He yanked the door wide and half stepped, half fell onto the rough wooden stairs heading up, reaching out to steady himself and catching his hand on what seemed to be an interior dead bolt. Seizing this opportunity, he slammed the door behind him, and just as he heard the scrabbling of hands on the other side, he snapped the dead bolt closed.

He quickly explored both sides of the door frame, found a switch, and flooded the tight passageway with light.

He bounded up the stairs, pursued by the repeated pounding of fists against the door.

At the top of the stairs was a long, unadorned corridor with doors on both sides, each leading, as he knew, to an assortment of small bedrooms, storage areas, and a bathroom at the end. Every other room had a garret window overlooking the lawn far below, but Dan recalled their all being small and placed high on the wall — enough to supply air and light, but hardly ideal as a means of escape.

Hitting another light switch on the way,

he continued jogging down the hall until he reached a trapdoor mounted in the ceiling.

As in a countdown to a launching, he heard Hauser battering the downstairs door with something far more solid and destructive than his fists or shoulder. It wouldn't be much longer now.

Dan checked the nearest room, found a half-broken chair parked against the wall, and pulled it under the trapdoor. He clambered up, wobbling atop its frail, spindly legs, and studied the overhead opening from close-up. It was larger and heavier than he'd expected, equipped with rugged hinges and a latch.

Fumbling nervously, aware of wood splintering below, Dan undid the latch and pushed with all his might against the square panel.

At the precise moment that the trapdoor yielded to his efforts, the chair collapsed beneath him, accompanied by a resounding crash at the foot of the stairs.

Hauser was heading his way.

Dan caught hold of the opening's edge, chin-lifted himself to where he could push the unhooked door with his head, and with some effort scrambled up and over the lip of the opening, surprised to find himself not in an attic but on the roof of the house itself. Just as he slammed the door back down, he saw his pursuer coming into view.

Unslinging his backpack and opening it as he ran, Dan crossed the flat roof to where it met the mansard slope downward and peered over the edge. Hopelessly far below, he saw the crown of a tree and only blackness beneath.

Dan glanced about for an anchor, found a nearby chimney, knotted a quick loop in one of his ropes, secured a carabiner to the harness around his waist, and — just as the roof-access panel flew back on its hinges and revealed a vertical shaft of light — Dan twisted around, took two steps backward, and dropped off the edge of the roof into the void.

Hauser was faster than he'd hoped. As Dan reached the gutter marking the boundary between the mansard slope and the sheer drop beneath it, he placed both his feet against the wall and pushed out, in order to effect a rapid descent by letting the rope fly almost unimpeded through his "beener."

Instead, the rope simply vanished, sliced through at its anchor point.

For a split second, Dan felt suspended in midair, before the tree's uppermost branches began tearing at his body in free-fall.

He reached out with both hands in desperation, caught several violent blows in his back and across his forearms, before finally grabbing hold of a branch thick enough to break his fall. Not slowly enough, being whipped across the face and body as he went, Dan tumbled from level to level within the tree's embrace before finally cascading out the bottom and landing in a heap on the cool grass.

Momentarily, he lay stunned on his back, wondering what might appear out of the night sky above him like a truck and crush him flat.

Then he gathered himself together, sat up without finding anything broken, and staggered to his feet.

He headed off, limping slightly, resigned that while he'd fended off Hauser here and now, he was going to have to make virtual ghosts of himself and Sally.

Starting immediately.

Chapter Ten

"Time rewards those who wait," Ron announced from the open doorway.

"I hate shit like that," Willy answered him, not looking up from the gun magazine he was reading.

"Nevertheless," Ron persisted, stepping into the VBI office and raising a hand in greeting to Lester Spinney, who was on the phone. "Parking Enforcement just let us know that they booted a car with Mass plates in the Elliot Street garage. Looks like it might be our dead guy's."

Willy opened his mouth to protest before Ron cut him off, laughing. "I know, I know. *Your* dead guy's. Wouldn't want to step on your FBI wingtips."

"Fuck you." Willy tossed the magazine onto his desk and got up.

"You ever figure out why he had Bariloche's name in his pocket?" Ron asked.

Lester had hung up by then and answered,

since Willy clearly wasn't going to. "Nope. The owner only gave us about five names of who might've been there that night — regulars or people he just happened to remember — I think he was mostly playing dumb, being protective of his high rollers."

Willy was already halfway down the hallway.

The municipal parking garage had been baptized the Transportation Center, in early hopes that commercial bus lines would use it as a depot, which — after the merest glance at downtown traffic patterns — they never had. It was a huge, hulking, oddly designed, multilevel structure whose otherwise acceptable redbrick veneer had been clumsily accented with small clusters of white brick, making the whole building look like it had succumbed to a case of acne.

But the building fulfilled its purpose, and had, by and large, addressed the parking concerns of the time.

They found the car facing the Elliot Street exit, a bright orange clamp affixed to its front wheel. Its lack of personality, even from a distance, said "rental."

The three men split up as they approached it, studying it from all angles, finally peering through the windows without touching anything, to see what might stand out.

"Anything on your side?" Ron asked.

Willy ignored him, but Lester responded, "Nope. You?"

"Nothing."

"You run this by anybody?" Willy asked at last.

"The rental firm," Ron told him, speaking over the roof. "The ID used in Boston was for Nate Sullivan. We plugged that into the system and of course got nothing. Did you want to call in the crime lab to process it?"

Willy was using his pocket flashlight to better see the interior. "Is Tyler around?" he asked.

J. P. Tyler was the police department's veteran forensic expert — small, self-effacing, and the man to see about prints, tool-mark impressions, serology collection, and the rest. The advent of DNA and a few other high-end scientific developments had eclipsed some of his talents, calling for more expertise or money than he or the PD could afford, but for most of the day-in, day-out basics, he remained a hard man to rival, and a credit to his chief, Tony Brandt. Most other departments had thrown in the towel by now, choosing to rely instead on an evermore hard-pressed state forensic mobile unit to do their evidence collection for them.

"Yeah," Ron answered, a little surprised. "You want him to do it?"

Willy straightened to stare at him. "No. I just wanted to make sure you were watering him regularly. Yeah, I want him to do it."

"For a homicide?" Ron persisted.

Once more, Willy didn't react as expected, choosing to explain instead, "I doubt we'll find much anyhow. The guy was stripped of ID, used a bogus name. What d'you wanna bet he didn't leave his diary under the seat?"

Ron was reaching for his cell phone.

Willy had called it correctly, of course. An hour later, J. P. Tyler, clad in a white Tyvek jumpsuit, backed out of the open car and unzipped the front of his costume to cool off.

"Anything?" Lester asked him. Willy had already wandered off somewhere.

"Just the same prints I lifted off your dead man," Tyler said. "But that's about it. For what it's worth, I collected soil samples from the pedals and carpeting and lifted a couple of threads off the driver's seat, but I wouldn't hold my breath. It's not a new car, so I'd guess a few dozen people have used it before the mysterious Mr. Sullivan. What I found could've just as easily come from them. The real world ain't *CSI*." He shook his head as he bent down to repack his tools and supplies, adding softly, "I hate that show."

Ron and Lester walked together across the parking lot toward the waist-high balcony overlooking Flat Street and the earlier homicide scene far below, by now a memory only. As usual, kids were clustered around the pedestrian bridge that spanned the water, trading stories and working their cell phones. It was blue-skied and sunny — the kind of beautiful day that helped give Vermont its reputation.

Both men leaned forward and rested their forearms on the rough concrete edge, enjoying the view. They could see Whetstone Brook sparkling in reflection, the co-op parking lot beyond, and the opposing hillside of the far bank, where South Main Street rose toward the cemetery on top of the hill.

Both Ron and Lester were family men, the first a local boy, the second from Springfield, up the interstate. Klesczewski had been with the Bratt PD, as locals called it, for his entire career, where Spinney had put in several years with the state police before transferring to VBI. But despite their never having worked for the same outfit, they shared a similarity common to many rural

177

New England cops — a quiet, nonmacho, practical-minded outlook, instilled as much by the practices of their departments as by the values of their region. Unlike the temperamental and iconoclastic Willy Kunkle, they were just hardworking cops, all but invisibly helping society stay on the tracks.

"You been kept up-to-date on this case?" Spinney began.

Ron let out a short, soft laugh. "Barely. Willy throws me a bone now and then."

Lester smiled knowingly. "I figured. Well, we got a name for our dead guy. Leo Metelica — a fingerprint hit from the U.S. Navy. And Boston PD just called to say they'd showed the photo we faxed them to the rental-car company."

"Nate Sullivan?" Ron guessed.

"Right," Lester said. "Which was weird, because it turns out Metelica used that alias before. Funny oversight for a guy running around with special bullets and a throwaway barrel. Anyhow, that was enough to make the connection and get Metelica's rap sheet."

"Anything interesting there?" Ron asked.

Lester laughed outright. "Like is he the Brattleboro town manager's long-lost brother? No such luck. I mean, these records are only as good as what people put into them, you know? Plus, in Massachusetts, there're all sorts of files that haven't made it onto any shared database. For all we know, Metelica had a dozen connections to Vermont or one of our hometown bad boys. But we *don't* know."

"You *think* he does?" Ron asked. "He was here for some reason, and he got killed by somebody. Too bad the Bariloche reference didn't work."

Lester nodded. "Yeah."

They were silently contemplative for a couple of seconds, before Ron asked again, "So what did Metelica's paperwork tell you?"

"Oh — right. The service record's pretty clean. He worked as a machinist's mate. Was slapped with a few infractions along the way, but got out with an honorable. Never saw any action, and never stood out for any weapons use."

"Not a SEAL, in other words."

"Hardly," Lester agreed. "Looks like he was a regular swabbie — just doing his time and getting out."

"He ever do time as a civilian?"

"Nothing hard. A little jail here and there. He mistook an undercover cop for a hooker once. That must've been disappointing."

"Not as disappointing as coming to

Brattleboro," Ron commented.

"True enough. We do have an address that looks current, in Lowell, Mass., that we'll probably check out — or ask the locals to."

"Tough town."

"Tough line of business," Lester said.

"Speaking of that, what about the restaurant owner?" Ron asked.

"Here? Of Bariloche?" Spinney asked.

"Yeah. Restaurants are supposed to be cutthroat."

"Jake Nessbaum. You know him? We interviewed him and checked him out. Nothing popped up."

Ron turned to look at his colleague. "Nessbaum. I do know him. Heard of him, I should say. This is like his third business or something. I was told that he opens a place up, makes it all the rage, sells out at just the right time, and starts over again. He's got to be pretty well off by now."

"The place is jammed every night," Lester said, as if in confirmation. "Looks like he's doing it again."

Ron considered that. "Maybe what you said about the gap between computers and paperwork applies here. High-risk business, unusually successful guy with immaculate timing, lots of cash floating around, and now a hit man found dead in the river with

Bariloche in his pocket. Even if Nessbaum's not in the computer for anything, you gotta wonder. Could be Bariloche, in other words Nessbaum, was exactly what was meant in that note — not that Metelica was supposed to meet anyone there."

Spinney remained staring out over the scene, nodding. "Can't say it doesn't have a ring to it," he conceded. "And it's not like we have a hot lead telling us something different. Still, Nessbaum was seen at the restaurant until closing. After that, his family vouches for him. If everyone's to be believed, I don't think he had time to slip out, get into a fight with a hit man, kill him, and resume his nightly schedule with nobody the wiser. It's possible, but . . ." He suddenly looked at Ron and asked, "Have you ever met him? Nessbaum?"

Ron was taken by surprise. "Me? No. I don't think so, anyway."

Lester nodded and went back to sightseeing, speaking to the view. "Let's just say that if you saw him, you'd have a hard time seeing him doing a kung fu on a trained killer."

"Got it," Ron said, before suggesting, "What about his employees?"

"Not a big group," Lester reported. "Kind of what you'd expect. There were a few ex-employees we interviewed, too, and the patrons you know about. A couple had records, some were basically kids, one was a snitch of Willy's named Kravitz, but none of them jump out as an obvious candidate."

Ron braced his chin on the palm of one hand. "Dan Kravitz? I remember him. Odd duck."

"Maybe," Lester agreed. "But Willy didn't see him for this."

Klesczewski made a face to no one in particular. "Well, I hate to be obvious, but somebody sure as hell did."

Chapter Eleven

Sally Kravitz was sitting in the back of the classroom, enjoying the fresh air coming in through the open window. The prep school was good for moments like this, more often than not — interesting teachers telling her stuff she enjoyed, in a setting more out of an English movie than reflective of reality.

Certainly any reality she'd ever known.

She glanced out the window across a picture-perfect lawn bigger than any park she knew of in Brattleboro, which boasted of more than fourteen thousand people.

Unbelievable contrast.

Not that she was complaining. She'd had a more interesting life than most so far, richer and more diversified than those of even her most privileged classmates, whose parents owned yachts and jets but who rarely stepped outside their bubbles. There'd been a couple of urban transplants last year from New York City, scholarship kids like her who'd had a hard time fitting into the school's air-locked social capsule. The three of them had enjoyed comparing big-city and small-town mean streets. One of the New Yorkers had cleared out after a year. The other, like Sally, had seen what there was to offer, and was still there absorbing everything that she could, expanding an already impressive collection of life experiences.

That was where Sally felt that she had an advantage over her peers. Her father had seen to it that she encountered more in her few years than many people received well into old age, all while making her feel safe and sheltered. His unique brand of adventurous, nomadic, protectionist parenting had presented her with a guided tour through poverty and privilege, happiness and woe, crime and serenity, loneliness and exuberance — all essentially without a scratch. She'd come to believe that her father, despite his personal demons, would remain the one anchor she could trust forever.

Living with Dan, she'd once told a friend, was like doing drugs with Yoda — the ultimate unorthodox trip of self-discovery.

Which is what made the sudden appearance of his face at the small window mounted in the classroom door so utterly appropriate.

Without hesitation, Sally rose from her seat, walked the length of the room, smiled politely to the teacher, and murmured, "Sorry. I'll be right back" — without being sure of any such thing — and left to meet her father.

"I'm really sorry, sweetheart," he began.

"Hang on," she whispered, taking him by the arm and escorting him ten feet down the hallway, out of earshot, before saying, "Please don't say we're leaving. I like it here."

He stared at her, his wise child, and managed to smile through the concerns that were fogging his mind.

"I'm not, but something is going on. I need to talk with you."

She studied his scratched and bruised face, ignoring the physical damage to watch for the expressions she'd learned so carefully over a lifetime. He was serious, very worried, and completely clear-minded.

Only then did she reach out and touch his cheek. "Holy cow, Dad. What happened?"

He stared at her as if she'd spoken in Latin. "Nothing," he said finally, slowly cueing in.

She got the message. Stick to the point. "So, talk," she urged.

"Are you okay?" he asked. "Has everything been normal over the past few days?"

She answered him directly. "I'm fine, and nothing's been weird."

"Have you noticed anyone watching you? Anyone unusual? This might've been from a distance, like at a ballgame or something. Maybe taking your picture? Someone trying to be just part of the landscape."

She shook her head. "Is this the man you mentioned in Bratt? You said he was creepy, maybe dangerous."

He was already nodding. "Yes, but he's not alone."

A door opened nearby and another student stepped into the hallway, no doubt headed for the bathroom. He looked startled to see them there.

"Hey," Sally said in greeting.

"Hey," he returned.

Sally led her father down a flight of stairs to the first floor, and from there onto the grassy expanse she'd been admiring earlier.

She pointed to midfield, anticipating her father's needs. "Out there. No one to eavesdrop and we can see everything."

He acquiesced, falling into step beside her.

They were twenty yards out when she said, "Tell me what's going on, Dad. What happened?"

He hesitated, not knowing how or where to begin. Not for the first time, he found himself caught between trying to be a good father and keeping the balancing poles of his inner world even. Sally was the one fully rooted point in a universe gone spinning. But he realized with excruciating precision that she was still a child, even with all her levelheaded poise.

"Does it have to do with the Tag Man?" she asked, sensing his dilemma.

He stopped dead in his tracks and stared at her. "What?"

She looked into his face, gently smiling. "Supergirl knew about Clark Kent, Dad."

His hand wandered to his forehead. He was at once touched by her knowledge and overwhelmed by yet another assault on his need for order.

"How long . . . ?"

She patted his chest. "A while. I kind of hoped it was you from the start, without really thinking about it. It was just so cool, you know?" Her face became serious as she added, "But I did wonder about the danger. I thought you might get shot or something, like a burglar. Is this something like that?"

He nodded slowly, recognizing that she'd given him a path he could follow. "Exactly like that. Somebody else figured it out, only he's a really bad man."

Sally suddenly straightened, her eyes widening as she spoke. "Oh my God. Dad. I heard someone was killed in Bratt, near the co-op . . ."

He merely nodded in acknowledgment.

She covered her open mouth.

"It was an accident," he said, confusion welling up. "He had a gun. He said he was there because of you. I just pushed him and he fell."

"Because of *me?*"

"I asked him why he was stalking me, and he said it involved you. That he'd been hired by people wanting to talk to me."

As he said all this out loud, he understood how nonsensical it sounded.

He shut his eyes for a moment. "Hang on, hang on. I know this isn't organized."

Again, Sally watched him, reading the signs. They knew each other well, these two halves of a draftsman's compass, and she knew to give him time to think.

He was clearly under a great deal of stress.

"I saw him at the restaurant," Dan started again. "He stuck out — you know how I notice things. He didn't act like a man at dinner. He was alone; he was on assignment somehow; the food was a cover; he left when he was done and not when the food was done. And I felt him watching *me*." Dan touched his chest.

"But you said he was hired," she prompted.

"Right. That was the weird part. And even if it didn't involve you, he knew that you existed. It's not like I'm on Facebook."

Sally burst out laughing at the idea.

He smiled through his nervousness. "Well, okay. You get the idea. Somebody had done their research."

She was back to being serious. "No one asked me, Dad. No one has even approached me — about anything. At least not in a while."

He pressed his temples with the heels of his hands. "I killed a man, Sally," he said softly, "because I thought he was going to harm you."

She reached up and took hold of his wrists, pulling his hands down. "Then you did the right thing, Dad." Her voice changed tone ever so slightly as she said, "I'm not challenging you, but why didn't you call the police? You didn't, right?"

He took a half step back, although not breaking her hold on him. "I was having a hard time explaining to *you* how this started, until you figured out the Tag Man part. How'm I going to do that with the police?"

He stepped up close to her — a proximity he never practiced with anyone else. "I have one job in this world, sweetheart, and that's to make sure you're okay. I don't crowd you, I don't question you, I try to be there when you need me, I give you advice when you ask for it and supply it when you need to know what I'm thinking."

"I know, Dad, I know," she repeated quietly as he spoke.

He continued. "All that goes away if the police get involved. They lock me up for what I've done, for the breaking and entering and for killing that man." He broke her grip to wave his arm around to include their surroundings. "And this goes away, too, once the school hears about your old man and what he does for entertainment."

This time, he cradled her face in his hands, looking closely into her eyes. "I live for you without trying to burden you with it. I know what that's like — to be crowded by people. I can't go to the police."

She leaned forward and kissed his cheek. "Thank you, Dad. I understand. I just had to ask."

He nodded, visibly helped by his own confession.

"So what *do* we do?" she asked.

"We disappear," he answered simply.

She tried to hide her disappointment, with mixed results. "Meaning I have to leave here?"

He'd anticipated that, knowing her needs to be far different from his own. "Just for a while," he said with hopeful emphasis. "Finals are mostly done. I'm sure we can work something out with your teachers, with your grades. Kids have to do this all the time." He squeezed her shoulder. "I am only talking about a little while, Sally. I promise. I know I can be a little high-strung, but you have to admit, this is real — or it's real until we can get to the bottom of it."

"We're not just running away?"

He shook his head repeatedly. "No, no." He looked around, as if suddenly feeling surrounded, and headed deeper into the field, saying, "Let's walk more."

She fell in beside him, surprised that he'd stayed put as long as he had.

"This man," he said. "The bad man I stumbled across. Not the one . . . who died. I think he's behind this. What I discovered about him was really frightening. There were pictures, keepsakes. In a suitcase hidden under the floor. I think he stalked young women, and maybe killed them."

Sally was staring at him as they walked.

"When, Dad? Where? I haven't heard anything about this."

He sighed with frustration. "I don't know. I've been trying to put it together. Figure it out."

He stopped again. "You asked what happened to my face. I went back to the house — where he lives. I wanted to see the pictures again. I only saw them quickly, the one time, and there were others I didn't see at all. I was going to copy them with my camera."

"What happened?" she asked.

"He was waiting for me," Dan explained, again reducing the truth to shield her. "He set up a trap in the house. I had to get out some way he didn't expect, and that's how I got cut up, falling into some tree branches."

"From out of a window?" she exclaimed, filling in the blanks.

He waved that away. "The roof. Anyhow, it worked. That's the point. But he was waiting, like I said, which tells me he's guilty of something."

Sally was looking reflective. "There was a string of murders years ago, wasn't there? Before I was born?"

"I thought of that," he told her. "I don't know. It's possible. That's one of the reasons I went back to copy the pictures. I was so thrown by finding them that I couldn't remember the details. I mean, they're burned into my memory — but to accurately describe the young women . . ."

"Maybe if you saw face shots of the victims from back . . . when was it?"

"They stopped in the late eighties," he said, thinking over her suggestion. "That's a good idea. There's a fair amount on them, in books and on the Internet. I've already done a little digging, but one of the things I found out is that since no one was ever caught, nobody's positive about the total number of victims, either. Some skeletal remains have surfaced that can't be identified; some women disappeared that were written off as runaways. It's hard to tell. And," he added, "there are probably half-a-dozen people that have been accused — none with anything approaching proof."

Sally shook her head. "God, it's like a zombie movie. Do you know anything about this guy?"

"His name's Paul Hauser. That's all I have. He works as a handyman, living in the basement of an old rich woman in Brattleboro."

"How did she find him?"

"I don't know. My guess is that he found her — made her an offer she couldn't pass up: free work for free room."

She glanced into the distance before musing aloud, "And now he knows about you and me — where we live, what we do, God knows what else."

"I don't think so," her father said.

She faced him. "What? Why not?"

"It's a long shot, but I got the feeling that while the hit man knew where I worked, he had no idea that I lived upstairs. He was waiting for me after work, hiding in that alley across the street. Why did he do that if he knew where I lived? He was planning to follow me home."

"Or he was waiting to ambush you in some dark corner, which is almost exactly what happened," she countered.

Dan shrugged. "Whatever. The punch line's the same: We have to move out of the restaurant and I have to quit my job. But I think we only have a tiny window to do so."

"What if they're already waiting at the apartment?" she pressed.

"I'll check it out," he told her, smiling to make her feel better. "After all, I have my ways. I can discover if anyone's watching the place."

She smiled back, but her expression was questioning. "I think the Tag Man thing is totally cool, even though it's made you

Public Enemy Number One with the wrong people, but why did you do it?"

He nodded, his smile struck away by the question. "Sweetie, you've got a pretty crazy father, not that you don't know that." He chose his words with care. "I was feeling the need for some kind of accomplishment, I think, on my own terms, not society's. And maybe I wanted to make a statement here and there, even if I was the only one to understand it." The smile returned as he added, "And it was also a lot of fun."

He stopped, looked around, and sighed slightly. She waited, knowing there was at least a little more to come.

"The shrinks would have a field day with it," he admitted. "It's probably devious, unhealthy, voyeuristic, and sociopathic, just for starters, not to mention illegal." He brought his attention back to her as he said, "But you asked why I did it, and I guess it was mostly because it made me feel in control."

Sally absorbed this quietly. Despite their unusual journey together, he had remained her sounding board, confessor, supporter, and guide, all wrapped up in one quirky, intelligent, sometimes marginally functional package. She wasn't about to argue with him, now that he finally needed her.

She stepped into his arms and gave him a tight hug, her words muffled by his chest. "I love you, Dad."

"I love you, too, sweetheart. I'm really sorry I got us into this mess."

She looked up at him. "Will you let me help when you think I can?"

"You bet. I put you at risk; the least I can do is let you defend yourself."

She nodded once. "Then don't worry about it. We'll make it work out."

CHAPTER TWELVE

Willy Kunkle looked around with a grimace. "Guess a dump is a dump, no matter where you live."

Lester glanced at the Lowell, Massachusetts, cop accompanying them, but saw only a smile greet the comment.

"You got dumps in Vermont?" the man asked. "You're kidding me. I heard it was all cows and trees and shit like that."

"You got the shit part right," Willy agreed.

They were in an apartment near Lowell's center, in a run-down section of town called the Acre, surrounded by a moatlike commingling of rivers, streams, and canals. It was all part of a hydropower system that had once fed a true manufacturing behemoth — hard as it was to imagine now, Lowell had been the nation's largest industrial center in 1850.

Of course, the standard capitalist folly back then of creating entire cities for a single purpose had ended here as it had everywhere else in New England, and modern Lowell — although benefiting somewhat from its proximity to Boston — remained largely a bruised and worn-out remnant of its former glory.

Not surprisingly, the late Leo Metelica had fit right in. Hollywood depictions of hit men in custom suits and decorator-designed penthouses notwithstanding, Metelica, like most of his ilk, lived in a neighborhood of crack houses, brothels, strip joints, and bars. And he did so as much out of familiarity as from economic need.

In this case, his apartment was located in a century-plus-old triple-decker, originally built for factory workers, now overlooking an alleyway clotted with trash. It consisted of one bedroom, a bathroom, and a living room with a kitchenette nook, all of it barely illuminated through three cloudy, narrow windows and a bare bulb hanging from the middle of the ceiling. The building's trademark exterior wooden staircase, zigzagging across its street-side facade, had been much patched and reinforced, but the clapboard had been covered with weather-streaked vinyl siding, reducing the entire structure to an awkward collision of decaying historical and tacky modern.

Willy and Lester were here on a search warrant secured through the Lowell PD, represented in the oversized person of Alvin "Big Al" Davis, one of 230 sworn local officers — a point made relevant only because by contrast, the entire Vermont State Police had but 90 more officers, grand total.

Not that Willy much cared or noticed. An ex–New York City cop himself, he found this environment to be reasonable and acceptable. Lester, however, was more in shock. He was a Vermonter born and bred, traveled outside only when he had to, and emotionally recoiled as soon as he crossed the border, feeling as much as seeing the press of millions of people all around him. Maneuvering Lowell's streets earlier to pick up Davis and the necessary search warrant at the bunkerlike police department, and then to proceed to Metelica's old address, had been enough to make him pray that this search would be a model of efficiency and that he and Willy wouldn't have to spend the night down here.

Willy was staring at him now, as Lester took in his surroundings. "Yo," Willy said. "It's not the Grand Canyon. You wanna stop admiring the view?"

Lester nodded without a word and passed into the bedroom, while Big Al loitered by the front door, watching.

It was a far nicer place than many they'd searched, despite the chaos and clamor of its neighborhood, sounds of which came in muffled through the dirty windows. Leo Metelica hadn't been neat or tidy by any stretch, or driven to wash dishes, vacuum, or make his bed. But he hadn't been a slob, either, or a packrat, and he had thought to take out the garbage before heading off to die in Vermont.

He had also apparently been either a man not to invite guests or not to care if they discovered what he did for a living. Strewn across what passed for the dining table was a copious assortment of gun-related paraphernalia, from cleaning rags and oils to reloading equipment and spare parts, including two more barrels for the missing .45.

Also, more telling to these visitors, stuck to the wall above the table were maps of Vermont and Brattleboro, downloaded photographs of the latter, and printed pages from Bariloche's Web site. There were no pictures of people, however, to indicate who might have been Metelica's intended target.

Nevertheless, Willy was pleased by the discovery. Up until now, the notion that this man had been a professional killer, sent to

Brattleboro to knock off one of its own, had been based entirely on educated intuition.

No longer.

"How're you faring?" Lester asked forty-five minutes later, stepping out of the bedroom bearing two rifles, which he carefully propped against the wall before peeling off his latex gloves in exchange for another pair. His hands glistened with sweat.

Willy was on his knees under the table, peering at a scrap of paper with the aid of a small flashlight. It was a receipt for some fast food, which he dropped back onto the floor as he spoke.

"Not bad. Got a few things worth checking out. What did you find in there?"

"A decent wardrobe and a better-than-average porno collection. He also liked war novels, gun magazines, and K-Y jelly." He nodded toward the guns. "Oh yeah. And a .308 Remington 700 with a Leupold scope and a .223 Bushmaster. Not to mention a pair of fifteen-power Swarovski binoculars that would make Bill Gates drool and a couple of knives to put Rambo to shame. I'm guessing a bit of penis envy going on."

Big Al let out a laugh from his station by the door. Despite his name being all over the legal paperwork, he'd been more than happy to watch from the sidelines.

"You find a phone?" Willy asked.

Lester shook his head. "Nope. You neither?"

"Probably used a cell," Willy mused, climbing out from under the table. "But if he did, then it's missing."

"Or he used a drop phone or pay phones. That would be quaint."

Willy looked over at Davis. "You still have pay phones around here?"

Davis frowned. "Few and far between, and none of them work. Local dirtbags seen to that."

Lester walked over to the dining table, which seemed to be where Metelica had spent most of his time when he wasn't in the bedroom either watching TV or pleasuring himself, or both. Willy had constructed a small pile of bagged evidence on one of the chairs, most of it consisting of shopping receipts from the trash, always a good source of time-and-motion information.

Lester pointed at it. "No computer, either?"

Willy glanced at him sharply. "Interesting point, Watson. And no mail."

They both looked around, reappraising their surroundings.

"Okay," Willy resumed. "We got a guy who either works for whoever hires him, or exclusively for one client, but it's still a job where he has to be contacted, like anyone else taking in orders for fulfillment."

"Nice way of phrasing it," Les agreed, following Willy's train of thought. "But how's he do it?"

"Right," Willy said. "What did the landlady say about how long he'd lived here?"

"Metelica? Maybe five years. She wasn't sure."

Willy addressed Big Al. "This neighborhood have all the usuals? Groceries, restaurants, Laundromats, one of those shipping places, maybe?"

"Most of that, yeah," Davis said, leaning against the doorjamb. "I don't know about any shipping place."

"Bars, though," Willy said, largely to himself. "I saw a couple on this block alone."

"What're you getting at?" Lester asked.

Instead of answering, Willy crossed over to Davis. "You do us a big favor and stay here while my buddy and I check out a couple of the local bars?"

Davis smiled lazily. "I've heard that one before." He then added, "Sure. I know what you're after. I'll give you thirty minutes. All part of the babysitting service."

"Want us to bring you back anything?"

The big man chuckled. "Tempting. I'll settle for a coffee that doesn't have anything swimming in it. Thanks."

Willy and Les got lucky at the second bar they entered — immediately across the street, named, without any attempt at originality, the Emerald Isle.

Even this early in the day, there were several patrons scattered near the two pool tables at the back, or at the far end of the bar. It seemed that everyone had an aversion to the front door — or the sunshine it briefly allowed in.

Willy and Les sat on neighboring stools and waited for the bearded barkeep to wander down in their direction.

"Name your poison," he said.

"Leo Metelica," Willy said without preamble.

"Never heard of him," was the hair-trigger response.

"You say that about all your regulars?"

"I don't know the man. You want drinks? Or are you on duty?"

The last was delivered with a faint smile.

Willy raised his eyebrows. "Whoa. Very slick. I can't imagine what gave us away. Why do all you guys like to fuck with us so much? Especially when you got a business hanging in the balance."

The man's eyes narrowed. "What's that mean? I just don't know the guy, is all."

Lester wearily rested his elbow on the bar. "It means that you're putting your license at risk for no good reason."

Willy removed Metelica's morgue photo. "Feast your eyes on your dead buddy, clever boy, and ask yourself exactly what you owe him."

The barkeep leaned forward, scrutinizing the picture without actually touching it. "What happened?"

"Off a bridge and onto the rocks. Really mashed the back of his head."

The man straightened back up. "Where?"

Willy replaced the photo, reached out, and simply hooked the index finger of his muscular right hand into the top of the barkeep's breast pocket — a tiny gesture gleaming with threat.

Kunkle looked deeply into his eyes as he spoke. "This is very simple. You talk to us about Metelica and we don't turn into your worst migraine. He's dead, and so is your business arrangement with him."

Still, the man hesitated.

Willy continued with his calculated gamble. "You were his answering service. It's an old gag with guys like him. They think it'll cover their tracks. Problem is, the poor sucker they choose ends up being called an accessory."

"I didn't do nothin'."

"So share what you didn't do and we'll go away."

The barkeep carefully unhooked Willy's finger and stepped back. "Wait here."

His shoulders slumped, he retreated down the length of the bar, reached under the cash register, and returned bearing a legal-size envelope.

This he dropped before them with a slap. "That's his mail."

"All of it?"

"Yeah."

It was too dark even to pretend to take a look, so Willy merely placed his hand upon it, taking possession.

"He used the phone, too," Lester stated flatly.

"Yeah."

"Did he receive calls or make them?"

"Both," the barkeep answered.

"How 'bout a computer? He keep a laptop here?"

He shook his head. "He used Internet cafés. That's what he told me — a bunch of 'em, so he couldn't be traced. And no, I don't know which ones."

Lester smiled. "We'll be getting your

phone records, anyhow. Now you can start sweating about who *you* might have called."

The man's face set hard. "I don't have anything to worry about. You people can fuck off."

Willy, against type, smiled pleasantly and slid off his stool, picking up the envelope. "I think we will. Thanks for your time."

The bartender turned his back and walked away.

Back in the apartment, all three detectives gathered around the contents of the envelope. Al Davis was gratefully sipping the coffee they'd brought back for him.

There were three cell phones, a note pad, an oil company calendar, a credit card, and a couple of pens.

Lester picked up the envelope and peered inside. "That's it?"

Willy put on a pair of gloves and opened one of the cell phones. He waited for it to power up before punching several of its buttons. He told Les, "Check out one of the others."

Lester aped his colleague, looking up after a minute. "Totally blank. It's a virgin. Yours, too?"

"Yeah." Willy picked up the third, snapping it shut moments later with disgust.

"What's the point?" Lester asked, staring

down at the pile. Willy had already revealed that the note pad and calendar were also empty.

Willy stepped over to the kitchen chair tucked under the table, pulled it out, and sat.

"The point," he said, "is that I think we better look at this guy from a different angle."

Les parked himself on the edge of the table, hiking one leg up. "Which one?"

Willy pointed generally around the room. "First I thought he was a slob — a low-brow with the brains of a newt. Now I'm thinking he was more like a good piano player with bad personal hygiene."

Lester looked at him, waiting, knowing how this worked. Big Al, of course, had no clue. "What?" he asked, drawing the word out.

"He only did one thing, but he did it well," Willy explained, unusually helpful for once.

"He's trying to say," Lester supplied, "that our host may have been a decent hit man, after all."

"Look at the guns," Willy explained. "Good equipment, well maintained. He laid his op out in an organized manner, complete with maps, pictures, and the rest. There're no phones, no computers, none of the giz-mos that most of these jerks love and we use to catch 'em." He pointed to the contents of the envelope. "Even when we found his remote office and grabbed that stuff, you can see how careful he was. No notes, no incriminating messages, and nothing on the phones. And even here, at home — the fridge is almost empty, there's little to nothing on the kitchen shelves, the trash is loaded with neighborhood fast food wrappers, there's dust on everything. What I'm seeing is a man who maybe slept here but who lived on the streets — eating, entertaining himself, running his business. I bet when he wasn't cleaning guns and whacking off, he was out. That's smart — it stops you from getting attached to a place, and from piling up possessions and electronic gadgets that can be used against you."

"But what about the phones?" Lester asked. "Why have three blanks in an envelope?"

"For grab-and-run missions," Willy mused. "We know he used the bar phone for his business calls. Fatso across the street told us that much. But look what we got: a calendar, a note pad, a credit card. That all tells me this is his travel stash. The piece of paper with 'Bariloche' written on it was the same as the pages on that pad."

Les was looking animated by now. "Cool — the credit card'll probably be blank, too, and I bet he left it behind because Bratt was just a short trip and he didn't feel he'd need it."

Willy shrugged. "I buy that."

"But," Les added, "assuming all that's true, here's my question: Where's the phone we should have found on him?" He tapped the empty envelope. "This is his gotta-go kit. You may not need a credit card, but you sure as hell want a phone — to report in, to get last-minute instructions, whatever."

Willy was already getting up from his chair, reaching for his own cell phone. "Jee-zum, Les — you're catching on. Let's hope the damn thing's still in the river and not wherever the gun is."

As Willy began punching in numbers, Lester turned to Davis. "Looks like we're heading out. We would sure love to take a look at that bar's phone records, though."

Big Al smiled. "No problem."

Late that same night, Lester and Willy were on the first floor of Brattleboro's municipal building, in the detective division of the police department with Ron Klesczewski and J. P. Tyler.

"You find anything on that?" Willy asked, looking at the cell phone they'd retrieved from the bottom of the Whetstone Brook, about one hundred yards downstream from Metelica's body, and now resting in the middle of the conference table.

J.P. cleared his throat. "Well, you were right about it being a throw phone. It's basically fresh out of the box. I did get a single number off of it, belonging to Benjamin Underhill, of Boston. I checked him out, but," he added, "it turns out the best information I got was already in-house."

Ron held up a stapled report before them. "Joe Gunther to the rescue — again," he said theatrically. "Joe volunteered to run a background check on Lloyd Jordan for me — he's one of the Tag Man victims — and interviewed a source in Massachusetts in the process. That person told him that Jordan used to work for or with Ben Underhill in the old days, before he retired here, and that Underhill is both part of the Boston mob and a really nasty guy, something J.P. confirmed with his record search."

"Underhill hired Metelica to whack Jordan?" Lester asked.

There was a momentary silence around the table before Willy said softly, "Maybe it's time to tell Joe to stop farting around and collect a paycheck."

CHAPTER THIRTEEN

"You are looking better," Eberhard Dziobek commented.

"I'm feeling better," Joe conceded. "It's a little confusing. Now part of my problem is I don't think about her all the time."

The older man nodded. "Guilt for not feeling guilty?"

Joe shook his head in wonderment. "Jesus. The way people screw themselves up, you should have enough work for two lifetimes."

"I am not complaining," Dziobek admitted. "Why do you think this is, though — this improvement? The passage of time?"

"Maybe. I'm also getting back to work, to a limited degree. I offered to help out my old colleagues at the PD, and I guess that's turned into a useful distraction. I just can't get over that she deserves more than to have me burying myself in the same old routine in order to forget about her faster."

"You do that a fair amount," the psychologist told him. "You head toward a truth and then you veer off at the last moment."

Joe looked confused. "What do you mean by that?"

Dziobek laughed at the question. "I think your subconscious knows very well, but I will explain. I believe that you enjoy your work as a police officer because it is good work; it helps people in need, it puts people in jail who deserve to be there, and it is good for your soul. It is also intellectually challenging, and it has little vestige of what could be called drone work. Every moment of every day is filled with the potential, even the likelihood, that whatever plans you may have had will be altered by some crisis, large or small.

"Having said that," he continued, "you diminish that description of your life by invoking a routine, as if you were an office worker fixing an endless row of broken Xerox machines in the basement."

He removed his glasses and rubbed them on his tie, no doubt merely smearing whatever had been clouding them in the first place.

"I am delighted that you are getting back to work. And while I do agree that it is comfortable for you to do so, I do not think that you should cheapen your self-healing by labeling it as an escape from your grief. You are leavening your loss with the worthwhile work that Lyn admired when she was alive. You are grieving *differently* than you were. That is all."

Joe smiled at what had amounted to the most forcefully stated opinion he'd ever heard from this otherwise carefully spoken man.

"Jeez, Eberhard, I thought folks like you were supposed to nod and say things like, 'Very interesting.' Not ream out your patients."

Dziobek took up a pad from the small table beside his armchair, poised his pen over its surface, and said sonorously, "Hmmm. Please go on . . ."

Sally Kravitz took a deep breath and rang the doorbell, as nervous as an actor on opening night.

A few moments later, the door opened to reveal a smiling elderly woman of generous girth who looked her up and down with obvious pleasure, a response Sally's father had been counting on.

"Yes?" the woman asked.

Sally smiled brightly and stuck out her hand. "Hi, I'm Nancy. Are you Gloria Jean Wrinn?"

Gloria shook her hand. "Yes, I am."

"I'm so happy to meet you," Sally continued, trying to forget the microphone she'd clipped to the front of her brassiere, and the fact that Dan was eavesdropping from a couple of hundred yards away. "I work for the state of Vermont, Agency of Human Services, Division of Indigent Residents." She reached into the canvas shoulder bag Dan had lent her and extracted a business card he'd also conjured up of the most bogus-sounding piece of bureaucracy Sally could imagine.

"She'll never buy this," she'd told him at the time.

"Trust me," he'd countered. "It's just the kind of craziness they do buy."

And she did. Gloria took the card and stepped back a foot. "How nice. And you're so young, too. Would you like to come in?"

Sally adhered to the cardinal order she'd been given. "Well, not actually, Mrs. Wrinn. I'm just doing a quick survey at the moment — kind of getting things organized for another visit later on." She reached into the bag again and pulled out a small clipboard with some documents attached to it. "Right now, all I need to know is if a gentleman named Paul Hauser is still living here."

Gloria's eyes widened. "Oh."

Sally blinked at the surprised reaction. "Are you all right?"

The older woman's hand fluttered like a hummingbird before settling on the door-knob. "Well, it's just odd, is all."

"How do you mean?"

"Paul used to live here, but he's gone. At least I think he is."

This wasn't what Sally had been expecting, although she suddenly began to make sense of why her father had come up with this whole charade to begin with.

"You *think* he is?"

"He vanished," Gloria explained. "Leaving a good many of his things behind, and a bit of a mess."

Sally filled in the blanks. "You think he just went on a trip or something?"

"I don't, not really," Gloria confessed. "It was just so unexpected; I'm not sure what to think."

"When was this?" Sally asked, slipping into her role, remembering what she'd seen on TV police shows.

"Three days ago, or nights, I should say, since that's when I think he left. Are you sure you wouldn't like to come in?"

Sally made an executive decision, imagining her father's blood pressure jumping. "Maybe for a few minutes. I think you'd enjoy sitting down."

Gloria smiled gratefully. "I would, actually. This has all caught me a little by surprise. I don't have much excitement anymore."

Sally followed her inside, remembering what Dan had told her of this woman's exuberant, globe-trotting life. She commented on the pictures and tokens crowding the ornate hallway and the coffer-ceilinged living room, where she was led. "It certainly looks like you had an exciting life once, and an amazing one. Did you collect all this on your own?"

Gloria laughed weakly, heading to an antique love seat and settling down. "Oh Lord, yes. I wish I hadn't, nowadays — it collects so much dust and I don't know what to do with it. Larry hates it; he's my nephew." She glanced about and sighed. "But it feeds my memories, and I do love to remember the old days . . ."

Her voice drifted off, prompting Sally to remind her, "About Paul . . ."

Gloria raised her hands in the air. "You see? Hopeless. Yes, yes. I'm so sorry. I simply can't keep on track anymore. It's a good thing I gave up traveling. Can you imagine what kind of trouble I'd get myself into?"

"Yes, ma'am."

Gloria lapsed into silence and stared into the middle distance for a moment, causing Sally to think that she'd have to prod her yet again.

But then she said, "I'm actually a little disappointed in Paul, to be honest. I know it sounds selfish, but I feel he's done me a disservice, leaving me in the lurch. I gave him a helping hand when people like Larry told me I was crazy, and that he'd probably cut my throat in the middle of the night, or rob me blind."

"Did he take anything when he left?" Sally asked.

"No. As I said, he actually left quite a bit behind — I think he took what he could carry on his back."

"Do you know where he went?"

"I have no idea."

"Family, maybe?"

"Maybe," Gloria agreed halfheartedly. "But he told me when we met that he had no one in his life — that they were either all dead or should be."

Sally nodded. "How *did* you meet?" She had no clue if her father wanted to know any of this — they hadn't rehearsed this possibility — but by now she was rolling on her own head of steam.

"He knocked on the door, just like you,"

Gloria told her brightly. "And by the end of the conversation, I'd offered him a room in the basement in exchange for his taking care of the place."

"So he was pretty likable?"

Gloria looked thoughtful. "I couldn't say that. Not truthfully. But I sensed that he was grateful enough that he'd never cause me harm, and I felt that it was long overdue for someone to show him a little kindness."

She stared down at her hands momentarily before saying, "I have traveled ever since I could afford to, and visited places that most tourists avoid, in part because I was interested, but also because I felt I needed to understand that not every place is like this." She took in the whole room with a gesture. "We Americans have it good, and I don't think most of us understand that. Maybe I was responding a little to that when I took in Paul."

"What did he say about himself?" Sally asked.

"That he was down and out, had no one to turn to, was willing to work for food. He saw that my grounds needed tending — my old gardener had retired and I hadn't gotten around to replacing him. He was a quiet man, and I respected his privacy and, as I mentioned, I sensed he needed a harbor that I could supply."

Gloria smiled impishly all of a sudden and added, "Plus, taking Paul in really irritated my nephew, and I love to do that."

Sally laughed out loud. "Really?"

Gloria joined her. "Oh yes. He's a real snob. Can't wait for me to die so that he can sell everything you see here and probably go out and buy a fancy car or something. The man's a fool. But he's the only family I have left."

Taking advantage of her father's inability to cast a vote, Sally decided to take a plunge. "Mrs. Wrinn, I do thank you a lot for what you've told me, and I'm really sorry that Paul left you hanging. But I do have my assignment for the agency, and I'd love to see if I can do at least part of it. Is there any way my colleague and I could take a look at Paul's old room, just to get an idea about him? We might be able to figure out where he went and do him some good — pick up where you left off, so to speak."

Her hostess's face brightened. "Oh, that would be wonderful. I am worried. It seemed so unlike him, and I'd like to know if he's all right. When I got home from visiting in Connecticut, I found a broken table from the upstairs hallway and a smashed door, and it looked like someone had been in my bedroom. Two of the windows were messed up. So anything you could tell me would be appreciated."

Sally thought to ask, "Did you call the police?"

"Why would I?" Gloria responded. "Nothing was missing. I have no idea how the table and door broke, but it didn't involve anything precious or valuable, and I didn't really care in any case. I didn't think the police could do me much good, to be honest."

Sally rose to her feet, still playing the young government worker. "Okay, well, then, if you don't mind, I'll round up my partner — he's doing paperwork in the car — and that way, we'll be out of your hair all the faster."

Gloria joined her, if considerably more slowly, saying, "Oh my dear. I don't want you gone faster. I've very much enjoyed your company."

Sally left her at the door and crossed to the side street where her father had parked the car he was using as a listening post. She tried reading his expression as she drew near, but couldn't quite get by the almost-polite smile he used to greet her.

"Nice job," he said. "Expertly done."

She cut to whatever was lurking beneath

the compliment. "But?"

The smile became more genuine. "I was getting ready to run over there just to kill you. But you did very well."

"So you'll come in with me and meet with this lady?" she asked dubiously.

He hesitated before asking, "She alone?"

"I think she is, and she's really nice. You think you could do that?"

"Of course, of course," he said distractedly, stashing his headphones and recorder back in their case.

She knew he'd do it — there was too much at stake. But she recognized his need to ready himself. This was a spontaneous moment, involving a person he'd never met — a double negative in his hyper-controlled world. But he overcame his phobias all the time, as she knew he was about to do again.

He finally put the case aside and gave her a fiercely cheerful smile. "Let's go to work."

Sally reached inside the open side window and picked up the small camera she assumed they'd want also. "Good deal," she said.

She called him John when she introduced him to Gloria at the door, and carried the brunt of the conversation as the three of them traveled slowly down the hallway to the kitchen that Dan already knew so well, and from there to the tucked-away staircase leading down.

There, Gloria stopped, saying, "This is as far as I go, I'm afraid. My legs aren't what they used to be. These stairs almost gave me a heart attack when I was trying to figure out where Paul had gone, so you're on your own. I hope that's all right."

"Perfect," Dan said, speaking for the first time since being introduced.

"I'll see you before we leave," Sally promised, already halfway down.

Before Gloria had even made it back to the kitchen, however, Dan cautioned his daughter, "Hang on. Slow down," as he caught up to her.

They halted at the bottom of the steps, by the closed door of the subterranean apartment.

"She checked once, right after she found him missing," Dan explained, his voice tense and low. "That just means that this would be the best place for him to hide out now."

"Oh," Sally said, surprised and at last a little frightened.

Dan stepped ahead of her. He pushed open the door with his foot and, knowing the light switch's location, merely reached in and flipped it on. There was no response from within when the light lit up the landing.

Dan and his daughter exchanged glances before he poked his head inside, half expecting to meet the business end of a baseball bat.

The room was empty.

"Okay," he told her quietly, his relief audible. "We're good."

Sally crossed the threshold gingerly, for the first time experiencing a hint of her father's odd predilection for other people's private environs, and glanced around the barren room.

"Gross," she murmured.

Surprisingly, despite his fastidious nature, Dan paid little attention, focusing instead on whatever story he could glean from Hauser's debris. Gloria had been right — it looked as if he'd departed with only what he could carry. Littering the furniture and the floor was the jetsam of a man packing in a hurry — and a man still bleeding from a recent injury. Dan noticed with satisfaction several drops of blood on the floor, along with a bloody tissue.

The overall effect was like following in a burglar's footsteps after he'd rifled through someone's belongings. Most everything they saw appeared scattered and disorganized, as if tossed aside in anger and frustration.

Dan liked the tone of that — a faint but lingering scent of despair. As he saw it, that gave him a little insight, along with a small advantage in what he saw looming as a high-stakes contest of wills.

"Dad?"

He turned toward Sally, having almost forgotten her presence. "What's up?"

She was looking at a loss, standing in the middle of the room, as if worried that something might rub off on her.

"What're we doing here?"

"Two things," he said, pointing at the floor. "First is to see if Hauser's suitcase is still there."

He dropped to his knees before a section of floor that Sally couldn't distinguish from the rest.

"There's a trapdoor?" she asked.

Instead of answering, he pulled out his Swiss Army knife and carefully slipped it between two floorboards. With a smooth flip of his wrist, he liberated a single board, and from there several more, to reveal a shallow hole underneath.

It was empty.

"That explains his traveling light," Dan said, sitting back on his heels.

Sally leaned forward at the waist and peered into the dark space at her feet, as if expecting something to leap out. "He took the suitcase," she confirmed.

"That's what people do in a crisis," Dan explained. "They grab the things they think they can't replace. Sadly, that usually means photo albums of loved ones — not pictures of dead people."

"So we're screwed," Sally said simply.

He rose easily to his feet, looking oddly satisfied. "Remember? I said two things. I didn't expect to find the suitcase. That would've been too valuable to lose, not to mention just a little incriminating." He thought back a moment to what he'd found in Lloyd Jordan's office, and mused, "I've never understood why people collect the things that could cause them the most damage, and then hang on to them instead of putting them in the fire. Weird, self-destructive habit."

Sally didn't bother commenting about self-destructive habits. She was still digesting the pure irony of what he'd said.

"What's the second thing?" she asked instead.

He looked around, forming a plan of attack. "People have no idea what they leave behind. And I'm not talking about fingerprints and hair follicles and DNA and the like. I mean the simple stuff — letters with return addresses, magazines with mailing labels, trash filled with information."

He stopped to face her directly. "We need to find something that tells us about this man — a connection we can follow to hunt him down."

He pointed to a spot near the door. "Start there and go through everything. If it's clothes, check labels and pockets; if it's a book or magazine, go through the pages to check for anything personal. Anything that catches your eye, put it in a pile in the middle of the floor."

"What about Gloria?" she asked. "We can't leave her dangling forever."

Dan gave her a lopsided smile. "Then we better get cracking."

Sally considered her father quickly before joining the treasure hunt. He was incredibly focused, zeroed in on his goal. Where she'd heard of an awful discovery and was now standing amid its source, fighting revulsion, she saw Dan as a man suddenly inspired, driven by the same influence as toward a valued prize. Sally shook her head slightly. She loved him dearly, but times like this reminded her of how differently he saw the world they shared.

There wasn't that much to go through. Any DVDs they found, they just added to the pile for later checking. As for the rest, it amounted largely to trash and garbage generated from fast food outlets within walking distance of the house. There were no files, no piles of bills, no photographs or letters, no computer or even a sign that one had ever been here. There was nothing of a strictly personal nature whatsoever.

With one exception.

Sally nervously knelt before the long edge of the bed and peered underneath, hoping to see only dust. That she did — along with a small rectangle of something pale, caught between the baseboard and the wall.

"Shoot," she said softly.

"What did you find?" her father asked.

"Probably nothing. It's kind of stuck against the wall." Sally tentatively began to reach out in order to grab hold of it, hoping her sleeve wouldn't rub up against anything.

"Hold it," Dan said, moving to the head of the bed and easily shifting the whole thing away from the wall. He sidestepped into the open gap, bent over, and straightened with a postcard in his hand.

"I'll be damned. I remember seeing this tacked to the wall last time. I thought he'd taken it with him. It must've fallen here."

He circled back around to her as she got to her feet and showed her a postcard of a lake. He read aloud, " 'Hey there! Greetings from the boonies. Remember how cold the water was here? Shrink your you-know-what. Hope you're not doing anything I wouldn't do. Bryn.' "

"Wow," Sally said. "There's a loaded message. It's addressed to P. Hauser at an address in Claremont, New Hampshire — apartment nine."

"The sender's name is certainly unique," Dan said quietly. "That could be helpful. What's the date on the postmark?"

Sally held the card closer and squinted. "Old. Looks like 1988, unless that's a six."

"And the lake? Where's that?"

She studied the faded legend in the upper left-hand corner. "Bomoseen."

"Western Vermont," Dan finished. "Not far from Castleton. Popular place to ice fish. Let's take that."

The postcard, it turned out, was the sum total of their relevant findings, assuming the DVDs came up empty as expected. A half hour after they'd hesitantly entered they killed the lights in Paul Hauser's abandoned room and made their way back upstairs.

They found Gloria Wrinn in her living

room, having prepared a fully loaded tea tray.

She looked up smiling as they appeared, their small collection of Hauser's belongings in a plastic bag.

"I thought you might enjoy some tea, after all your work," she said, gesturing them toward the couch opposite hers. "How did you fare?"

Dan answered for both of them, surprising his daughter. "Not all that well. He either didn't have much to start with or took everything he valued and left the rest."

Gloria was pouring two cups of tea and now handed them out, indicating the cookies, cream, and sugar by twiddling her fingers over the tray. "Feel free, please. I don't want to have to eat those myself. I'm not too surprised by what you say. When he moved in, he was carrying everything in a backpack."

"And a suitcase?" Dan asked leadingly.

She looked at him anew. "Yes. And a suitcase."

"I could see where he'd stored one, from the dust mark it left on the floor," Dan said easily.

"You're very observant," Gloria commented quietly, her gaze steady.

"That's why we keep him around," Sally

said brightly, suddenly concerned that Dan had overplayed his hand. "Lord knows, it's not his personality."

"Nancy told me Hauser didn't talk about himself much," Dan said, remembering the name Sally had used in her introduction an hour earlier.

"No," Gloria agreed. "He was a loner, all right."

"Estranged from his family, or what there was of it?"

"That's what he told me."

"What about friends? Did anyone ever drop by when he was living here, or did you ever see him with anyone?"

Gloria, still smiling, merely shook her head.

"How about Lake Bomoseen? Did he ever mention that? Or maybe Castleton or Fair Haven? Those're both in the same area."

Gloria sat back on her sofa and studied them with a kindly expression. Sally braced for the worst, for the first time missing the usually taciturn father she was forever urging to talk more.

"Where did you say you both worked?"

"Agency of Human Services, Division of Indigent Residents," Sally recited, her heart skipping.

Gloria nodded. "Ah yes. Indigent Residents. Such a very Vermont thing, to have a branch of government solely devoted to the homeless. It's such a wonderful state that way."

"Well, ma'am," Sally said, feeling her smile brittle and false. "We like to think we try."

"And hard, too," Gloria concurred. "You've been spending so much time on just one, and he's not even around anymore."

Dan, the perpetual worrier, started laughing. "You're not buying this, are you?"

Gloria's smile broadened. "Not really, but I am intrigued." She pointed at him. "You could be the police, but your partner is far too young. You might be criminals, but you've been too obvious, and nothing about you strikes me that way. I can't figure it out. Is it Paul? Are you after him for some reason?"

"We think he may have committed a crime," Dan said simply, hoping it would be enough. His daughter was speechless, staring at him.

It was. Gloria nodded thoughtfully. "You may be right. I did mention that he struck me as a bit odd. What do you think he's done? Or can't you say?"

Dan was grateful for the out. He shrugged

and gave her an apologetic look. "I am sorry, but you apparently know how that works."

He felt his daughter's gaze on him as he continued. "That being the case, Mrs. Wrinn, is there anything you can remember about him that might help? Some comment about his past or his family or any friends he might have mentioned? Or where he came from, for example?"

"Well," she answered, "as I told your sidekick . . ." She interrupted herself and pointed a finger at Sally. "You were very good, by the way. Very convincing." She returned to Dan. "He didn't go in for that much. For what it's worth, whenever we did speak about the weather or local events — maybe an election or something — he always spoke like a native, as if he'd been familiar with the region and the locals all his life. You know how most people refer to their origins pretty early on in a conversation? He didn't do that. I always got the feeling this was home."

"Brattleboro?"

"No. Not quite," she disagreed. "More generally than that. Maybe even from New Hampshire, since he said a few things about Vermont that were less than generous."

Sally's memory returned to the postcard

with that reference and snapped her out of her trance. "Claremont?"

"Could be," was the response. "I don't know that for sure, but it would fit."

There was a slight lapse in the conversation before Dan stood up, prompting the other two to follow suit, and walked to the entrance.

"I want to thank you for your time, Mrs. Wrinn, and apologize for our discretion. I am so glad you understand the position we're in."

"I understand no such thing," Gloria said pleasantly, pointing again at Sally. "If it weren't for her, I never would have spoken with you. But I knew she was a straight shooter, even if she was following a script."

"What made you suspicious?" Sally asked, shaking her hand but feeling a little stung.

"You assumed I knew nothing of state government," Gloria told her. "In fact, I do, or certainly enough to know that there's no such thing as the Division of Indigent Residents, much less enough money to fund two investigators to work for it."

"And yet you let me keep going."

Gloria patted Sally's hand. "I was curious."

Dan was shaking his head. "All kidding aside, I'm very worried about this man. I

235

think he may be dangerous, and I definitely want him held accountable."

Gloria nodded. "Will you ever tell me what it was all about?"

"I will," Sally quickly answered, seeing her father frown slightly. And, as if to drive home an unspoken subtext, Sally leaned in and gave Gloria a quick kiss on the cheek. "Thank you. Mrs. Wrinn."

The old lady smiled and fixed Dan with her eyes. She had understood their pecking order if not their goal. "You take care of her," she ordered.

"Yes, ma'am," he answered fondly.

CHAPTER FOURTEEN

It was quiet in the squad room, despite the small crowd, with everyone looking at the desk nearest the window, featuring as it hadn't in months the one man each of them liked to think of as a mentor, publicly acknowledged or not.

Joe Gunther took a sip from his coffee mug and gave them all a small, somewhat sad smile. "Long time," he said softly.

"Welcome back," Lester responded quietly.

The full VBI squad was there, including Sammie, who'd found a babysitter, and Ron Klesczewski, J. P. Tyler, and their chief, Tony Brandt, from downstairs.

"I'd like to start off by thanking each of you for your support," Joe told them. "Throughout all this, it's been a pretty big thing for me to know you were there, on the job."

"You've done it for us enough times,"

Sammie said.

"Whether we liked it or not," Willy grudgingly added.

Joe raised his eyebrows. "Point taken." He took another sip and put his cup down. "But now we've got a small problem to solve." He nodded at Ron. "Which is no longer as low-key as just running a background check on a victimized local resident."

"I guess that's fair to say," Ron acknowledged.

"Guy's as crooked as a dog's hind leg," Willy groused.

"True?" Joe asked.

"Not if what we've been told is accurate," Lester said. "He *was,* if we believe Abijah Reed, but assuming that Jordan did take out a little insurance against his former playmates, in exchange for retreating from Boston and that business, I'd think he'd be working overtime to walk the straight and narrow."

"Old dogs and new tricks," Willy shot back. "No way he's straight. It's in the blood. He's definitely up to something."

"That's what you always say," Sammie told him.

"And I'm usually right. Besides, if he's so lily-white, why did his old Boston buddies sic a triggerman onto him?"

"Before we all get ahead of ourselves," Joe interrupted, "what do we actually know? That Metelica is dead and appears to have been a hit man on assignment, targeting someone who frequents Bariloche."

Willy sighed wearily.

"That Metelica got a phone call from Ben Underhill while he was on that assignment," added Ron, well used to his old boss's Socratic style.

"That Jordan and Underhill once had a relationship," Sammie joined in.

"And that Jordan eats at Bariloche," Willy said, returning to the fray. "I got a look at the restaurant's receipts. Turns out Jordan and the trophy wife eat there a lot."

"That night?" Joe asked.

Willy grimaced, slightly caught out. "If he was, he paid cash, but he did that too, sometimes. I asked, once I got them to remember that he came there at all. He's a lousy tipper, big surprise."

"Not to be obvious," Tony Brandt said from the back of the room, "but since you're writing a checklist, you might want to add that somebody killed Leo Metelica."

There was general laughter to that. "Oh, yeah," Lester cracked. "Knew we were forgetting something."

"Good point, though," Joe said. "We shouldn't lose sight of our primary purpose here. All this chatter about the mob and Underhill and our obsession with Lloyd Jordan."

"Not an obsession if Jordan killed the guy," Willy said sourly.

"Granted," Joe agreed, while Sammie silently rolled her eyes. "Your hypothesis is that Underhill took out a contract on Jordan but that Jordan got the jump on his killer instead."

"Just because it's straightforward doesn't mean it's wrong," Willy told them.

"Why now?" Ron asked. "Hasn't this hands-off arrangement between Jordan and his mob pals been in place for years?"

"Maybe Jordan's running low on funds and put the squeeze on," Willy said. "What the hell do I know? Maybe Underhill got tired of having a pebble in his shoe."

"But why ambush him at the restaurant?" Lester asked. "Downtown, high visibility, not sure of the timing — or even if the target would be eating out that night."

Willy was scowling by now. "Hey, these guys are fucking animals. All of a sudden, they gotta think rationally?"

"Someone was rational enough to hire Metelica," Joe said quietly.

Willy shook his head. "Fine. One of you can come up with something else. I heard somebody wanted to hang this on the restaurant owner."

Joe held up his hand. "Hold on. Let's not get derailed. There is something rising to the surface with all this — something we've been missing."

He rose from his chair and perched on the windowsill — a position they'd all grown accustomed to and were pleased to see him resume.

"We mostly agree that Metelica was hired to kill somebody and that whoever that was turned the tables on him. Any arguments there?"

Silence greeted him.

Joe continued. "So, what follows is that one planned surprise resulted in an un-planned surprise replacing it."

Willy murmured "Jeez" loud enough for everyone to hear it.

Joe smiled. "Bear with me. We've talked about a few variables that Metelica had to deal with. Would his target come to the restaurant that night? Who might be with him? What time might he leave? How would he leave? By car parked right outside the front door, or by walking a distance into the darkness, which might make him available to being picked off?"

"Making the whole proposition look weaker and weaker," Brandt commented. Even Willy's expression had changed from angry to merely sullen.

"Maybe, maybe not," Joe reacted. "That's less my point than the fact that so many variables mean more time needed to address them."

Willy suddenly looked up, his mood instantly reversed. "The motherfucker had a motel room."

Joe laughed. "Bingo. If Metelica was caught off guard, and not even a toothbrush was found in his car, it suggests he has a room somewhere in town with all his stuff still in it."

Lester was already getting to his feet. "Assuming it isn't all in a Dumpster by now."

It took them most of a day to locate Leo Metelica's motel. Not that they actually located his room. Lester had been right about that. Metelica's possessions had been removed a few days earlier, once management had concluded that he'd skipped.

But they weren't in a Dumpster. They'd been placed in a large garbage bag and relegated to a storage room, following the motel's policy of keeping such items for a month before disposing of them.

Joe, Willy, Ron, and Lester made for a large group in such a space, so Joe asked the counterman if the empty breakfast nook off the lobby might be used for a preliminary inventory of the bag's contents.

Lester poured their discovery out across two small tables shoved together, under the placid gaze of a muted, wall-mounted TV set in one corner, and a row of silent and empty coffee and cream dispensers, two waffle irons, and several pedestaled cake holders designed for doughnuts, crullers, bear claws, and other standards of the American diet.

There wasn't much in the garbage bag — a small overnight bag, barely larger than an old-fashioned doctor's case, a toilet kit, a few changes of socks, underwear, and shirts, and a plastic folder closed with a rubber band.

Knowing that they'd be putting it all under close scrutiny later on, Willy wasted no time, quickly and expertly opening the folder with his latex-enclosed right hand.

What fanned out before them was a map, some photographs similar to what they'd found at Metelica's apartment, along with a single, close-up portrait of a man wearing a black watch cap and black turtleneck. The man pictured was either distracted or unaware of the lens, which was angled high, as might befit a surveillance camera.

"I'll be goddamned," Willy said, almost to himself.

"You know who this is?" Joe asked.

Willy was staring at the image as if willing it to confess. "I should. I've been working him as a CI for years. That's Dan Kravitz. He must've been the target — not Jordan. What the hell?"

"I don't know, Dad. I'm starting to understand why you live alone."

Dan appeared from the back room. "The accommodations not up to prep-school standards?"

She laughed. "It's better than living in a van, for sure. As for the academy, I think they keep their lawnmowers in something like this."

Dan had found them an empty hunting cabin, northwest of Brattleboro, high in the hills and deep in the woods, on loan from a friend of Dan's he hadn't identified and Sally hadn't asked about. She was long used to her father's ways, and his eccentric taste in living arrangements.

"Speaking of vans," he said, leading the way to the rear door, "I thought it was time to upgrade our transportation."

"Oh God," she said. "What? A sixty-eight Beetle with a flower-power paint job?"

He stopped shy of the threshold and looked back at her. "I had no idea you were so versed in nostalgic iconography."

She pushed him gently. "Show me the heap, Dad."

He threw open the back door and gestured with a flourish. "Ta-dah."

Her eyes widened at the sight of an old but well-maintained Land Rover, complete with spare tire mounted on the hood.

"Cool," she said, circling the car and running her hand along its flanks. She looked happily at her father. "You have really traded up this time."

"Well," he cautioned, "it's only a loaner, so don't get too attached, but I thought it might be a good idea to drive something not associated with us — or me, at least."

That lowered her high spirits. She grew more serious. "You think this guy is that good?"

"I think it would be foolish to assume otherwise."

The hard-thinking logician in her responded with a nod. "Right." She then smiled again, patting the Land Rover like an oversized pet. "Kind of funny to be anonymous in something that sticks out like this."

He shrugged and rattled the keys. "So let's enjoy it while we can."

"Really?" she asked. "Now? Where're we going?"

He waved the postcard back and forth that she'd found in Paul Hauser's room. "How 'bout Claremont?"

Claremont was somewhat larger than Brattleboro, and utterly different in character. Once a mill town, across the river from Interstate 91, it featured some splashier architecture than its southern neighbor's — like an impressive Italian Renaissance town hall — but also a stretch of depressingly abandoned factory buildings, hulking and useless, that generally caused more debate than action about urban rehaul and improvement. To the east, straddling Washington Street, was also a commercial strip that rivaled Brattleboro's Putney Road in its tacky abandonment to fast food restaurants, shopping outlets, and motels. In all, to Dan Kravitz's taste, Claremont had its points, but lost significantly in terms of flair and uniqueness. To him, it simply existed, and as such remained no more than a place to drive through.

But then, he considered himself a bit of an expert in driving through — both places and people — and conceded to having become a hobo/snob.

The address on the postcard was perhaps predictably located along Washington Street's oldest and most downtrodden stretch, where the miracle had left that mile, yielding to newer, larger, more frequented commercial attractions down the road. The building in question appeared to have once been a motel, long ago converted to apartment units, or maybe just a failed prefab stack of apartment-size boxes, done quickly in an effort to offer some cheap housing.

Affordable or not nowadays, its budget-minded genesis starkly stood out on its weather-streaked, exhausted surface.

Sally craned forward in her seat to appreciate the entire structure as Dan pulled up into its weed-choked parking lot.

"Wow — nice place to call home, just in case you had too good a day at work."

She turned suddenly to face her father. "Why're we here, anyhow? This is ancient history, right?"

Dan killed the engine and joined her in surveying their surroundings. "It's a long shot," he agreed. "Given what little we've got, I'm hoping somebody here dates back to when the postcard was mailed."

She raised her eyebrows. "We're going to knock on doors?"

He stepped out of the car and smiled back at her. "We'll start with the most reasonable one first — see what that gives us."

The manager thankfully lived on site, as Dan had been hoping, and even had a sign on his door advertising the fact. And though no one answered when Dan rang the bell, he and Sally were still standing there when a voice rose behind them.

"Who're you?"

They turned to see a small, thin man wearing a single earring and no hair. In his hand he carried an antique wooden carpenter's box, filled with an assortment of old hand tools.

Sally smiled broadly. "Hi. We were looking for the manager."

The man's narrow face remained pinched and severely set. "Why?"

This was not Dan's strength, dealing with potentially hostile people. Sally approached him with her hand out in greeting. "I'm Sally. This is my dad. We're kind of on a history-hunting trip, looking for my long-lost uncle Paul."

The man shook her hand reluctantly, not quite willing to be outright rude.

"So?"

Sally pointed at the wooden toolbox, her face brightening. "I'm sorry. It's just that my gramp had one of those. I used to love that thing. Are you a woodworker?"

"No."

She carried on, unsure of her direction. "Me, neither, not that I'm not interested, but it's harder than it looks. That's cool, though. Where did you get it?"

He glanced at it as if surprised to find it in his hand. "My grandfather. Who did you say you were?"

Sally crouched down to study it closer up. Startled, he took a half step back.

"I'm Sally. This is my dad," she repeated, looking up. "This really is just like Gramp's. And the tools're old, too. You like working with them?"

He considered the question seriously. "They feel good in the hand," he conceded. "Better than the newer stuff."

She straightened and tilted her head slightly. "I'm sorry."

His brow furrowed. "What?"

She indicated the toolbox. "That must've seemed a little weird, is all. My getting all worked up about it. It's not like we know each other. Kind of rude, really."

He passed his hand across his bald pate,

his confusion plain. "No, that's okay. It triggered a memory, right? No crime in that." He bowed ever so slightly at the waist and added, "I'm Jonny Bombard. I'm the manager. Who did you say you were looking for?"

"Paul Hauser. My aunt Sylvia died last week — that's my dad's sister. She was once married to this guy who we think lived here for a while, and they were really happy until things went wrong over a stupid misunderstanding and they never talked again and it totally broke her heart —"

Dan saw his cue and steeled himself to talk, touching Sally's elbow. "Sweetheart. Give the man a break. Not everybody's as enthusiastic as you."

"No, that's okay," Bombard said. He thought for a moment, his eyes downcast in concentration. "Nah," he finally conceded. "Doesn't ring a bell. When did he live here?"

Dan answered, "In the eighties sometime."

Bombard's mouth dropped open. "The *eighties*. Are you kidding me? I have no clue who lived here back then. I thought maybe you were talking about a year ago or something. People pass through here like it was a motel, sometimes."

"Is there anyone who *might* know?" Sally implored. "Someone who's lived here longer than most?"

Jonny watched her face, as if gauging her sincerity. "Look," he relented. "There is a guy. Used to be manager before me. Norm Myers. He's old, though. I don't know what he's got left, you know?" He tapped his temple with his index.

"Where's he live?" Sally asked.

"Vermont. On Kendrick's Corner Road, near the Springfield airport — at least he used to. It's not far from here." He pointed off into the distance, adding, "Due west, ten, fifteen miles. He worked here for more years than anyone knows. I think maybe he even owned the place when it was new. Something like that."

"How do you remember where he lives?" Dan asked, typically struck by the sudden detail.

"He came by a couple of times when I first signed on," Jonny explained, now readily talkative, largely because of Sally, who was pretending to hang on his every word.

"That was about ten years ago. Some niece or daughter or whatever drove him here. A trip-down-memory-lane thing. It was actually kind of handy because he knew stuff that turned out to be a big help — service panels, utility lines, shit like that. I didn't know much about running a building back then. I guess it was less run-down in his day — at least that's the way he made it sound." He added after a moment, "Nice old guy."

Bombard suddenly smiled at Sally, which startled her enough that this time, she took a step back. "Reminded me of my grand-dad, like you said."

"That's neat," she said softly, genuinely touched.

"Anyhow," Jonny returned to Dan, "I think Norm's your man. The way he was talking, he knew all the tenants like he was a dorm parent or something. Really into it." He eased past them both and opened the door to his apartment. "I've got something with his address on it somewhere. I kept it in case some other piece of this pile of bricks falls apart I can't fix."

Joe, Willy, and Ron reached the top of the narrow staircase and fanned out across the pristine wooden floor of the large room above the Bariloche restaurant.

"It's like a ballroom," Ron commented.

"Might've been," Joe told him. "Back when the factories were going full guns, there were a bunch of dance halls around town, to keep the workers entertained."

"I bet," Willy cracked, looking around.

"Not like that," Joe corrected him. "Look at the chair railing." He pointed to a broad horizontal strip of wood running around the wall, about four feet off the floor. "See the regularly spaced, slightly dark smudges? That's from the hair pomade the men used to wear. They sat along the walls on Saturday nights, leaning back and waiting for their turn to dance with the girls, maybe passing a bottle around, maybe not. From what I was told, it wasn't usually rowdy. Everybody was too tired from six days of work."

Willy crouched in the middle of the floor to get a better angle on whatever might still be resting on its polished surface — any scuff mark, piece of fabric, or scrap of paper. There was nothing. The room might as well have just been reconstructed for a museum exhibition, and awaiting a shipment of period furnishings to match Joe's narrative.

"Well," he said admiringly, given his own cleanliness issues. "It's pretty obvious Dan wasn't too pressed for time to leave this place like a surgical room. We got zilch here."

Joe nodded in agreement. "Except that the restaurant owner said he was here one day and gone the next, like a ghost in the night."

"Or a man on the run," Ron suggested.

Willy fixed his boss with a look. "Did you check out his daughter, Sally? At school?"

Joe nodded slowly, still glancing around. "Soon as we figured out Dan was Metelica's target." He smiled sorrowfully. "Call me hyper-vigilant nowadays when it comes to collateral damage. But she's vanished, too. At least it doesn't look like she was grabbed — her father phoned right after they noticed her missing to sort out some final-exam issues, but that was it."

Willy stood back up. "That settles it. If he cleared the kid out of there, we're in for the hunt of our lives. That girl means everything to him — if he's got her under his wing, he's good to go to hell and back, and we'll probably never be the wiser."

CHAPTER FIFTEEN

The address Jonny Bombard had given them on Kendrick's Corner Road belonged to a simple, tidy, one-story ranch with a garage at one end and a mother-in-law extension at the other. The name on the mailbox said "Harrison."

"You think?" Dan asked his daughter.

Sally hitched her shoulders. "Jonny said it was a woman driving Norm around. Could be her married name."

Dan pulled into the driveway, turned off the ignition, and made to step out of the car when a woman appeared on the home's front stoop.

"May I help you?" she called out, her expression open and friendly.

Both Kravitzes swung out onto the gravel driveway. This time, Dan took the lead, since Sally was all but hidden by the hulking Land Rover as she walked around its hood into view.

"Yeah, hi," he said, flapping a hand at Sally, "We're Jack and Maddy, from the Manaqueetoc Water Control Group. We've been hired by the city of Claremont to map the water lines over there. Jonny Bombard — at the building complex that Norman Myers used to run — told us that Norm was the man to see when it came to things like that."

"At least where it concerned that neighborhood," Sally threw in for form, recovering from the novelty of seeing her father's theatrical debut.

But the woman in the doorway was showing no suspicions whatsoever, even though Sally was wondering where in hell her father had cooked up that one. Sally had learned early on to front for her father by carrying the load of most social interactions. To see him as poised as he'd been since all this began had revealed a whole new person to her — and proved how much he felt was at stake.

"Norm's my dad," the woman told them, coming forward to shake their hands. "I'm Peggy Harrison. He lives with us nowadays." She pointed to the extension attached to the house.

"Unfortunately," she then said, "you just missed him. He's taking his annual pilgrimage to see the wreck."

Dan and Sally exchanged glances.

Peggy interpreted the gesture. "Sorry. It's a huge local thing. Nobody else knows much about it. There was a plane crash on Hawks Mountain, back in the forties. It was a really bad night: a military plane got lost and flew right into the mountainside. It was terrible. Everybody onboard died. All the locals climbed the mountain in the dark to see if they could help. My dad was part of that, as a young man. It's haunted him ever since, so every year, he revisits where it happened." She then admitted, "It's a little weird. I never got it. But it's a big deal to him."

Sally remembered what Jonny had said about Norm's mental health, and was groping for how to broach the subject, when Dan asked, "He can do that? Alone? Jonny said he was a little worse for wear mentally."

Peggy's eyes widened, but she was smiling as she said, "He did, did he? Well, maybe it doesn't take one to tell one. I would've called Jonny a moron. No, my dad's a hundred percent. He's old, but he's wiry and as sound as a bell. Plus, he's been doing this for over sixty years. He'd more likely lose his way to the bathroom than get lost on Hawks Mountain."

Dan was agreeably nodding his head. "I heard about that crash," he said. "It was a B-29, I think. A heavy bomber. What they called a Superfortress."

"That sounds right," Peggy agreed.

Dan turned to his daughter and explained, "Same type of plane that dropped the A-bomb on Japan, at the end of World War Two."

Peggy was still speaking. "So I'm afraid you won't get to see him today, unless you want to chase after him."

Dan looked at her, surprised. "We could do that? He wouldn't mind? I'm asking because we are on a tight schedule, and heading up north at the end of the day. Coming back would seriously mess up the calendar."

"No, no. That would be fine," Peggy said. "Dad would love to share this with somebody. I'm afraid I'm a big disappointment to him there. Let me get you a map."

She vanished inside the house and re-emerged with a single sheet of paper, which she handed over. "It's incredibly easy. You have to ask permission of the people whose property you'll be crossing, but Dad already did that, so if anyone challenges you, just say you're with Norm Myers." She laughed. "They know him by now almost as well as I do. You'll have fun. It'll only take a few hours, it's a beautiful day, and you two look pretty fit."

It was a beautiful day — a true advertisement of Vermont's best features — and after a quick glance at Sally, Dan accepted Peggy's suggestion, made his farewell, and drove them both to the jumping-off place in the heart of Perkinsville village.

"The Manaqueetoc Water Control Group?" Sally asked as they climbed out of the Land Rover and got themselves oriented at the foot of the first sloping field they were to address. Hawks Mountain — carpeted with trees, devoid of any signs of humanity, loomed above them like the menacing thing it had once been so long ago.

Dan smiled slightly. "I liked the sound of it."

"What is Manaqueetoc?"

He checked to see that the water bottle he'd attached to his belt was secure. "Beats me."

Hawks Mountain lay at the heart of an official wildlife-management area, which helped preserve its pristine condition, so it wasn't more than fifteen minutes later that Dan and Sally found themselves as surrounded by trees as they might have been in Colonial times — excepting, as Dan pointed out, that Vermont had been clear cut of forests by the mid-1800s, making all of this woodland a second-growth crop, if not more recent.

But it was still old and sheltering, and wonderfully quiet, and the higher they climbed, the more often they caught glimpses of the valley below and to the east, including — Sally noticed with sad irony — a clear view of the Springfield airport, its paved and slightly elevated runway gleaming in the early-summer sun.

What they didn't see for well over an hour, however, was any sign of Norman Myers, who they now both realized had either left home a lot earlier than they'd been told, or was built like a billy goat.

It turned out to be the latter. Just as they encountered the first amateur paper signs, covered in plastic wrap, announcing the beginning of the general crash site, Dan saw a red shirt bobbing far ahead of them, like a cardinal flitting amid the green foliage.

He put on a little more steam to close the distance, not bothering to admire a couple of mangled metal objects lying by the side of the trail — far too large to be carted off by souvenir seekers. Finally, he placed his hands around his mouth and called out, "Norm? Norm Myers?"

The slender, white-haired man far ahead stopped and turned, his face as welcoming as his daughter's had been earlier.

"Hi," he said simply.

Sally tried guessing her father's mood, no longer so sure how to play her role now that Dan had become such an extrovert.

As if reading her thoughts, Dan stepped right up to the man and made the introductions — truthfully, this time.

"Hi, Norm. I'm Dan and this is my daughter, Sally. Peggy told us how to find you. I hope we're not interrupting. I understand that this is a special yearly pilgrimage for you."

Norm was visibly impressed.

"You know this place?"

While Sally shook her head, her father said, "I read about it, but I've never been."

Norm turned to the scene. The surrounding trees stood farther back here, creating an area like a forested box canyon — open at one end, enclosed on two sides, and faced at the head wall by a steep and forbidding cliff that launched straight up to the top of Hawks Mountain, 150 yards or more overhead.

The entire setting had a faintly cathedral air, which in turn was given meaning by the presence of several objects noticeably at odds with the peaceful backdrop.

Norm pointed to one of them. "One of four engines. All of them are still here, and parts of the landing gear and undercarriage." His finger moved up the cliff. "Up there, on the ledge. If they'd just been a few hundred feet higher up, they would've missed it." He added, "Not that it probably would've mattered."

"Why not?" Sally asked.

"This isn't the highest peak in the neighborhood. Ascutney is a lot taller, and just a few miles north. The way the pilot was poking around, looking for a landmark, I guess he was going to hit something, sooner or later. Still . . . You never know."

Norm walked a little farther into the shrine. As their eyes adjusted to the environment, differentiating the rocks from the trees from the scattered dull-metal reminders, they became increasingly aware of how much debris remained. A true sense of the disaster materialized, causing Sally to suddenly recognize that the glade they were occupying had most likely been formed less by nature and more by a cataclysmic and fiery explosion of unimaginable proportions.

"I was there," Norm said simply. "When it happened."

"That must have been horrible," Sally sympathized.

Norm turned and smiled at her. "Changed my life. I was a young man then — 1947. Full of beans and ready to take on the world. I was angry that I'd missed the war. Just a couple of years too young. And I was filled with . . . I guess you'd call it resentment. I felt I could've been a hero, that I would've had amazing stories to tell, and a sense of being rounded out somehow. The guys who had served and come back didn't talk about it, and pretty much brushed me off, and I couldn't figure that out. I thought they were putting me down. At that age, everything's about you, you know?"

He focused on Sally more closely at that and immediately apologized. "No offense."

"None taken," she said. "You're right."

"So that night," Dan brought him back. "You got a small taste of reality?"

Norm nodded. "Good way of putting it." He looked around. "It's hard to tell now. It's so peaceful and there's not much left. But the explosion was really huge. Middle of the night, raining like crazy. The whole world shook with a rumble. I was listening to the radio in my bedroom when my window lit up like the sun had come out of nowhere. I knew what it was — or at least I had a pretty good idea. We'd all heard the plane going over a couple of times, like it was looking for something, and those engines made a hell of a row. Just a few seconds before the explosion, they went out, like you snapped a switch. I remember sitting up, all tingly, wondering what was going on, and then, *boom*." He raised both his arms overhead as he said the last word very quietly.

"You came up here that night?" Sally asked.

"Nothing could've held me back," Norm told her. "Everything I was telling you welled up in me like nobody's business. This was it, I thought. This is my shot at a real story. An incredible adventure. I mean, here it was, after midnight, still pouring, black as the bottom of a well, and we had no problem knowing where to head. There was that much fire. Thousands of gallons of aviation fuel, burning hundreds of trees . . . You can't even imagine."

Dan turned in a circle, as if admiring a museum display. "All right here," he murmured.

"It was like everything I'd ever been told about Hell," Norm said. "The old Bible version — fire and brimstone and burning flesh. Even after all the time it took us to slip and slide up the mountain in the dark and the rain, there were still pools of gasoline burning like bonfires, and huge pieces of plane everyplace — including the whole tail section, and bodies and body parts . . . It was huge and it went on forever. There didn't seem to be an end to it. We ran from place to place, trying to find somebody to help, but behind all the crackling fire and hissing steam and the shouting from all of us, there was a silence."

He looked at them both intently. "It was like the dead were making more noise than we were, you know what I mean?"

Dan thought of Hauser's albums. "Yeah. I do."

Sally, however, with no such scarring memories, was of a more practical mien. "So what happened?"

Norm blinked at her. "Here? We collected what we could of the bodies. The army came and finished it up, blowing up the wreck and carrying away a lot of the mess. Nature did the rest."

"They blew up the wreck? Why?"

"They didn't want it seen from the air," he explained. "Big impact like that would've been visible for years, and been reported by other flyers again and again. I think it was a sign of respect, too."

"And a reflection of the Red Scare era," Dan put in, his voice low. "People worried about secrets."

Norm shrugged. "Probably. In any case, there's not much left from that night."

"And what about you?" Dan asked, sensitive to a kindred spirit.

The old man's smile was sad. "Like I said, changed my life. What I saw here, and what I saw in the faces of the men who climbed with me, told me a lot. I realized what an idiot I'd been, believing all that John Wayne crap." He glanced at Sally. "Sorry."

"That's okay."

He continued. "Korea started up a couple of years later. I was the right age this time, and given how I'd been thinking, I was a natural to serve. But I didn't. I'd had nightmares ever since, and begun drinking by then, too." He was staring at the ground and shaking his head. "Good thing I didn't fight in the war, the way I reacted up here. I probably would've been shot as a deserter."

"Oh," Sally said.

Dan joined her. "I don't think you're being fair to yourself. You were a kid, and this mayhem came from out of the blue. Men in battle don't go there straight from listening to the radio in their bedrooms, Norm. There's a process that hardens them."

"Oh, I know," he said vaguely, wandering a few steps.

Dan was aware that they were overstaying their welcome, especially with such armchair psychology. Norm Myers's course had been set long ago. He didn't want anyone telling him that his reaction to all this had been perfectly normal. On that level, it was akin to telling a pilgrim to Lourdes that God is dead.

Dan veered him back to more tangible matters. "You may not have gone to war, but you did well — a daughter who's happy to keep you nearby; an apartment complex that you knew like the palm of your hand. People think well of you."

Norm gave him a blank stare. "Apartment complex?"

"Yeah. In Claremont. Back when. I think maybe you even built the place. Is that right?"

Norm scowled slightly. "What about it?"

Dan decided to give up the subtle approach, for fear of losing everything. "I'm really sorry about this, Norm — interrupting your privacy and everything — but did you ever have a tenant named Paul Hauser? It's really important that we find him."

Norm looked like a man waking up from a dream — and none too thrilled at the interruption. His earlier mood of drifting reminiscence became soured by reality. "I had a lot of tenants. Most of them weren't worth remembering."

Sally was watching his connective tissue of age and memory and private pain, stretch and tear apart.

"What about Bryn?" she asked, sensing little to lose.

The older man looked at her in surprise, the darkness clearing from his face. "Bryn? Oh sure. He was a character. But he wasn't a tenant."

Dan followed his daughter's lead. "My mistake. Guess I messed that up. Sorry."

Norm Myers was happy to go there. "It's because of that crazy name. Took me forever. Bryn Huxley-Reicher, with a hyphen. I always said it sounded like a British lord, or maybe one of the guys in the Charge of the Light Brigade. He isn't like that at all, really, but it sounds like it from the outside — until you meet him."

That made Dan hopeful. "You're using the present tense — you still see him?"

"All the time. He almost lives at the American Legion hall in BF."

"Bellows Falls?" Sally asked.

"Yeah. On Rockingham — across the street and down from Nick's."

CHAPTER SIXTEEN

Joe studied the front page unhappily. PO-
LICE SEEK MAN AS WITNESS. Dan Kravitz's
face confronted him, he thought a little
resentfully.

He couldn't blame him. From what Willy
had said, and from what they'd discovered
since, Kravitz was almost fanatically private.

"You think it'll work?"

He glanced over the top of the page at
Sammie Martens, who was back at her office desk, if only for another hour. She'd
just hung up the phone, which had been
ringing ever since the paper's appearance.
She was still on maternity leave, but was
transparently yearning to return to work.
She claimed to be trying out babysitters,
leaving them with Emma for a few hours at
a time — supervised by a set of clandestine
video cameras, at Willy's insistence — but
Joe knew the trial separations to be as much
for her as for her daughter.

"It better," he said. "We've tried every-thing else. The man's like a friggin' ghost, drifting all over town without leaving a trace. That another I-know-him call?"

"Yeah," she said without elaboration. They had received ten of those so far, from people who hadn't seen Dan recently but knew him personally, or knew *of* him. "Do you know where he is now?" Of course not. "Oh, is that what you wanted to know?"

The phone rang again. This time, Joe picked it up.

"Gunther. Vermont Bureau of Investiga-tion."

The voice on the other end was elderly, tentative, and female. "Hello?"

"This is Joe Gunther. Vermont Bureau of Investigation."

"Are you the people looking for Daniel Kravitz?"

"That's correct, ma'am. Do you know where he is?"

"No, I don't," she said. "But he was here just a couple of days ago."

That was some improvement, Joe thought. "Where are you?"

"At home." She gave the address.

"He came to your home?" Joe asked, entering the address into his computer and requesting a cross-reference. The name that

270

came up belonged to a Gloria Wrinn.

"Yes," she was saying. "With a young woman. They pretended to be from a state agency that I knew didn't exist. They were asking about a tenant of mine."

"Is this Mrs. Wrinn?" Joe asked.

"Why, yes," she answered, surprised.

"Are you at home right now?"

"Yes, I am."

"This is very interesting, Mrs. Wrinn. Would it be all right if a colleague and I came right over to speak with you?"

"Of course."

Joe hung up and looked at Sam. She was already reaching for her jacket.

Forty minutes later, Joe placed his empty teacup on the low table before him and addressed their hostess.

"Mrs. Wrinn, did either one of them tell you why they were so interested in Paul Hauser?"

She reached into her cardigan pocket as she spoke. "John — that was the name he used — said they thought he'd committed a crime."

"They said they were cops?" Sam asked, startled.

"No, no. From the Division of Indigent Residents."

"What?"

Joe started laughing as he read the business card Gloria handed him. "This is classic." He gave it to Sam and asked Gloria, "What was the crime supposed to be?"

"He didn't say."

He pointed to the card. "You believed that?"

"No, but I knew they weren't dangerous, or at least Nancy wasn't . . ."

"Nancy what?"

"She never gave me a last name. She was the one I met first. Knocked at the door and introduced herself as running a survey of everyone on their indigent residents list. She was very sweet. After she interviewed me about Paul, she brought in John, and I allowed them to go through his things."

"You didn't think you'd need Hauser's permission?" Sammie asked.

"Honestly?" Gloria asked with her eyebrows raised. "No. He left me high and dry. I suspected that he was up to something underhanded before he disappeared."

"What was that?" Joe asked.

"I'm not sure. I knew that someone had been in my bedroom when I was away recently. It had been cleaned up, but you can always tell when things aren't exactly as you left them. I also found a broken table from upstairs that had been hidden in the basement, as if Paul thought I wouldn't notice it was missing, and the doorframe to the top-floor staircase was split. People always assume that old folks are idiots."

"Okay," Joe resumed. "So you let them go through his things. Did you go with them?"

She shook her head. "I accompanied them to the top of the stairs. Paul lived in a separate apartment I have under the kitchen. I don't go down there very often anymore, because of my legs. I don't move as easily as I used to."

"I understand," Joe said. "But let me get something straight: They came here asking what you knew about Hauser. Is that right?"

"Yes."

"And they asked to see his apartment?"

"That's correct."

"Did they tell you about the apartment or did you bring it up in conversation?"

Sam glanced at her boss, realizing how much she'd missed him during the past few months.

Gloria hesitated. "I don't recall."

"How about when you showed them where it was? Did you lead the way?"

Her eyes froze on his face. "Oh, my goodness."

"What?"

"Well, I really didn't. I mean, we all went together, I remember — kind of in a herd — but now that I think of it, John knew exactly where to go. I remember him holding the door open for me at the back of the kitchen, which leads to the downstairs. There's no way he should have known . . ." She lapsed into thoughtful silence.

Neither Sam nor Joe said anything, letting her gather her wits.

"He'd been here before, hadn't he?" she finally asked.

"It looks that way," Joe agreed. "Was there anything else that tells you they knew more about Hauser than they were letting on?"

"He asked about Lake Bomoseen."

The two cops exchanged looks. "Bomoseen?" Joe asked. "In what context?"

"Whether he'd come from there, or had family there. The girl asked about Claremont, New Hampshire. The conversation was generally about where Paul might have been from, I think in part because I said that I thought he was a local, more or less. From this overall region, in other words."

Joe looked at his partner. "You have any questions?"

Sam shook her head and he returned to Gloria. "I'd like to ask you an enormous favor, Mrs. Wrinn, and you should know that you'd be entirely within your rights to turn us down."

"Go ahead," was the ready response, "although I think I know what it is — you'd like to see Paul's room, too."

Joe laughed. "Well, you're absolutely right. We would. But there's something else: We'd like to follow up on what you said about somebody having been in your bedroom, and breaking a table from the upstairs hallway. It's sounding as if something happened in this house while you were away that set these people against each other, and we would sure like to know what that was."

She was already nodding. "Of course. Of course. I'd like to know myself."

Joe and Sam stood, smiling. "Outstanding," he said. "I'll get a team in here right away and we'll get to it."

"There is one last thing that I almost forgot," Gloria suddenly added.

"Yes?"

"The man — John — made a point of mentioning that Paul had a suitcase, and asked if he'd left with it."

"Did you know what he was talking about?" Joe asked.

"Oh, yes. Paul was carrying it when he first came. It was just strange, is all, how John mentioned it. I think I'd made some comment about how Paul traveled with everything on his back — I don't remember my own wording anymore. But John specifically added, 'and a suitcase,' or something like that. And when I looked at him oddly, he explained that he'd noticed how a suitcase had left a mark in the dust of Paul's room."

"So the suitcase meant something special?" Joe ventured.

"That's what I thought."

The smile returned to Joe's face as he said, "You've been great, Mrs. Wrinn. This has been a huge help. I'll make that phone call now and rally the troops."

Bellows Falls was a good example of how the march of history can alternately make a place successful or maul it underfoot.

Its geography tells most of the story. It is located on a point of land within a dramatic bend of the Connecticut River — complete with a waterfall, resulting hydropower, and one of the nation's earliest bypass canals, all of which once made it both picturesque and commercially viable. A go-to place.

That had been long ago. Since then, the interstate had been laid out like Hadrian's Wall to the west, complete with a couple of slightly-too-distant exits, introducing a subtle suggestion that this once-vibrant village was now a place to speed past without thought.

That, of course, was open to interpretation. As with any town, Bellows Falls — or BF as locals call it — was accessible with ease; it was even the immediate area's commercial hub. But it was hard to argue that where the river had once made BF a destination point, so the interstate now largely passed it by.

The village had spirit, however, and stubborn lasting power, and most modern boosters were happy to think that the worst times — involving crime and poverty and economic blight — were things of the past.

Dan Kravitz agreed. He'd been coming here for years, on his restless peregrinations, and had even called it home a couple of times, once when Sally was a child.

The American Legion building on Rockingham Street, just off the eye-catching downtown square, was not representative of the latter's architectural grace. A single-story, largely windowless brick building, it had the appearance of something constructed to withstand a nuclear attack. But it was a home away from home to many, and perhaps a place where a person could pretend, if only for a while, that the outside world had indeed ceased to exist.

That certainly seemed true for the man at the end of the long bar, who looked as attached to his seat as a potted plant — turnip-shaped, with a tangle of hair standing in for the leaves. In response to Dan's whispered inquiry, the barkeep said, "That's what's left of him," before returning to his soapy sink.

Dan led Sally down the length of the nearly empty room. He sat by one side of their target while she sat by the other. The large man barely took them in.

"Bryn?" Dan asked. "Bryn Huxley-Reicher?"

"Like there're two guys named Bryn in the room."

Huxley-Reicher had both pudgy hands cradling a half-empty glass of beer, and Sally was suddenly struck by the similarity between his fingers and his rounded lips, which had barely moved when he'd spoken. In fact, all she could see of him seemed to be constructed of rolls of flesh-colored material — like the Michelin Man stripped of all his white outer coating. It was simultaneously fascinating and revolting. It made her happy that her father once more had taken the lead.

"Good point," Dan said. "Where's the

name from?"

"Parents."

Dan nodded. He could be like that. For years, he'd had Willy Kunkle believing he could speak in little more than grunts. For that matter, he knew his own daughter thought him a social misfit. But in a world where people spoke too much and said too little, silence was a good way to find out a lot without asking a single question.

Or simply to be left alone, which Dan knew worked for him, and suspected was the case here. Bryn Huxley-Reicher did not appear to be a man much interested in anything.

"Norm Myers says hi," he tried.

"You could fool me."

"He's doing his annual thing at the crash site."

The thick lips compressed for a second before Huxley-Reicher reacted. "That is so crazy."

"You ever been?" Sally asked.

The large man finally moved slightly, turning his head to take her in. "That look likely to you?"

"Doesn't look like you could get out the door nowadays," she said cheerfully, abandoning her embarrassing first reaction for a new tack. "But you got around once, and

279

Norm's been doing his thing for more'n sixty years."

Huxley-Reicher swiveled his head all the way back to Dan. "Where'd you find her?"

"I'm his daughter," she answered. "My name's Sally." She stuck out her hand, both to undercut her prejudice and out of a darker need to discover what it would feel like to shake this man's hand.

Bryn hesitated. It appeared that he had settled for a limited repertory of social interactions, none of which involved physical contact.

But her approach and her gender made the difference. He cautiously unfolded one hand and awkwardly extended it to her, a bit like an offering with an uncertain future.

Her smile widened. His hand was incredibly soft and warm and pleasant to grasp, akin to cupping a baby's bare butt.

"It's a pleasure to meet you, Mr. Huxley-Reicher."

He half smiled back wondrously. "Really?"

"You know how it is," she said, her father all but eclipsed by now on the far side of this huge human being. "You get into a routine, always seeing the same people, pretty much saying the same things, narrowing your focus more and more until even you get bored by you. It's nice to get out sometimes — do something you never tried, or meet someone you'd normally never meet. Like you and me. It doesn't have to be like bungee jumping, right?"

He was laughing by now, or at least shaking in a way that made it appear as such. Certainly, his eyes were almost closed and those lips were smiling.

"You talk a mouthful, you know that?"

"Gets me in trouble sometimes," she admitted. "I usually end up hurting someone's feelings." She laid a hand on his forearm. "I didn't do that, did I?"

He shook his head, glancing down at her hand but not touching it.

"No," he told her. "You're a breath of fresh air."

He suddenly straightened and looked around, seizing his glass more firmly. "Tell you what," he said. "Let's move over to that booth, so we can see each other."

Dan and Sally slid off their stools, while Bryn began a slow and cautious maneuver that caught the attention even of the barkeep, who glanced over in fear.

"You okay, Bryn? Where're you goin'?"

Huxley-Reicher ignored him, perhaps didn't even hear him. He placed his feet on the floor and tested it momentarily, as if gauging the sea swell beneath a deck. He grunted approvingly and began shuffling toward the booth across the aisle. The barkeep, his mouth open and hands dripping, stared as if the moose head on the wall had begun to sing.

It was a bit of a journey, and Sally even helped some by placing her hand on their new friend's elbow, not that she could have done much had he started to fall.

But Bryn's expression told of his satisfaction and sense of achievement as he lowered himself before the table with the grace of a large ship sidling up to the dock. He sighed happily as his companions slid in opposite him.

The bartender continued watching in amazement for a moment before offering, "You guys want something?"

"A couple of Cokes?" Sally asked.

"On my tab," Bryn added.

"You kidding?" the man asked without thought, before immediately adding, "Got it, Bryn. No sweat. Comin' right up."

The big man's smile broadened as he looked at Sally. "You're a smart girl." He shifted over to Dan at last to say, "You're a lucky man."

"Don't I know it."

Comfortably situated at last, Huxley-Reicher studied them inside a single angle of view, without having to move his massive head.

"So, what do you want? It's not to say hi from Norm. He can do that himself."

"It does involve him, though," Sally continued, having figured out that this conversation was now hers to carry to the end. "You two go pretty far back, right?"

"That's something you already know."

She laughed suddenly. "This is cool — like *Law and Order.*"

He looked baffled. "Why're you people here? You're not cops."

Dan's impatience got the better of him. As grateful as he was to Sally for winning Bryn over, his own anxieties were beginning to well up.

"We're after Paul Hauser. You know him?"

"Paul?"

"Yeah. I need to talk with him."

Bryn shook his head. "Peter, not Paul."

"What?" Sally asked.

"I know *Peter* Hauser," the big man explained.

"A brother?" Dan asked.

"Yeah. I never met Paul. I heard about him, like a thousand years ago, but Peter was the one I hung out with. Peter's dead. Well, not dead-dead, but he's in a home, totally out of it. A vegetable."

"Why?"

"Some blood-shortage thing. I guess it was an accident or something. Starved his brain. Anyhow, it messed him up big time. He just sits in a wheelchair, staring at wherever they point him. Pathetic."

"How long ago did you see him last?" Sally wanted to know.

Bryn pushed out his lower lip. "Years. It's not worth the effort, and it takes everything I got just to cross the street nowadays."

"Back in the day, though," Dan asked, "when you and Peter hung out, what did he say about his brother?"

"He didn't like him."

"Why not?"

"Pete thought he was weird." Bryn tapped his temple with his fingertip. "Talk about the elevator not reaching the top. I guess he tortured animals and shit like that."

Dan was scratching his forehead, in need of details. "Can we start with some basics? I'm just trying to get a full picture here. What do you know about the family? Mom, dad, siblings — stuff like that?"

"Dad was a postal worker. Mom was a teacher. I think there was a car crash or something. Whatever it was, Mom was pretty messed up and Dad ended up a drunk, cheating on his wife, losing his job, abandoning the family. Peter was fine but Paul went through the wringer. I think Pete told me that his brother was messed up before then anyhow, though, so maybe that had nothing to do with it."

Dan thought back to the pictures of the young women, tortured and splayed, and was inclined to differ.

"How old were the boys when this happened?" he asked.

"Little enough. I don't know. Under ten, maybe?"

"How bad did it get at home?" Dan persisted.

Sally turned to look at him, struck by his urgency. She'd been told that her mother had died in childbirth, and had wondered about that, although never actually asked, as she gathered was typical of kids like her. At times like these, however, given the father she'd been handed, she had to wonder if some of his questions weren't rooted in a more dramatic story than the one she'd been told.

"I think it was pretty bad," Bryn was saying. "Pete and I met in high school, near Castleton, and I guess a lot of this was still happening at home."

Sally would have left it at that, but her father kept right at it. "A lot of what, exactly? The drinking?"

Bryn played with the mug between his hands before answering. "The drinking wasn't it. Hell, both my folks drank — my dad till he passed out every night. I don't think Pete's father was the only one stepping out."

"Mom cheated as well?"

Bryn sighed before admitting, "I came over to their house once. Pete hadn't showed up when he said he would, so I rode my bike to his place to find out why. He wasn't there, but his mom was, and she came on to me pretty strong. It was really awkward."

"You talk to Pete about it later?"

"Nah. Too embarrassing. But he asked me if I'd come by, and I fessed up then — kind of. He just came right out with, 'Sorry if she put the moves on you,' or something like that. He said she was sick and did that a lot to people. That's what made me think that Pete's home life must've been pretty tough."

Sally had rested her chin in her palm, mesmerized. "That's one way of putting it."

"What was Pete like?" Dan asked.

"He was a good friend."

Neither Dan nor Sally said a word, respecting his meditation.

Bryn eventually continued. "He was a

little driven, like he had something chasing him down."

"A risk taker?" Dan inquired.

"Yeah. Right. Jumping off rock quarries when he didn't know what was under the surface; running onto the ice without checking how thick it was; driving too fast. Just basically pushing the envelope. But he was fun, and he watched your back, and he was the best friend you could have."

"And you needed a friend like that," Dan filled in. "Given your own situation."

Bryn stared at the beer before him. "Yeah," he said almost soundlessly.

"What happened to Paul?" Sally asked. "Weren't you all in school together?"

"No. He went somewhere else. I never knew why or where. No one ever talked about it."

"But you and Pete kept in touch," Dan proposed.

"Kind of. We tried. You know how it is. I'd visit him when he lived in Claremont sometimes. That's how I met Norm."

"Norm doesn't remember him."

"Yeah. No doubt. Pete didn't live there long, and didn't like Norm much anyhow. I'm the one who hit it off with Norm. After Pete left, I kept coming back just to visit."

"Did Norm ever meet Paul?" Sally asked

impulsively.

"I think he did, yeah," was the surprising answer. "I don't think he knew his name. Hell, he forgot Pete's soon enough. But he told me once — actually, it was kind of strange . . . You remember when all those women were being murdered along the Connecticut River?"

Dan felt his face flush as he leaned forward. "Yes."

"Well, nobody knew who was doing it, and the cops were running all over, getting nowhere. Norm and I were sitting out front of his place, just watching the world go by, when he said that he wouldn't be surprised to hear that my buddy's brother had done the deed, or something like that. Even then, he'd forgotten Pete's name. But that's who he was talking about."

"So he'd met Paul?" Dan sought to confirm.

"Must've. And it must've been more than just in passing."

Dan looked at his daughter, who supplied the words, "So he knew Paul, after all."

"I guess."

"We need to talk to him again," Sally said.

"At that conversation you had with Norm," Dan asked. "Did you follow up about Paul being the Connecticut River Valley killer?"

Bryn shook his head. "I don't think so. I would've forgotten all this if you hadn't brought it up. It wasn't a big thing, and I didn't give it much thought. I just assumed they'd bumped into each other one time when Paul was visiting Pete. I mean, you meet people all the time you think might be capable of walking into a restaurant with a gun, right?"

Dan's memory returned to meeting Leo Metelica and his gun right after leaving a restaurant. "Right."

"Did Pete ever say anything like that about his brother?"

"He might've. I don't know."

Sally laid her hand on his forearm again, urging him on. "Bryn."

"What do you people *want?* The guy was a friend of mine."

"Peter or Paul?" Dan asked.

But Bryn didn't vary. *"Pete,"* he emphasized. "I *told* you."

"All right, all right," Sally soothed him as the bartender looked over from across the room. "We're sorry. For what it's worth, we've never met Paul, either, but we think he may have done something frightening, and we want to make sure everybody's okay."

"This is all pretty crazy, you know?" Bryn complained.

"I know, and it's not fair to put you through the wringer because you happened to know a guy once."

"And maybe you're feeling a little guilty for not visiting him much now that he's down and out," Dan suggested, reading into Bryn's mood.

Huxley-Reicher looked up at him, slightly startled. "You're right, you know? I think about him — the times we had. I didn't have many friends." He waved his hand around. "I sit here all day, people come and go and say hi. They're good guys, maybe, but they don't give a damn. I'm just the fat man at the bar. They all pat me on the back like I was a damn Saint Bernard. Not one of them knows me."

"But Pete did," Sally filled in.

He looked incredibly saddened by that. "Yeah. He did. And now it's all inside him, and it'll never come out."

This time, Dan stuck his hand out for a shake. "We'll get out of your hair, but I want to thank you for your time, Bryn. You didn't have to talk to us."

Bryn nodded silently, shook Dan's hand without great interest, and didn't look up as they slid out of the booth and took their leave.

"It's so sad," Sally commented as they hit the sidewalk.

But her father wasn't listening. He was rooted in place, watching a small truck leave its parking place a short distance down the street. Its license plate was too dirty to read.

"What's wrong?" she asked, seeing his suddenly pale face.

"I think that was Paul Hauser," he said. "I know it in my gut. He was watching us."

CHAPTER SEVENTEEN

Lisbeth Jordan saw him crossing the broad expanse of lawn — a slightly rumpled older man with a nonthreatening manner. She straightened from her gardening but didn't get to her feet, simply resting her gloved hands on her thighs, a trowel dangling from her fingers.

"Hi," she greeted him. "May I help you?"

He crouched opposite her, a row of tomato plants between them, and nodded with a smile. He had a kind face. "I hope so. My name's Joe Gunther. I'm with the police." He stuck out his hand. "Don't worry about the glove. My father was a farmer."

Nevertheless, she removed one glove and shook his hand, enjoying the solid feel of his palm against hers — an impression mirrored by his overall appearance.

"Is this about the break-in?" she asked. "Have you found who did it?"

It was a reasonable question, but stated

without urgency. Despite what Joe and his colleagues had learned since Lisbeth had first met Ron Klesczewski, she had no reason to know how much the stakes had grown, especially in terms of her husband's involvement.

"No," he said candidly, reaching into the warm dirt and sifting it through his fingers. "I'm a woodworker, myself," he added, watching the dark soil pouring back into the bed. "But I used to love to watch my father when he was out in the field, surrounded by his land. He reminded me of a sailor, all-knowledgeable of the currents and the weather and the movement underfoot. The land really spoke to him. He could hold a handful to his nose and decipher its contents. He even tasted it sometimes."

He shook his head and wiped his hands together, smiling in a slightly embarrassed way. "Sorry. Suddenly brought me back. You do all the gardening yourself?"

"I try to. Lloyd keeps telling me to hire somebody, but I enjoy it."

Joe glanced around. "You're doing very well, from what I can see. This all shows a lot of care."

Now it was her turn to reach out and grasp a handful of soil. Her voice was wistful. "It makes me feel like I'm doing *some-*

thing constructive, even if it's a tiny thing like growing a plant."

Joe looked beyond her at the huge house looming like a wanna-be Tara. He took a slight chance interpreting what he thought he heard in her voice. "This can all get a little overwhelming, can't it?"

She followed his gaze, as if expecting the house to have inched toward her while her back was turned. "Sounds kind of stupid, doesn't it?" she asked. "Poor little rich girl."

"That's not what I'm thinking."

She gave him a quizzical look. "You're not like any policeman I've ever met."

He laughed. "I get that sometimes. Probably been at it too long. You met a lot of cops?"

"No," she conceded. "Enough. You are kind of everywhere, when you think of it. Not a day goes by when most people don't see a police officer somewhere." She added, laughing, "Usually when they don't want to, of course."

He joined her. "You think I don't slow down when I see a cruiser by the side of the road? We all do it."

Her eyes dropped then, drawn by a passing thought. "All creatures of habit, aren't we?"

"We create habits," he qualified. "And

make assumptions about who and what we are. Until the rug gets pulled out from under us."

"That's happened to you?"

He shifted his weight and got down on his knees, as she was, so that they looked like they were praying to each other. He was enjoying her effect on him. Virtual strangers could be comforting that way, he knew, which maybe explained some of the confessional's appeal.

"More than once," he allowed. "Even recently. A close friend of mine died unexpectedly. Shook me up."

"I'm so sorry." Her voice verified the truth of that. "This was a personal friend? I mean, not another police officer?"

"No, no, although I've had that happen, too. This was a woman I kind of lived with. Well, not really, but we saw a lot of each other."

She surprised him then by reaching out and stroking the back of his hand, just once, saying, "That is so sad. You loved her. I can tell."

He remained still, his eyes on the middle space separating them, filled with a sudden upwelling of emotion. A bad idea, he told himself. God, what a bad idea. What the hell was he doing?

"Can I get you something?" Lisbeth asked, getting ready to rise if necessary. "Something to drink, maybe?"

He held up a hand. "No. I'm all set, thanks. Stupid."

Her voice was stronger than he was expecting. "No, it's not."

He looked up at her, surprised.

She continued. "I think what you're feeling is the way it should always be. I envy you that, even with your loss." She waved at the acreage around them. "I'd trade all of this for —"

Her voice stopped momentarily before she pasted on a smile and said in a false tone, "Good Lord. Listen to me."

He saw an opportunity to both get back on track and show respect for her honesty. "I *was* listening, Mrs. Jordan. I meet a lot of people in this job, but I rarely get to really speak with them. There's all sorts of heartbreak out there. It's too bad we're either too tough-minded or distracted or messed up to be more open about it. So, don't apologize."

After a telling pause, she said in a near whisper, "I'm not complaining."

"But you're not happy," he suggested, slowly getting back on course.

She frowned briefly before admitting,

"Things didn't turn out the way I thought. I suppose that's been said before."

"Had you known each other long before you married?"

"No," she said mournfully. "It was your classic whirlwind romance." Again, she half turned and took in the house, this time dismissively. "I didn't come from this. My parents live in a suburban ranch in need of a new roof. Lloyd seemed like a visitor from another planet."

Her voice trailed off.

Joe figured that he probably wouldn't get a better opportunity. "What do you know about your husband, Mrs. Jordan?"

Her expression was mournful as she corrected him. "Lisbeth. Call me Lisbeth. He calls me Liz, but I don't like it. And I'm not Mrs. Jordan. Not in my mind, at least. Very little, to answer your question."

She hesitated, and he let his own silence fill the void, suspecting what might be going through her mind.

"That night," she finally asked, "it wasn't just about some creepy guy breaking into houses, was it?"

"Why do you ask?"

"Lloyd," she said simply. "He changed. I could tell something had happened."

"Changed how?"

"He's edgier, more short-tempered. He needs a lot of time alone, and to be honest, I'm happy to give it to him. He can be an angry man."

"Has he ever hit you?" Joe asked.

"No." But her answer was slow, revealing that she considered it a possibility.

"But he hasn't said anything." It was more statement than question.

"No," she repeated.

"Lisbeth," he said. "I need a favor."

She looked into his eyes. "About Lloyd?"

"Yes. I would like permission to bring some colleagues of mine into your house and check a few things out — maybe even in his office. When he isn't here."

"I could do that?" she asked, which he found a telling question.

"You can let us in every place that you control and can access," he said carefully.

She nodded. "Sure."

He watched her closely. Her back was straight and stiff, as if braced. Her jaw was set and her eyes were steady on his.

"You have access to his office?" he asked pointedly.

"He told me once that everything he owns is mine," she said.

"If what you say about his temper is true," Joe counseled, "you might want to give this more thought. By helping me, you could be putting yourself in danger. I don't want to minimize that."

"I'll be fine," she told him. "We don't have all that much left between us anyhow. He doesn't think I know, but I'm pretty sure he's seeing someone else. This whole thing is just a matter of time."

Her back had slumped as she spoke and, by now, she once more looked like the kneeling penitent.

There were five in their party the following day, counting Ron, including Sam, Willy, Joe, and J. P. Tyler, who as usual had brought his oversized evidence bag.

Ron gave Lisbeth his friendliest smile. "Hi, Lisbeth. Joe said you'd be expecting us. I'm really sorry to be bugging you again."

She looked at Joe and gave him a brave smile, stepping back to let them in. "I thought that might be it when Lloyd said he had to make an emergency trip to Boston."

Ron laughed self-consciously. "Yeah. A little sleight of hand."

In fact, they'd asked one of Boston's finest to call Jordan for an interview down there. They'd even watched him drive off earlier in the day, and had assigned an officer to tail him.

Once inside the house, Joe made introductions, making even Willy shake hands.

At that point, after signing the carefully worded consent search form they handed her, Lisbeth told them, "I know you have your job to do. I've decided that since I don't know why you're here, I don't want to know. I think it'll be better that way. So, I'm just going to hang out in the kitchen and cook something and let you get on with it. If that's all right."

It was. Ron and Sam had discussed that they would probably keep Lisbeth company while the rest of them checked out Lloyd's office, but now, instead, the two of them let her be and went up to the master bedroom, to revisit Lloyd's personal effects there.

Willy, J.P., and Joe repaired to their primary point of interest.

"A man's desk is his command post," J.P. announced as he circled Jordan's yacht-size version. "And this guy looks like he plays the role with a vengeance."

After studying the surface of the chair quickly but carefully, the diminutive forensics man settled into the seat and surveyed the world before him, ignoring the laptop computer for the moment.

"Jesus Christ, J.P.," Willy told him, beginning to check behind the books and paintings along one wall. "What the hell? You bucking for a promotion?"

"This is where he calls the shots," Tyler explained. "I'm thinking that if there's something he really cares about, I'll be able to see it from here."

"Very Sherlock, Sherlock. Turn on the stupid computer — that's where everybody keeps everything."

Tyler wasn't about to be bullied. Also, while highly qualified to deconstruct computers and their contents, he remained at heart an old-fashioned man. Joe sidled up behind him and surveyed the same scene over his shoulder, studying the pattern of strewn-about paperwork. He pointed to an area to the right of the desk's surface. "There," he said. "What's that? Looks different somehow."

"Right," Tyler agreed, clearing the spot and running his fingertips across the polished wood surface.

"What?" Willy asked.

"There's a panel designed to look like the rest of the desk," Joe explained. "But the paperwork on top of it was neater than the rest — easier to move."

Tyler had risen and was scrutinizing the

place. "Yeah," he confirmed. "The cracks here aren't just inscribed. They go through. It's well done, though — beautiful craftsmanship."

He dropped into the knee well and pulled a small flashlight from his pocket. "I got a latch here . . ."

Willy and Joe saw the panel suddenly drop an inch and slide from view under the rest of the desktop. A blank, flat TV screen rose with a gentle whirring sound and tilted to face them.

"Cool," Willy said. "Double-O-Seven via Neiman Marcus. What a joke."

There was a control panel under the screen, which J.P. studied for several minutes.

Willy, quickly bored, began checking out the rest of the enormous desk.

Tyler finally pressed a button that got the screen glowing. "That's a start," he murmured. Surfacing from the black background, a message floated up: **Password.**

"Shit," Joe said.

"No, no," J.P. said. "Most people make this easy. Plus, it's only him and his wife in the house, so it could be as easy as this." He punched in "Lisbeth."

The message box read, **Not a Valid Password. Try again.**

"Try 'Liz,'" Joe urged. "That's what he calls her."

Tyler typed it in with the same results.

Willy's voice drifted up from over the far side of the desk, where he was crawling around looking for more secret compartments. "Christ. You guys are such dopes. It's 'Susan.'"

J.P. and Joe exchanged looks. *Jordan's girlfriend,* Joe mouthed without a sound.

Tyler tried it and saw the screen come alive. What appeared was a series of eight small photographic rectangles.

"I'll be darned," J.P. said. "He's got a surveillance system." He quickly worked the controls and cycled through all the screens, making each full-size, including the one showing them around the desk.

Willy stepped in beside Joe to watch. "Hold that one," he ordered and moved across the room to where the shot's angle indicated the source of the camera. The other two saw his face loom enormously on the screen.

"Ugly, Willy. Wicked ugly," Tyler said.

Kunkle ignored him. "Hidden camera," he announced. "I can barely see it from three inches out. I bet they're all that way. The son of a bitch is a paranoid snoop, probably hoping to catch his wife or the maid doing Christ knows what. That thing have an archive?"

Tyler was already searching. The screen came up with a calendar legend. Joe leaned forward and tapped the date of the Tag Man break-in as Willy returned to join them.

They watched all eight frames as Tyler keyed in an approximate time of day.

"Jesus," Willy said, watching where and how the cameras had been positioned. "What a freak. He looks at his own wife taking showers."

Tyler moved the time up a notch. They saw most of the screens turn dark, except for the bedroom.

"I bet he tapes them having sex, too," Willy added. "Seems like the type."

Not that night, however. The three men saw the couple settling in, reading or watching TV for a while, and eventually extinguishing the lights.

Tyler added a couple of hours to the log. There was a movement on one of the screens, and they saw the camera's diaphragm automatically adjust to brighten the image. A slim, athletic figure dressed entirely in black began moving from screen to screen, going through the house with the sure-footedness of a cat, sitting on furniture, checking out rooms and their contents, and helping himself to whatever was in the fridge. At one point, he glanced unknowingly into one of the cameras, and they all witnessed a full-face shot of Dan Kravitz.

"You little bastard," Willy said.

"Damn," Joe added. "This is making sense."

Tyler, less engaged in the case's intricacies, looked up at him. "How?"

"In a nutshell? Dan is the Tag Man; the Tag Man gets tagged in turn by Lloyd; Leo Metelica gets hired to rub out Dan; Dan kills Metelica instead."

"Except that it doesn't explain shit," Willy grumbled. "Why's Dan doing this? What did he do here that got Lloyd so bent out of shape?"

"There," Joe said, pointing.

On one of the screens, they saw Dan enter this office and begin to search it with astonishing efficiency, and in the near dark as well.

"Jesus," Tyler said admiringly. "We ought to sign him up. Look at him go, and without disturbing a thing."

"He's a detail freak," Willy explained. "With attitude. He sees stuff the rest of us don't even notice. That's why I've been using him all these years."

He suddenly pointed. "There — that's the

shot we found in Metelica's motel room. Jordan just printed it from the video."

They watched Dan sit down at the desk, turn on the computer, and get through its password protection as if he owned the device. He spent about thirty minutes perusing its contents before killing the power and moving on.

"Guess nothing turned him on," Joe commented.

"Here we go," Willy said, as Dan extracted the desk drawer and checked its back end. "The mother lode."

Dan separated a packet of papers from the drawer, slid the latter back into place, quickly examined the contents of the packet with the help of a flashlight, pocketed a few items, and replaced everything as it had been.

Joe straightened his back as Dan left the office. "There's your Kewpie doll," he announced. "The thing worth killing for."

Seeing Dan finally return to the bedroom and leave his calling card Post-it note next to Lisbeth's sleeping body was almost anticlimactic.

Joe tapped J.P. on the shoulder. "Okay, slide out of there. Let's see that drawer."

Tyler did as asked, and Joe mimicked Dan by removing the drawer. Not surprisingly, there was no packet to be found.

"Jordan's either burned it or it's in a bank vault by now," Willy suggested.

"It's got to tie into what Abijah Reed was telling me about Lloyd's connection to the Boston bad boys," Joe said. He pointed at the computer. "As things develop, maybe we'll come back for the contents of that with a search warrant. I seriously doubt that her permission to search trumps his own personal password protection. In fact, we all know we've seriously pushed out those boundaries already."

Willy smiled at his boss's manner. He'd been appreciating Joe's gradual resurfacing since Lyn's death. Not only was he as attentive to detail as ever, but there seemed to be an added element — a small sense of release, as if the Old Man, as Willy called him, had been cut loose in some way by the death of the woman he'd loved. Willy considered his own evolution — now sharing a house with the mother of his new child — and wondered if he wasn't witnessing a rebirth of sorts in Joe, perhaps stemming from the belief that he had little left to lose. It was a bittersweet thought — while Willy could celebrate the resurgence of Joe's powers, even he could recognize its genesis as a sad thing.

Of course, there was also the unexpected irony — was Willy witnessing an ongoing shift here, where he was becoming more centered, while Joe was drifting free?

They replaced everything where they'd found it and walked to the office door.

"I'd hate to be Dan right now," Willy said with uncharacteristic sympathy, possibly influenced by his musing. "Between us looking to throw him in jail and a bunch of crooks hoping to kill him. He's got to be wondering how what he stole can save his butt."

In fact, Dan had more immediate concerns. "Make sure you got everything," he urged Sally.

"I got it, Dad." She sighed, stepping back into the small front yard with what little she'd bothered even to bring into their new home in the woods. "What're you going to do about the Land Rover?"

"I'll call the owner and let him know where to get it. He knew it might end up like this, where he'd have to scrounge around a little to find it."

She looked at the surrounding trees, trying to imagine how far they might be from anywhere civilized. "And we're going to get out of here how?"

He gave her a broad smile. "Oh, we're not done with the car quite yet. One last short trip, with the assumption that we're being followed."

She shook her head and headed for the vehicle. "That is so not cool."

He interrupted what he was doing to stop her and place his hands gently on her shoulders. "I am really sorry for all this, for what I've gotten you into."

She placed her hands on top of his. "Dad. You are totally crazy and you've given me an upbringing that would've lost you custody of me if anybody had been paying attention. But it's worked — I love you, I have learned from you, I am better because of you, and that's just going to keep going. Who cares if it means the occasional psychopath will try to take us both out, right?"

He kissed her cheek solemnly, ignoring the one-liner. "I love you, too, sweetheart."

Lester Spinney was waiting for the whole group as they stepped back out into the Jordan driveway. He held up his cell phone. "Got a call I thought you'd like to hear about in person," he told them.

Joe made sure the big front door had closed behind them. "We get a break?"

"More of a monkey wrench. We have

309

another body, about forty minutes north of here."

"Dan?" Willy asked, concerned.

Lester gave him a surprised look. "No. It's an old guy named Norman Myers."

They all stared at him, waiting for details.

"He was found dead near Perkinsville, in the woods. The thing is, when the detective interviewed his daughter, who lives with him, she said that she'd given directions on how to find him to two people. They fit Dan and Sally Kravitz to a T."

Joe turned to J.P. and Ron. "Thanks for your help here, gents. It looks like the rest of us are heading north."

The local medical examiner was not pleased. "We *are* going to send him up for an autopsy," she said, "if he hasn't decomposed by then."

Joe's mouth fell open as Willy burst out laughing. "I like that. Why haven't we met before?"

The woman in question smiled and shook hands, saying, "Lisa Westfall. Sorry — seemed like a good line."

Willy was still laughing as he crouched beside the man lying facedown on the ground. It was true, of course, all joking aside — they had asked the team processing

310

Norm Myers to freeze the scene until they got there, which had stretched the whole procedure out by two more hours. They deserved a couple of barbs.

"I'm the one who's sorry," Joe explained to Westfall. "We're thinking this may be related to another case we're working on. Sort of made it important to take a look."

Westfall patted his shoulder, unaffected. "Totally relaxed. My husband tells me I should get paid for busting people's chops. It's an instinct." She bowed slightly. "Take your time, Joe. My body is your body."

Joe crouched down beside Willy, who was laughing again. They were on Hawks Mountain, not far from the open fields extending out from the base of the slope. Norm's body was pointing downhill, as if he'd been returning from a hike. "What do we have?" Joe asked.

Willy became thoughtful. "Well, you know what they say — every scene's a murder till proven otherwise. I gotta say, though, I'm not so sure this one isn't."

"Based on what?"

"Gut, mostly," he admitted. "You got a few choices in a deal like this: sudden heart attack, where the guy slows down and crumps; a violent attack, where the evidence of foul play afterwards stares you in the face;

311

or something in between, where you just sense that something's wrong."

"And that's where you are," Joe suggested.

Willy looked over his shoulder. "Lisa?"

Westfall raised her eyebrows. "What's up?"

"Anything about all this strike you one way or the other?"

"You mean natural versus not?" She pulled on her earlobe and conceded, "There's nothing that says not, but it's particularly neat and tidy, even for a natural. The way he's perfectly stretched out, arms by his sides, legs straight out. I'm not saying it wasn't a massive coronary — and those can drop you like a steer in a meat plant — but it almost looks staged."

"Anyone get hold of this guy's doc yet?" Joe asked.

The Vermont State Police detective who'd responded initially stepped forward. "I did. He was fit as a fiddle. Took no meds, had no problems. The doc said no way would he sign the death certificate. This was a complete surprise, despite his age."

"Why was he out here?" Joe asked.

"Annual pilgrimage," the cop said simply. "Kind of a ritual with him, dating back decades, like an anniversary."

"And what did the daughter say about the people who came looking for him?"

"Perfect description of the two you're after. That's why I called. But they gave her different names and fed her a line about being from Claremont and working on some bogus water-line project. They said they needed to ask him what he knew about the old apartment complex he built over there years ago."

"And she just sent them after her old man? On that?" Willy asked incredulously.

The detective smiled. "She gave 'em a map."

Willy glanced at his boss. "That should be an easy interview."

Joe rose from crouching beside the body. "Yeah." He looked at Lester, who'd accompanied them here. "I'm going to take Willy to meet the daughter and then probably head over to Claremont to find out more about this apartment building. Let's stay on the safe side with all this and treat it like a homicide." He addressed the detective. "There been much scene contamination?"

The man shook his head. "I had the kid who found him describe what he did and where he walked; same with the first trooper who responded. I've kept a lid on who did whatever since. I can write all that up in a report for whoever comes next. That going to be the crime lab?"

Joe pursed his lips for a second before saying, "Yeah. They're not going to like it, given the lack of clear evidence. But I want to do this by the numbers. I think Willy's right. Something funny happened here."

Dan's voice was mournful as he pulled the Land Rover over to the side of the road, just within sight of Peggy Harrison's modest home on Kendrick's Corner Road.

"Damn."

"What?" Sally asked, turning around and looking out the rear window, thinking that he'd seen someone following them.

"That car." He pointed ahead.

She swiveled forward in her seat and squinted into the distance. There was a nondescript sedan parked in Peggy's driveway.

"Cops," Dan said tersely.

"You sure?"

"Yeah. They stand out almost as much as marked cruisers. Besides, you can see the extra antenna from here."

He put the vehicle into Reverse and began backing up. "I guess we won't be asking Norm any details about Paul Hauser," he said grimly. "Or anything else."

"You mean he's dead?" Sally asked, startled.

"I wouldn't be surprised, the way things're going. But I'm not going to drive up there and ask." He hesitated before adding, "Time for us to pull the vanishing act of a lifetime."

She slid down in her seat slightly, for the first time beginning to grapple with the size of the threat pursuing them.

CHAPTER EIGHTEEN

Lloyd Jordan sat in his darkened office with his hands resting on the arms of his chair, his legs crossed casually, in the same feigned calm that he'd used back in the bad old days, when his life had sometimes felt as if he were riding a bicycle along the edge of a cliff — thrilling, but perilous.

This time, however, the thrill was missing.

He had wondered about being summoned to Boston, the meaningless interview with a cop who had so little knowledge of him and so little enthusiasm for the questions he'd been posing. The man had even glanced at his watch once, as if maintaining a schedule. In all his years of being interviewed by the police, that was the first time Lloyd had ever seen one of them check the time.

It had felt like a tell at the time — that twitch or giveaway gesture one gambler inadvertently gives to an observant opponent. But why? Lloyd wasn't in any game that he knew. He'd left the city confused and uncomfortable.

Until he'd returned home.

His gaze returned to the closed-circuit monitor sticking out of his desk like a half-buried headstone. There was no bank of small, square screens representing the cameras around the house, however. The shimmering image was of an operations time log, and it told Lloyd that someone had been viewing the contents of this system while he'd been in Boston.

The police, according to his idiot arm-candy wife.

Fucking bimbo.

Now they knew at least part of what he knew — that someone had rifled his desk and stolen some of its contents.

But what else?

Had they made an identification, as he'd finally been able to? Had they tied that half-wit Leo Metelica to a contract to take out Dan Kravitz? Had they then gone back a step and somehow drawn a connection between Metelica and Lloyd? Wouldn't they have arrested him by now if they had?

Apparently, they'd made some discoveries about him. But — just as clearly — they were also still fishing.

So, what did they know?

He looked down at his right hand and found it clenched into a fist. Deliberately, he opened it up and flattened it, draping his fingers over the edge of the chair's arm, almost as if they belonged to someone else.

Gotta get back into the swing of things, he thought — reacquire the smell for blood he'd once regarded as his most valued asset.

He pulled his attention away from the screen's unnatural radiance and glanced about the opulent room. When they'd moved in here, he'd taken enormous pride in this extravagance in particular. He had seen it as the prize of his labor, the reward for a hardscrabble life filled with violence and human filth. He'd swum against the sewer's current, all the way back to the rich folks' palace.

Now he felt it had merely made him soft and vulnerable. He'd been deceived by the mythology of it just as surely as he'd been betrayed by the human bauble now lying in his bed upstairs — crying and bruised from the slapping around he'd meted out.

It was time to get his muscle tone back, call in some favors, and get just a fragment of his old operation up and running again.

And it was time to go after Dan Kravitz himself.

■ ■ ■ ■

"Undetermined?" Joe said into the phone, trying to keep the frustration from his voice.

One of his oldest and most cherished friends, Medical Examiner Beverly Hillstrom, was on the other end of the line.

"For the time being. We'll have to wait for the toxicology results, as always, so it isn't my final finding, which will most likely be 'natural,' but I'm just warning you of what to expect, Joe. I uncovered nothing in this case which leads me to believe that Mr. Myers died of anything other than having overly exerted an ancient anatomy."

"No conveniently broken neck or knife you might've missed?" he asked jokingly.

Hillstrom, however, for all their years of collaboration, was not a kidder. Her voice remained straightforward and serious. "He was a borderline healthy male, given his age, with an aversion to doctors and medicines. His organs were old and not in prime shape, albeit perfectly functional. There is such a thing as a truly natural death, in layman's terms, where the body simply fails for no apparent reason, basically as a result of a series of coincidental and minor mishaps. I cannot say that this wasn't such a case. To use your own terminology, I found no smoking gun. If someone murdered him, they were either very lucky or very good."

"How so, 'very lucky'?" Joe asked.

"They may have done something to him that left no trace, or at least left nothing behind for me to discover — the medical equivalent of leaping out from behind a door and scaring someone to death. Even someone without an acute heart condition might die of fright, as melodramatic as that sounds.

"But," she cautioned, and he could almost see her finger in the air, "I am not suggesting any such thing, since you supplied me with no context. Have you uncovered anything at the scene suggesting even the presence of another human being?"

Joe had the crime lab report on his desk, as a painful reminder. "No," he told her. "It's a popular trail — too much traffic to tell one way or the other if he was alone."

"Well," she said sorrowfully, registering his disappointment, "I'll probably be calling it a natural, then, as I suggested, and listing the cause either as presbycardia or 'old heart.' It's not used often, but I like it for this."

"All right, Beverly," he conceded. "Thanks for the update. Take care of yourself."

Joe replaced the phone and looked across the VBI office at his entire team, Sammie included, who had once again found a baby-sitter.

"Dead end?" Willy asked with a smirk, pun intended.

Lester groaned quietly.

"Afraid so," Joe conceded. "She'll most likely be ruling it natural."

"We've worked around that before," Sammie lobbied. "We don't necessarily need a finding of homicide to make a case. We still got Dan crawling around Lloyd's place, stealing his stuff, and planting his stupid Tag Man Post-it. And we got Metelica targeting Dan on Lloyd's orders before getting killed himself, clearly by Dan and probably in self-defense."

She hesitated, gathering her thoughts.

"Right," Willy interjected. "And right there, you already got a problem, don't you? We're only pinning Metelica on Dan because it suits us. We have no proof. Not only that, but Norm's death — which I'm still calling a murder — puts us in the same pickle. We *think* Dan and Sally went after Norm on that mountain, but then what? I mean, I like Dan, and Jordan's an asshole, but it's Dan who keeps showing up in the wrong place at the wrong time. Hell," he threw in, his exasperation plain, "*we* were the ones who gave Jordan an ironclad alibi by sending him to Boston with a tail."

Willy continued, riding his rant to its natural conclusion. "And what about Hauser? What the fuck is that all about? And why is Dan so fired up to find him? It's all crazy stuff — a complete mess. All due respect, what we really got is Dan sneaking around on a video. Period."

In the ensuing dead silence, Joe quietly stated, "Dan is the Tag Man," his voice startling in contrast to Willy's stridency.

There was a telling silence in the room, which Willy filled with, "So what? I just said that."

"So, he's how we got into all this. How many houses has he hit that we know of? Six?"

"Maybe," Lester said. "That's Ron's department."

"Yeah," Willy answered more confidently. "Six."

"All high-security," Joe recited. "All hyper-rich; all occupied at the time of entry; all left precisely as they were found with the exception of Post-it notes and some eaten food — including the alarm systems, which were as functional afterwards as they were before being breached, except for Gloria's, of course."

Willy was getting antsy. "What's your point? We're circling the same hydrant."

"Think about it," Joe pressed on. "We've now seen Dan in action — a fully filmed documentary of the Tag Man at work, thanks to Lloyd's automatic cameras. And what did we learn? That Dan doesn't just sneak in, eat people's food, leave a note, and split."

"He cases each joint — top to bottom," Lester suggested.

Joe looked pleased. "Exactly. He sticks his nose into every drawer, closet, shelf unit, nook, and cranny — like he's taking inventory. And what's the result? Nothing. What was reported missing or disturbed in every house except Lloyd's?"

"Nothing," Sammie echoed.

"Right," Joe resumed. "I interviewed Merry Hodgkins. She's a neatnik like Willy and Dan —" Willy scowled at the reference — "and she has an eye for when and how her belongings might have been disturbed. She wasn't as thorough as Lloyd's cameras, of course, but she gave me a general picture. Dan went through her place like a hyperactive safety inspector, including reading the contents of her computer. She even thinks he stole her investments homework, to make a little cash on the side. But that's it.

"My point," Joe said directly to Willy, whose body language was nearing explosion, "is that, as far as we know, Lloyd is the only one Dan physically ripped off, and we know that because Jordan totally wigged out as a result.

"But ask yourselves," Joe went on, "what other house have we associated with Dan Kravitz that's also related to our investigation, as Tag Man or not?"

After a telling silence, Lester said tentatively, "Gloria Wrinn's?"

Joe, who'd been walking back and forth before his desk, now settled on its edge. "That's it."

Willy fixed him with a stare, suddenly enlightened. "Shit."

"What?" Lester asked.

"We've been looking at what Dan wants us to see," Willy explained, adding, "Dan Kravitz isn't just eating caviar and leaving Post-its. He's collecting data — investment tips, blackmail information, Christ knows what else."

He stopped suddenly.

"Like what?" Lester persisted. "Is this why all the fuss at Gloria's?"

"He didn't leave a Post-it or eat any food," Sam protested. "We don't know if he was even there except when he went by with Sally."

"Sure we do," Willy argued, making Joe smile at how fast his brain could adapt. "There was that deal with the broken table and the evidence J.P. found where Gloria's windows had been messed with, and the damaged door to the top floor. And, Sam," he suddenly added, "you were the one who told us that Kravitz knew where Hauser's room was, proving he'd been in the house before."

He looked back at Joe. "And the suitcase he asked Gloria about? What was in it?"

Sam was rubbing her temples. "Dan knows what's in Hauser's suitcase? How?"

Joe shrugged. "That's what I'm suggesting. Just as Dan stole something from Lloyd, and may have copied information off of Merry's computer, he could have visited Gloria's place without leaving his Tag Man calling card. The whole Post-it note thing might be something he does only now and then, for fun. Given how careful he is, he could've broken into fifty houses around town without ever leaving a trace, and," he threw in for Willy, "maybe stealing a little something from all of them — either unnoticed or too embarrassing to be mentioned."

He resumed pacing. "Gloria said that Dan, or 'John' as she knew him, claimed that he knew about the suitcase because it left a mark in the dust of Hauser's room. We know that's baloney because J.P. checked it out when he examined the whole house. Also, J.P. found the empty secret compartment in the floor, the same size as a suitcase, which Dan probably found before him."

Willy filled in the rest. "Meaning Dan went through its contents, just like he goes through the contents of everything. I can vouch for that. The man is always touching stuff and rearranging it. I think he counts, too, like trees he passes or parked cars, or people in a restaurant. That's what made him such a great snitch — he notices every-thing."

"But what did he find?" Sam asked point-edly. "We have to assume that whatever it was, he didn't take it the first time — or maybe he didn't take enough of it — 'cause he apparently came back for more."

"I think he finally got interrupted," Willy suggested. "The broken table? The beaten-up door? Then all of a sudden, for the first time we know about, Dan masquer-ades as a state employee to get access to a house he's already visited. I'm betting he was doing his Tag Man bit, like Joe says, but at long last got caught, probably by Paul Hauser, and they had a knock-down, drag-out fight. I don't know where Norm Myers fits in, but that would at least explain why Hauser took off without a word and why Dan is trying to find him."

Lester let out a small laugh. "Jeez Louise. This thing's like a kid's game. Dan's trying to find Hauser, we're trying to find Dan, I'll bet my pension old Lloyd's wishing he could find Dan, too, and Christ knows what Hauser's up to, or why he's running for cover. Did we ever check out his background?"

"Yeah," Joe answered him. "He doesn't exist on paper."

"Meaning an alias?"

"Meaning anything you want," Willy said bluntly.

"All of which brings up a point," Joe mused.

"That we're up a creek?" Willy asked.

"We're in shallow water," Joe conceded. "I'll give you that. But I meant that our biggest obstacle is that most of the players have run to ground — Dan, Sally, and Hauser. For those three, we can issue be-on-the-lookouts for law enforcement eyes only, and keep our fingers crossed that someone'll be seen at a bar somewhere, or picking up groceries, or stopped for speeding, and that we'll get lucky. In the meantime, we're left with Lloyd and whatever smoking gun it is that Dan stole from his desk."

"We are?" Sam asked.

"By proxy — Ben Underhill, the Boston mob, everything that Abijah Reed told us. We need to collect enough evidence there so that we can start pressuring Lloyd. He's our wild card — Dan stole from him, and he's going after Dan."

"While Dan's going after Hauser," Lester reiterated.

"All the more reason," Joe said, "to get in on the chase."

"How?" Willy asked bluntly.

"We just got Lloyd to drive all the way to Boston PD on some feeble excuse. That tells me that the peace arrangement between Lloyd and Underhill's bunch needs constant care and feeding, and that Lloyd is twitchy about its overall health. If we figure out how to stir all that up, who knows what might come slopping out?"

"Or who might get killed in the process," Willy suggested sourly.

CHAPTER NINETEEN

Dan waited for the train to pass and the flimsy gate to lift, drove their latest borrowed car a few hundred feet along the cracked macadam, and veered left onto a broad expanse of remarkably flat pasture, where he rolled to a stop to give Sally a better view.

Both her hands were hanging on to the edge of the door, the window rolled down, and her eyes wide. "Oh my God, Dad. This is amazing. It's like a really old movie set."

She had a point. Across a weed-choked, picturesque pond was a hunkered-down, enormous shoebox of a building, all glass and weather-stained steel, surrounded by the vast acreage of an empty parking lot large enough to double as a decent-sized airport.

"What is this place?" she asked.

"It *used* to be the Green Mountain Race Track," he explained. "And believe it or not,

I used to work here."

She twisted around to face him. "Here? As what?"

"Just a grunt," he said dismissively. "It opened in the early 1960s as a Thoroughbred- and harness-racing track — it had stables enough to put up over eight hundred horses in its day. Quite the deal. Then, in the late seventies, it switched to greyhounds. That lasted maybe fifteen years, and it's been looking for a purpose ever since."

He pointed out the window past her. "We're parked on the actual racetrack right now."

She half jumped in her seat and cracked open the door to better see. "We are?"

Looking closely, she could just make out the oval outline of the old track beneath them. It made her feel odd, as if a galloping herd of horses might suddenly come thundering upon them from behind.

"Holy cow," she said. "This is really cool."

He put the car back into gear and slowly drove clockwise around the oval, circling the pond and getting closer to the ever-looming building dominating the scene.

"I'm pretty sure it's still the largest indoor stadium in Vermont — over five thousand seats behind glass, in a heated environment.

Talk about your creature comforts. Makes sense, though. This far north, why bother building something so big that's open to the elements, right?"

"I guess," she responded vaguely, bending far forward to take it all in. Perched atop the rigidly rectangular structure was something akin to a two-story penthouse, complete with bay windows. She pointed them out. "Those the sky boxes?"

"In part, before they were called that. If I remember, one of them actually housed the cameras that recorded the races. Not sure about that. Looks a little worse for wear, doesn't it?" he added, joining in her scrutiny of the place.

Having rounded the sharp end of the track, they were now parallel to the building's enormous glass front. Behind its glittering surface, just visible behind the reflection of the Green Mountains across nearby Route 7, they could make out an orderly tiered mass of wooden-backed empty seats — and imagine this now ghostly structure once seething with crowds and exploding with noise.

Sally glanced over at him, her expression wry. "Our new home, I'm guessing?"

He smiled brightly through his guilt. "The caretaker's a pal. Maybe we can talk him into one of the sky boxes. Make it all feel less empty."

She laughed without conviction. "I don't know, Dad. It's starting to sound like *The Shining*."

He laughed, but he didn't tell her that his suggestion about using one of the uppermost vantage points had more to do with security than isolation. He glanced around, pretending to be enjoying the flat, empty acreage, while in fact watching for his biggest fear, the malevolent threat of Paul Hauser.

Lisbeth Jordan's voice had sounded weak and timid on the phone — not at all reflecting the poised young woman Joe had met while kneeling before her tomato patch.

He understood why when he entered the Thai restaurant in the center of town — built with a vengeance, he thought, on the former site of his beloved if bedraggled Dunkin Donuts. He spied her sitting at a far corner table, her back to the door, and, he discovered as he rounded the table to sit opposite her, wearing sunglasses.

It was eight fifteen at night.

He forewent the usual polite amenities, studying her face instead. One cheekbone had too much rouge, especially for someone as careful as she.

"What happened?" he asked.

"That's not why I called you," she answered. There was a bowl of soup before her, untouched.

He nodded. "Okay."

"I want to know why you're after Lloyd."

He chose to wait her out, suspecting that she had something to add.

She did. "When you and I last met, I said that Lloyd and I didn't have much holding us together anymore. That problem's been solved."

"I can't give you ammunition for a divorce, Lisbeth."

She glanced down at the table between them, her mouth tightening as she concentrated.

"I understand," she then said quietly. "Of course you can't."

"I suspect you already knew that," he suggested.

She didn't answer at first, apparently making peace with the inevitable.

"I guess I did," she finally conceded.

"Which doesn't mean that you still can't talk to me."

"About what?"

"You and Lloyd."

She smiled thinly. "Now you're a marriage

333

counselor?"

"I care about your safety," he told her, adding, "and I won't say I'm not interested in Lloyd."

"You want me to rat him out."

He barely shook his head at the comment. He'd had these kinds of conversations before, in more and less subtle variations. He wasn't complaining, though. More often than not, they proved worth the effort it took to conduct them, and he needed all the help he could get right now.

"You called me, Lisbeth," he said, signaling for the waiter. "I think you're the one who wants to rat him out. You just don't know what I might need to hear."

He ordered a Thai iced tea, as close as they came here to a milkshake, and very good for all that.

She didn't argue his point, countering instead with one of her own. "How can I know, if you're not going to tell me what you've got on him?"

Joe shifted his approach. "I take it he wasn't very happy with your giving us access to the house."

Instinctively, she brushed her cheek with her fingertips, as if checking to see if her makeup was still in place. "No."

"What did he say?"

"Relevant?" she asked. "Not a lot. He basically concentrated on my overall intelligence and the sum total of my importance to his life, neither of which came to much."

Joe liked this woman. Earlier, he'd been struck by the image of someone who'd sacrificed too much of her integrity and pride for the material comforts she seemed to be enjoying. But he was beginning to reassess. She had spine, and — beneath her hurt and pain — he suspected she also had a longing for freedom, and maybe for just a bit of revenge.

He could work with that.

"You mentioned that you thought he was seeing another woman," Joe said. "Any idea who?"

"No," she answered flatly. "I intercepted a message — handwritten, like a note in school. I thought it was almost childish, and kind of rare in this electronic world. Especially with Lloyd. He's into the gadgets."

Unsurprisingly to Joe, who figured that Lisbeth had put more thought into this meeting than she was letting on, she reached into her pocket and slid a small piece of paper across the table to him.

Simultaneously, the waiter returned with Joe's iced tea and asked if either one of them wanted anything more. They didn't.

Joe ignored his drink and picked up the note. " 'Make it the Sunoco,' " he read. " 'Same time and place.' Where did you get this?" he asked.

"Jacket pocket," she answered simply. "Not too original. I think he just forgot about it."

He held it up between them. "Any ideas?"

She shrugged, frowning. "I was guessing they hooked up at a gas station somewhere and shared a ride to a motel, like a routine. But there are Sunocos everywhere."

"Does — or did — Lloyd have a schedule?" Joe asked. "Like a regular weekly event or outing that he might've used as a cover for this?"

Again, she shook her head. "He didn't need an excuse. He does pretty much what he wants and doesn't bother explaining. I stopped asking a long time ago. It just pissed him off anyhow."

Joe mixed the cream and tea together before taking a sip through his straw. He used the time to think for a moment.

"Lisbeth," he asked, licking his lips, "did you tell him you found the note, or that you suspect him of cheating on you?"

"No."

He nodded. "Good. If it's okay, I'd like you to keep it that way. Can I keep the note, incidentally?"

"That's why I brought it."

"Do you have access to the phone bills in the house?" he then asked.

"Cells or house?"

"Whatever."

"I pay my own cell bills; he does every-thing else."

"And he keeps the bills to himself?"

"Yes. Sorry. I bet those would be interest-ing, wouldn't they?"

"They often are. You wouldn't be able to get to them?"

She laughed bitterly. "Not likely. My guess is he's attached a grenade to his office door by now."

Joe took another sip and slid the note into his breast pocket. The phone bills weren't a big issue, assuming he could persuade a judge to issue a search warrant for them. "That reminds me," he said to her. "I think you should know about something that we discovered at your house. It's a safety issue, really."

"What?"

"Your husband has a very sophisticated camera system throughout the house, which he monitors from his office. I tell you this so you won't try to do anything at home that you don't want him to know about."

Her brow furrowed and she looked stunned. "Where are they?"

"Pretty much everywhere."

He left it at that, and his brevity gave her what she needed to know.

"Oh my God," she murmured. "That bastard. That means the bedroom, too, doesn't it?"

"Among other places."

She reflected on that for a moment before saying, "I knew it. I just had a feeling. The things he had me do — like there was a mirror. Only there wasn't one."

She slipped her fingers up under her dark glasses and rubbed her eyes briefly. "Jesus, I wish this would end."

He thought about reaching out and patting her arm, or extending some other sign of sympathy, but he didn't. As solidly as he was in his professional mode at the moment, he couldn't ignore his nearly perpetual grieving. While Lisbeth Jordan in no way resembled Lyn Silva, she was roughly the same age, and of similar build. To see her distressed brought Joe back to those intimate moments he'd had with Lyn, including ones where she, too, had expressed pain or confusion, and he'd been able to render some solace.

The mere thought of that sharpened his

sense of loss.

"It will," he said blandly instead, and moved on. "Was there anything else you thought might be helpful?"

She straightened slightly at his change of tone, dropped her hands back to the tabletop, and looked at him. "What?"

"I was just wondering if you had anything else?"

She appeared momentarily confused. "I, ah . . . No. Will the note be helpful?"

"Maybe." He forced himself back onto even keel. "It might give us something to work on. If you could keep your eyes open for anything else, without endangering yourself, that would be very handy."

"I doubt that'll happen," she said. "He's left."

Joe's eyes widened slightly. "Where to?"

"You think he told me? Ever since he found out about you people, he's been tearing around the house like his feet were on fire, either locked in his office or making whispered phone calls on his cell. Then all of a sudden, it was a fat duffel bag and out the door with tires squealing. I have no idea where he went or when he'll be back. He didn't say one word to me."

"What's he driving and what's the license plate number?" Joe asked.

She told him the registration. "It's his stupid Hummer. Like driving a battleship. Wherever he's going, it's not the city."

Joe looked up from writing in his pad. "He considered that his country car?"

"I guess," she said dismissively. "Although he's so paranoid about every nick and scratch, I don't see him actually leaving the pavement in it."

"That's interesting, though," Joe continued. "The implication being that he's headed somewhere rural. What's he use for his trips to Boston?"

"The Bimmer."

"And it's still here?"

"Sure."

"You have the keys?"

"Sure."

Joe smiled slightly. It was a good bet that Lloyd's office was now as clean as the proverbial pin, and that his computer was safely tucked into the Hummer beside him. But Joe knew from experience that when you were under pressure to head out the door, you didn't often think of those surrogate homes away from home that too often got filled with the trash and details of everyday life.

"Lisbeth," he asked, "when Lloyd was preparing to leave, did he go to the Bimmer at all, maybe to get anything like a GPS or a map?"

"Not that I know of, and the GPS is built in anyhow. The only time I was aware of his using the garage was when he left. He might have grabbed something then, of course . . ." She hesitated before correcting herself. "No, then the BMW keys wouldn't have been in the kitchen, and I saw them there before coming here. Why?"

"Specifically?" he answered. "I have no reason whatsoever. But to help figure out what Lloyd's been up to and where he's been, I'd like to get into that car, if you'll allow it. Most GPS units keep a record of past trips."

"Of course."

The bartender at the Emerald Isle in Lowell looked balefully at Willy, who this time was accompanied by Big Al Davis instead of Lester. Typically, counter to official protocol, Willy had traveled south alone.

"What do *you* want? I already gave him my phone records." He pointed at Al, who merely smiled.

Willy pulled a photograph from his pocket. "Don't get cranky now. I came all the way down here just because you were such a sweetheart last time."

"Fuck you."

"See? It's all about attitude." Willy looked at Big Al with a bright expression. "Just what we were talking about, wasn't it? People who help people are the happiest people in the world." He looked back at the barkeep, adding in a far darker tone, "Because they don't fuck with the people who can make their lives a living nightmare. Especially over nothin' at all." He laid the picture on the bar. "Like this. Ever see him?"

The bartender stared at Willy, ignoring the snapshot. "This gonna get you outta my hair?"

"In fact, it is."

The other man smiled bitterly and picked up the photo. "Then I'll give you everything I got."

He squinted at a face shot of Lloyd Jordan in the dim light, holding it close, as if he were trying to discern a counterfeit twenty.

"Yeah."

"Yeah, what?" Willy asked him.

"Yeah, he was here. That's what you wanted, wasn't it?"

"Cute. So you have no clue."

The barkeep rolled his eyes. "Fuck. Can't win for losin'. He came in here with Leo, all right? Made a big fucking deal about my not having Glen-something-or-other for a single-malt scotch. La-di-fuckin'-da."

"You remember when this was?"

The man simply stared at him.

"How 'bout the circumstances?" Willy persisted. "Any details."

"Middle of the day. Slow time — 'nother reason he stuck out." The bartender pointed to a far booth. "They sat there, talked quiet. Shut up whenever I got near, like they were planning a bank heist."

"You overhear anything at all?"

He shook his head.

Willy tapped the picture with his fingertip, content that what the bartender had told him matched what they'd extracted from the GPS unit in Lloyd's BMW. "He ever here before or since?"

"Nope."

"They look like they knew each other well?"

"How the fuck would I know?"

"When they met; when they walked in. Body language. You know."

He actually did know, and nodded. "They knew each other. The snotty guy was here first, sat at the booth, did his bullshit with the scotch. Leo came in after and they greeted like they went back a while — casuallike. No big deal."

"You said you didn't hear anything," Willy stated. "You see anything happen between them?"

"An envelope," the bartender answered without hesitation. "Rich guy slid it over to Leo, who just put it in his pocket. Not the first time I've seen that here."

"In general or with Leo?"

"Leo. You already know he used this place like an office. What did he do, anyhow?"

Willy was surprised. "What did Leo do? I thought that was against some bartender code of ethics, asking questions like that."

The man shrugged. "He's dead, right?"

"Right," Willy agreed. "Which means I'd have to kill you, too, if I told you. What a shame, huh?"

Chapter Twenty

Julie Johnson unlocked her office, removed her damp raincoat, and hung it on the clothes tree by the door, spreading it out slightly so that it might dry more quickly. She was a careful, fastidious woman, which helped explain her success as the school's comptroller, and the happiness of her well-tended, if unambitious, husband at home.

She frowned slightly at the scene outside her second-floor window. She wasn't fond of rainy days. She appreciated what it did for the grounds — and nature in general — but remained unhappy at the untidiness of it all.

That having been said, she saw no irony in her next gesture, which was to check on the moisture of the rubber plant adorning her desk. It was, of course, perfect.

Wiping her fingertip carefully on a tissue, she circled the desk, deposited the tissue in the trash can, settled into her chair, and turned on the computer before her, content in the sense of order so compulsively mirrored in the entire room's layout. It was one of the school's prized humorous tidbits, how the custodians never had to dust and vacuum the comptroller's office, since she did the job herself with the care of a cleaning crew.

She listened with satisfaction to the computer waking up, enjoying the orderly rhythm of all its components getting ready to observe her commands.

In the process, however, she failed to hear the slight sound of the small bathroom's door opening just out of her line of sight.

She did, however, feel the sharp sting of a knife being held against her throat.

"Mrs. Johnson, do not move. Do you understand me?"

The voice was male, adult, and bone-chilling in its calmness. Despite her normal readiness to criticize or at least question, Julie knew enough now simply to pay attention.

"Yes. What do you want?"

She could just make out the shape of a man wearing a hood over his head in the thin reflection on the polished computer screen.

"We'll get to that. Are you expecting any

visitors?"

"No."

"Does your secretary have a habit of walking in without knocking at this time of the morning, maybe to offer you coffee or deliver the mail?"

Julie frowned. What in Lord's name? She struggled to stay focused. This was absurd. It was eight o'clock in the morning, for heaven's sake.

"She will come in sometimes. I don't drink coffee, and I pick up my own mail." She moved slightly and complained, "What is going on here? What do you want?"

The response made her squirm in her chair. The knife bore down harder and she could feel a trickle of warmth course down past the collar of her blouse.

She began to shiver.

"Page the outside office," the man's voice said, "and tell them that you're about to place a very important phone call and that it's crucial that you are not to be disturbed — that it'll only be about a quarter of an hour."

"That's crazy," she protested. "I never do anything like that."

The knife moved painfully. "Then you better make it believable."

"Right now?"

The voice showed its first impatience. "Are you that stupid?"

"Okay, okay," she protested, and reached for the phone.

She did as she'd been told, wrestling to maintain a normal tone, her brain beginning to fill with increasingly wild notions of what was about to happen. She was actually grateful when her secretary simply acknowledged her comment and hung up, so she didn't have to worry about her rising panic giving her away.

Nevertheless, she'd started trembling, and she could feel sweat breaking out all over her.

"What do you want?" she whispered plaintively.

He ignored her. "Pick up the phone and open a line. No need to dial. We just want the button to light up."

She followed instructions again and placed the receiver on the desk.

"Are you paying close attention?" the man asked.

"Yes."

"Good. This is what I want. You get on that computer and you get me the mailing address, phone number, and anything else related to getting in touch with Sally Kravitz's father."

Julie couldn't stop herself. She tried to twist around. "What . . ."

He pulled her head back by the hair and moved the point of the blade from her throat to her cheek, right in line with her right eye. She gasped in pain and surprise.

"Have I not made myself clear?" the man asked.

"Yes," she managed to get out.

"Is there a problem, then?"

"No."

He returned her to her previous position. "Then get to it. Sally Kravitz. Father's name is Daniel."

Her fingers jittery on the keys, Julie tried several times to enter the information before succeeding.

"It's a post office box in Vermont."

He leaned over her slightly, trying to decipher the abbreviations and general format of the screen before them. "Is there a phone number?"

"It says it's an answering service. We get that sometimes. Our parents can be very self-protective."

"You ever had any problems with Kravitz paying his bills?"

She nervously scrolled down the screen. "No. She's a scholarship student, so most of the tuition has been waived, but he's always met the deadlines on incidentals. There's a note here from the academic dean that Sally will be doing some makeup exams later in the summer, due to a family emergency."

"How does Kravitz pay his bills?"

She checked before saying, "By money order." Her voice betrayed her surprise.

"Show me the address," he ordered.

Reluctantly, she reached out and touched the screen — something she hated to see other people do. She generally gloried in the pristine shininess of flat glass before her.

She could sense the man memorizing both the address and the phone number.

"What else do you have on how to reach Kravitz?" he demanded. "Bank accounts, references, next of kin — anything at all?"

She tried shaking her head and then froze, feeling the knife, and answered instead, "Nothing. It all gets entered here."

"How about in a medical emergency?"

"That's a different database. There are confidential restrictions."

"Don't bullshit me, lady. Money makes the world go around. If the infirmary has better contact information on the parent than you do, it'll be the first time in history."

Julie had to concede. "There would be an

indicator on our screen. There isn't one."

He laughed. "I knew it. You financial people are always the end-all, be-all. Regular sharks."

Julie didn't understand his meaning. She merely sat there, frozen, her hands flat out before her, waiting for what might come next.

"How 'bout an e-mail address?" he asked.

She scrutinized the form. "Yes." She recited it aloud.

"Good. Send him this note. Ready?"

She went to the appropriate page. "Okay."

"Dear Mr. Kravitz," he dictated. "We've hit a problem in arranging for your daughter's makeup exams and have mailed the appropriate paperwork to your post office box by express mail. Unfortunately, due to circumstances beyond our control, if we have not heard from you in the next three days, your daughter's standing at this school will be compromised. We deeply regret any anxiety and inconvenience this unavoidable imposition may cause."

Julie proofread what she'd written, struck by its sophisticated wording. She heard all sorts of language used on campus, from the maintenance crew to the richest of parents. If she were to receive such an e-mail herself, she thought, she'd be inclined to believe its contents utterly.

It only further drove home the most confounding of her many questions: Who *was* this man?

The knife left her neck with the warning, "You move, you die."

She barely breathed. There was a rapid movement behind her, a frightening ripping sound, and then a flash of duct tape passing before her eyes. She felt a broad band being applied to her chest, just under her breasts, pinning her arms and body to the chair. Instinctively, she struggled. He smacked the back of her head hard, making her eyes tear.

"Stupid bitch. I told you not to move."

A second swath of tape was slapped across her mouth, then a third cut off her vision. Finally, she felt her swivel chair being turned away from the desk, followed by her lower legs being bound to the base of the chair. Instinctively, she clamped her knees together as she sensed him crouching before her to do this.

"Don't worry, lady," she heard him say. "I couldn't care less about that."

She felt an abrupt emptiness then, and realized that his body heat had disappeared, like a radiator being shoved out of the way. She heard a sound by the door, heard it open quietly, and then could only imagine as he turned left and walked down the short hallway, away from the secretary's open area, toward the private entrance that Julie used when she wanted a little discretion.

She sat there for a moment, assessing the truth of being truly alone. And alive. Even if disheveled and bleeding and taped to her chair.

Then she began to weep.

Lester and Sammie sat side by side in the darkness of the gas station's back room. They were beside Route 2 in Massachusetts in a place appropriately enormous for the heavy traffic it bore — a combination deli, grocery store, coffee shop, and service station. The nonstop bustle of dozens of people was muted by a heavy, locked door.

Before them was a large flat-screen monitor and a DVD player. Sam was holding the remote.

"What was the time on that printout?" she asked Lester.

He checked the document that J.P. had extracted from the GPS in Lloyd Jordan's BMW and read off the time stamp opposite the Sunoco's address.

She uttered something unintelligible, followed by, "I knew I'd screwed it up. Not enough sleep."

"Emma still working up a storm every night?" Lester asked.

Sam scrutinized the remote as she spoke, trying to decipher which button to hit for fast-forward. "Not a storm. She quiets right down once I'm feeding her, but it's still every few hours. She's a peaceful baby otherwise."

Lester was smiling in the dark, nodding. "My daughter was like that. My son? Hell on wheels. Screamed for weeks. Have no idea why we didn't murder him. I guess as soon as you're about to, they do something cute to buy a little more time. Amazing process."

Sammie was laughing.

"How's Willy faring?" Lester asked.

With almost anyone else — except Joe, of course — she might have read into the question. But Lester was a nice man, and she took his curiosity at face value.

"Good," she said, her eyes glued to the screen. "He gets up and brings her to me, changes her diapers, plays with her. He's a good dad." She quickly cut him a glance, adding, "And he and I'll both shoot you if you repeat any of that."

Les was also transfixed by the whirring images before them. "My lips are sealed, but I'm not even remotely surprised. I

354

always thought Willy was a softy at heart."

Sam let out a bark of laughter. "You're an idiot, Les. Willy's heart is as dark as the bottom of a well. But he loves that child and I guess he tolerates me as her mother."

She tacked on, "And that goes for me, too, 'cause most of the time, I could kill him."

Les opened his mouth to answer, but then pointed and said instead, "There."

She immediately froze the image to reveal Lloyd Jordan standing just inside the gas station's entrance, looking around. He crossed to the coffee dispenser, poured himself a cardboard mug full, and retired to a small corner table with a direct view of the front door. The time on the screen matched not only what J.P. had discovered from the Bimmer, but one of the receipts that Willy had found in the trash of Leo Metelica's Lowell apartment. It was that coincidence that had brought them here, accompanied by a Mass state trooper and the warrant he'd prepared for them. The trooper had stepped outside to use the men's room and get some coffee.

Sam didn't go to fast-forward again, instead making them wait as long as Lloyd did for his appointment. Lester didn't speak; neither of them wanted to miss a single detail. Through the following eight minutes, they watched Lloyd nurse his drink, glance at the flow of people coming and going, and occasionally consult the clock on the wall. He seemed relaxed, however, with his legs crossed and his body slightly slouched. For a man about to meet a contract killer, it seemed like just another day at the office. Eventually, he pulled a folded newspaper from his back pocket and laid it on the table beside his elbow. He did not open it.

"Ooh," Lester commented. "Real spy stuff."

Leo Metelica appeared the same way Lloyd had earlier, stopping at the door and casting about. He saw his contact immediately, of course, but ignored him to continue his survey, eventually also using the coffee machine before ambling over to the table next to Lloyd's and settling down. He made a show of checking his watch and looking around some more, before at last acknowledging Lloyd with an unheard question. Lloyd pretended to listen politely, pointed to the newspaper inquiringly, and then handed it over with a smile.

Leo took the paper but didn't actually open it up, placing it flat on his own table and pretending to read the headline facing him.

"Sure," Lester said again. "That looks normal."

Lloyd stood up after that, straightened his back, left the eating area without a backward glance, and paid for the coffee on the way out the door.

Leo watched him leave, surreptitiously checked the inner fold of the paper for the envelope Sam and Les assumed was there, and then followed Lloyd's suit, shoving the paper into his pocket in the process.

"Voilà," Lester announced, retrieving their copy of the DVD. "That oughtta play well in court."

Sammie nodded and added, "Not to mention get us a warrant to access the Hummer's OnStar location finder. I'm looking forward to telling Lloyd that his own pretensions pointed us straight to him."

Lloyd loved his Hummer. It was huge and gleaming black, trimmed with enough chrome to qualify it as pure bling. As a kid, he'd watched Cadillacs and their ilk purring through the neighborhood, carrying cold-eyed, self-satisfied bigwigs with bodyguards and nervous women. He remembered his mixture of contempt and envy and remembered as well his ascribing the former to youthful ignorance as he became rich enough to buy fancy cars himself.

But he never drove this tank to town. Not the big town, in any case. The BMW was tasteful by Boston standards, but the Hummer? Even Lloyd could still not completely rationalize its use on his old home turf. The part of him that had become what he'd once envied still housed a fragment of the kid who could recognize a male ego in need of toys.

Now, however, he was feeling pretty satisfied with himself. His plan was working to perfection. After a day-and-a-half stakeout — another good reason to have chosen the roomy Hummer — he'd seen Kravitz arrive at the post office and disappear inside just long enough to allow him to stroll down the sidewalk, pretend to fumble and drop a book he was carrying, and stick two separate homing devices onto the rear of Kravitz's rusty Subaru sedan as he bent down to retrieve it, all in one smooth swoop.

Very sweet.

Back behind the wheel and relocated virtually out of sight, he could train a pair of binoculars on the post office's front door and see his target cautiously step out, watchful and on edge, all as expected, and reluctantly get back into his vehicle.

Lloyd smiled to himself. Poor bastard. He

had no choice. The empty post office box had to have told him that the e-mail was a hoax — a way to get him out into the open. But what to do? He had to return to his darling daughter, wherever she was. She was Dan's whole life, even if she didn't have her father's smarts — all his efforts to be invisible within society blown by a kid who couldn't stay off Facebook. That's how Lloyd had discovered where she attended school, and how he'd been able to tip over the first domino in locating his nemesis. Talk about irony.

"What to do? What to do?" Lloyd repeated, watching Dan's car pull away from the curb.

The trip to Pownal took most of the day. Dan drove around half of southern Vermont, up long hills with spectacular back views of the road behind, along dirt roads capable of throwing dust a hundred feet into the air, down dead ends along which he eventually double-tracked, all to catch anyone potentially tailing him.

And all to no avail. Through every such maneuver, Lloyd merely hung back, following the small blip representing Dan's car on his video display, and giving the sucker miles of room. He'd even assumed Dan would eventually stop and check for bugs, which is why he'd deposited two of them, and was delighted when his console informed him that the more openly placed of the pair had been removed and thrown to the side of the road. This, Lloyd had calculated, would lessen enough of Dan's mistrust to make him start thinking about heading home.

And it worked. By mid-afternoon, Lloyd saw the blip representing Dan leave Route 7, cross the railroad tracks at the old Green Mountain Race Track, and come to a stop behind the ancient stadium.

"I'll be damned," Lloyd muttered in admiration. "The man does know his rabbit holes."

As events would have it, however, Lloyd's pride in his hardware was shared by the trio of Joe Gunther, Willy Kunkle, and Lester Spinney, who were following their success with the BMW's GPS unit by latching on to the Hummer's On-Star locator beacon and using it to lead them to precisely the same spot.

But they weren't the only ones.

Despite Dan's care and hard work, his efforts to disappear and to offer his daughter shelter ended up merely highlighting the paradox that sometimes those most eager to

360

fade away often became the most eagerly sought.

And so it was that Paul Hauser, with no technology or subterfuge, was also in the neighborhood, having been here ever since the Kravitzes had first arrived.

He might have lost Dan in Gloria's house during the chase to the roof, but Hauser hadn't given up. In the manner to which he'd adapted his life — in his own way, as ghostly, quiet, and self-effacing as Dan — he'd been tracking the latter all along.

Dan was the only living soul who had ever seen the contents of that suitcase, and to Paul's thinking — which had taken on a peculiar shape over the years — that made him a man who needed to be stopped.

CHAPTER TWENTY-ONE

Dan sat in the rickety aluminum lawn chair and gazed out at the panorama before him. He was inches from the plate glass window of the stadium's highest vantage point — the uppermost of the stacked sky boxes that Sally had noticed upon their arrival. These were really like small apartments, seemingly placed as afterthoughts on top of the building's vast flat roof, six cubes arranged in a perfect double row.

The view was impressive, as the front wall of each of them was all glass, and perched well over one hundred feet above ground level. Below, as in an archaeological dig of an ancient Roman sports arena, the vague outline of the racetrack's enormous oval was just discernible in the overgrown grass and weeds circling the stagnant pond. Beyond were the railroad tracks gleaming in the setting sun; still farther off was Route 7, thinly traveled and as white as an ironed flat ribbon; and finally, the remnants of the Green Mountain foothills, petering out on their way to becoming the Berkshires in Massachusetts. Overhead, the sun to Dan's back had colored the clouds a virulent and gaudy swirl of variegated pink, which changed in shade and tone as he watched.

He'd been troubled earlier, after traveling all the way to the post office to retrieve the school's mail and finding nothing. But right now, a day later, faced with this overwhelming beauty, he allowed himself a moment's relaxation. He'd noticed nothing around the post office, had seen nothing in the rearview mirror, despite the endless switchbacks and false turns on his way back, and had disposed of the tracking device he'd found attached to his car — a discovery that, while alarming in itself, had both confirmed his concerns and partially addressed them.

He rose to his feet to see Sally next door, to make sure that she, too, was enjoying this natural light show. The sky boxes were interconnected by a back hallway that also led to a staircase down into the vast stadium itself. The rooms had been a mess when he and Sally had arrived, but they'd swept and tidied up two of them, and moved a few pieces of somewhat functional furniture from elsewhere in the building to vaguely emulate a pair of living quarters. It wasn't great, but he was hopeful that it would hold until the next development — whatever that might be.

He wasn't thrilled to have been reduced to a wait-and-see position, feeling but never seeing suspicious movement all around him, and unable to distinguish reality from any figments of his already sharpened wariness.

He left his room, marched down the few feet to the next door, and entered his daughter's room, already speaking her name, "Sally . . ."

He got no further. The room, as flooded with pink light as his own, was empty.

He frowned and reflected for a moment. Rick, his contact here and the place's caretaker, should have left for home by now. He'd greeted them warmly earlier, and he and Sally had immediately hit it off, he being just the grizzled type of old-timer that she loved to chat with.

That being said, she wouldn't have necessarily known of his work hours, and might have gone down to swap stories.

Dan headed for the stairs and the hangar-sized main hall just below, filled with its thousands of banked wooden seats, all seemingly transfixed by the spectacle he'd just been enjoying. In the almost disturbing total silence, he listened intently, straining to hear some evidence of his daughter's wanderings.

Far below, on the building's nondescript back side, Lloyd Jordan got out of his car, which dwarfed Dan and Sally's latest loaner, walked up to a narrow glass employees' entrance, and — without hesitation — picked up a rock and smacked it through the glass in one smooth movement. He reached through the resulting hole, triggered the door latch, and let himself into a narrow hallway with small, abandoned offices off to both sides.

He had no clue what the name of this place was, although its purpose once was clear enough, nor did he care. He was sick of the crap that had befallen him, and now that he had its source within reach, he was eager to start rebuilding his life. Not to mention that time was of the essence. If this loose cannon ever shared what he'd stolen with certain Boston-based parties, Lloyd would quickly become an endangered species.

He had little left to lose.

He reached a T-intersection with another, longer corridor that ran the length of the stadium, turned left toward a flight of steps he saw far in the distance, and marched off as if he'd been here a dozen times before.

But he was in for a surprise. Taking the steps two at a time, he surfaced into a single room the size of a football field, packed with hundreds of tables and chairs, located behind and beneath the ramped army of seats facing the racetrack. This was the stadium's once jam-packed food emporium, now lined with shuttered stalls with fading signs advertising hot dogs, burgers, and soda. Through several wide, sloping bays across from him, he could see the staired entries to the stadium's seating and glimpsed the view overlooking the racetrack.

"Jesus," he murmured. "What the hell?"

He'd been functioning as if on autopilot until now, responding simply to what appeared before him — Dan at the post office; the blip representing Dan's car; watching the caretaker leave for the day. Now, abruptly, he was at a loss, feeling like the sole inhabitant of an empty factory.

Which is when he heard the regular thumping of footsteps resounding above him and echoing through the distant bays.

Running on soft-soled shoes, he bolted toward the wall of fast-food cubicles and flattened himself out of sight beside one of the ramps, just as the overhead footsteps rounded the corner to enter the food-service area.

He watched as a teenage girl jogged past him unseeing, headed toward the very staircase he'd used to get here.

"Rick?" she called out into the stillness. "You still here?"

Lloyd checked to see if anyone was following, and then soundlessly slipped in behind her, reaching out.

Paul Hauser worked his way along the treeline bordering the stadium's employee parking lot, grateful to be in motion at last. Neither an athletic nor a young man, and certainly not one to seek the outdoors, he'd been living out of his hidden car for days, after tailing Dan and his daughter here from Bellows Falls. The strain of waiting and watching had plumbed his reserves. His inner resources were slim at best, and he was ruled by random thoughts, colliding images, and seething flashes of anger — a jumble of lunacies in conflict. He could function in the world, if not held to exacting standards, but even that balance was known to wobble when he was upset or dislocated, both of which he was now.

Dan Kravitz had done him significant

harm, throwing off his ability to fake nor-
malcy. Now, all Hauser could see clearly
was that by eliminating Dan, life would
return to what it had been.

Which was why he needed to move now,
at last, in part stimulated by the anomaly of
the mysterious man leaving that huge car
and entering the stadium. As if investigating
some God-given sign, Paul had to find out
what was going on, and he needed to see it
for himself.

And take action if necessary. Not for the
first time, his hand wandered to his waistband, to make sure the gun there hadn't
somehow shifted beyond his grasp.

Dan heard Sally's distant voice call out,
although he was unsure of her wording. He
wasn't inclined to shout in turn, and try to
catch her attention, so he merely continued
his descent from the building's roof, traveling along the broad, deeply set steps of the
tilted viewing deck, noticing as he went how
quickly the light was fading with the setting
of the sun. By the time he'd reached the
second-story tier of seats, dark shadows
were already cascading in from the far
corners of the space around him.

This was also when he heard a crash
and a sharp, high-pitched scream, instantly

cut short.

"Sally?" he shouted, and began to run.

"Damn," Sammie commented, craning forward over the dashboard and squinting into the sun's remnants. "That place is huge."

Joe was at the wheel. "My brother loved coming here, way back when they ran horses. In its day, it was a major deal."

"But, Gramps," Willy cracked from the backseat, "didn't everybody ride horses when you were a boy?"

Lester burst out laughing as Sammie twisted around to glare at him.

But Joe smiled as he trundled the SUV across the train tracks between the highway and the racetrack property and approached the gargantuan hulk that had caught Sammie's attention.

"Hey, Techno-Man," he addressed Lester. "What's your GPS reading? Is Lloyd's land yacht in the front or the back of this place?"

"Back," Les responded immediately. "And he's still not moving."

"That one's not either," Willy commented, his voice serious.

"What?" Sam asked.

Willy's arm appeared between them, his finger extended. "There's a car parked in the bushes over there, half hidden."

She swung her head and stared. "Where? How can you see that?"

"I was trained to," the ex-sniper answered grimly.

"You see anyone inside it?" Joe asked.

Lester had already extracted a pair of night-vision binoculars from a canvas bag at his feet. Of them all, he was the one who most enjoyed the latest tools of the trade. He quickly brought the glasses to bear as Joe slowed to a crawl.

"Empty," he announced.

"Unless the guy's on the floorboards," Willy said.

"Check it out?" Sam asked.

Something was playing on Joe's sense of urgency to keep moving.

"You get the registration?" he asked.

"Yup."

He sped up. "We'll do it later," he said simply.

Earlier, unknown to them, Dan had given his daughter the scenic tour, traveling the ghost of the old racetrack proper, and thus circling the pond. Joe stuck to the broad, paved access road leading to the northern parking lot, where they could see the narrow end of the building in the distance, looking vaguely like a snub-nosed cruise ship, beached and left to rot in the rapidly growing gloom.

Sally was staggering, fighting to keep on her feet as the man who'd grabbed her half dragged her downstairs by the hair to where Rick kept his office. In his other hand, he held a knife to her throat.

"One word," he said in a whisper. "One sound, and I cut your throat."

As they dropped below the dining area, she thought she heard a sound far behind them. Her father's voice?

She tried feebly to break away, only to have her neck snapped back by another violent yank.

The man's face was so close to her own, their noses were almost touching. "You stupid or something? You *want* to die?"

She stared at him.

He stopped at the foot of the staircase, back in the corridor that led to the exit and his car beyond.

"Answer me," he insisted. "Or better still . . ." He let her go and stepped back suddenly, pulling a large pistol from under his jacket.

She staggered against the wall and stood staring at him.

He waved the gun toward the stairs. "You

want your *dad* to die?"

She opened her mouth to protest when he swung the gun around like a snake's head and almost hit her in the teeth with it.

"Quiet," he hissed.

"No. Please," she pleaded, barely audible.

"Then move your ass. *Now.*"

He shoved her roughly by the shoulder and she began to stumble in the direction indicated. They heard another shout from upstairs, this one closer and clearer.

"Sally."

Hauser took advantage of the abrupt darkness between the woods and the back of the stadium to step clear of his cover and enter the parking lot. Like a dim fire far away, the sky's lingering pink tinge barely colored the gap overhead.

His eyes were fixed on Dan's and Lloyd's parked cars, and beyond them the small door with the broken glass. A movement inside — the smallest flash of something pale — caught his attention.

For no reason beyond his own obsession, he saw only what he chose to.

"Dan Kravitz," he murmured. "Dan Kravitz," and he pulled the gun free of his waistband.

■ ■ ■ ■

"There," Willy said from the backseat. "Straight ahead."

Joe accelerated and ignited his high beams starkly revealing a shabby-looking man in the middle of the parking lot, growing in size as they approached. He twisted from facing the parked cars to the left to looking straight into their headlights, his eyes wide and disoriented.

Then he suddenly returned to his original position.

At that same moment, they saw movement at the door — a girl in a white shirt, followed by a man holding something dark.

"Gun," Sammie shouted, as a flash of light erupted not from the twosome but from the man standing in the open.

No one fell by the door, but as the man there raised his own gun to return fire, the shooter swung around once more and brought his weapon to bear on Joe's car, firing twice. As Joe slammed on the brakes and yelled, "Get out. Get out," they heard a thud strike the engine block and saw a star explode in the middle of the windshield.

Despite his disability, Willy got out first, diving into a tight roll and coming up on his feet, drawing his gun from its holster.

"Don't move. Police!" he yelled, as Sammie landed beside him, on her stomach with both hands outstretched, clutching her .40-caliber. Joe was still skidding to a stop ten feet off to their side.

The man before them looked momentarily confused — his gun arm straight out but his weapon silent — until the Hummer's slamming door startled him.

He fired a third shot in their direction, the bullet whining over Sammie's head, before both she and Willy opened up, dropping him onto the pavement like a laundry bag cut from a rope.

At the same moment, the Hummer burst into life and, squealing tires spewing twin plumes of burning rubber, pulled away, heading south down the parking lot.

"Get him, Joe," Willy shouted to his boss, before realizing that their car had been crippled, a thin cloud of steam rising from under its hood.

Just inside the stadium door, unseen by all, Dan Kravitz steadied himself against the wall with an outstretched hand and stared at Paul Hauser's motionless body, theatrically frozen in the police car's lights.

Sally was gone, in the fraction of a second.

He'd seen Jordan throw her into his car and peel out while the bullets were flying. He fought to keep breathing.

He raised a fist in frustration, as if about to strike the wall, before the shouting outside brought him back to the present, and to what needed to be done.

Without hesitation, he faded backward into the darkness, vanishing as he knew all too well how to do.

Joe was crouching by the fender of the crippled car, gun in hand. *"Who's hit?"* he shouted into the night. *"Talk to me."*

"We're good," Sammie said. "Willy, too."

"I'm okay, boss," Lester answered from the vehicle's other side.

Gingerly, his adrenaline pulsing, Joe stood up. He thought he understood what had happened, if only because he could now rerun it in his head: Jordan gone with Sally; what was presumably Hauser down and not moving, his gun within sight and far from his hand; and as for Kravitz, no sign, but also not considered a threat.

It was done. He didn't know the hows or the whys, but it was done — or appeared to be.

"Okay," he called out, before reaching in through the car window. "Secure everything.

I'm calling for backup and a shoot team and a BOL on Jordan and his Hummer. I'm also going to pass along this bastard's On-Star information. Let's do this by the numbers. We have a kidnapping still in motion."

The mission was clear — the sightlines truer than they often were in police work — and as Joe began to work the problem with both radio and cell phone from his improvised command center, watching his team spread out and get busy, he felt a calm settle back within him at last, like the yearned-for return of an old and intimate companion.

His pain and his longing and his chasm-deep regret notwithstanding, he felt in that moment his battered hull roll back onto an even keel. He knew himself then to be a man perhaps in mourning, but a man intact.

CHAPTER TWENTY-TWO

Dan stepped inside his inner sanctum — neat, white, windowless, as organized and clean as a museum exhibition — and closed the door behind him, pressing against it with his shoulder blades. He was hot, flushed, his heart hammering, his hands trembling — having a full-blown panic attack.

From the moment of Sally's abduction, now four hours ago, he'd been struggling to stay centered.

But the weight of his doubts about his own sanity was pulling him down. He felt trapped halfway up an endless set of stairs, saddled with a rock-filled backpack that only grew heavier as he ascended.

"Sally, Sally, Sally," he whispered, as he had been compulsively for hours, using her name as a guiding light. He was down to his own basic elements now, of repetition, of orderliness, of trying to exert control over anarchy. As he'd driven a truck that he'd stolen near Pownal, after fleeing the race-track, he'd steered solely with his left hand, using his right to arrange and rearrange the maps and pens and general trash that he'd found scattered across the seat beside him — almost hitting the ditch several times in the process.

All the while repeating his daughter's name.

He blinked several times. Here in his room at least, everything was as he'd left it — every object touched by him, placed by him, brought here by him. Functionality was addressed, the role of each item clear and defined, the very pattern in which they were displayed refined through constant trial.

There could be no perfection in Dan's life — no real hope of release from the tensions of his world. But this room, at least, was better than almost anywhere else.

And if there was any hope for Sally, this was where he might achieve it.

That very notion cleared his mind slightly. He stopped mumbling her name, took a deep breath, and shook out his hands — like a pianist preparing to play.

He'd been stricken by what had occurred at the racetrack, but not solely because of Sally. Seeing Hauser and Jordan in the same place at the same time had come as a complete surprise. All his thoughts had been given to the former, whom he'd seen lurking, after all, outside the American Legion in Bellows Falls. The logic had fit: Dan had stumbled over the man's murder album, and in so doing had disturbed a hornet's nest.

But Lloyd Jordan?

Dan crossed his immaculate room, sat in his wheeled office chair, and rolled over to his filing cabinet, where he'd placed the documents that he'd stolen from Jordan's office but only glanced at cursorily.

Part of him felt like an idiot, that he'd never fully addressed the code protecting the content of that material. But ironically, it wasn't his habit to pry unnecessarily.

Lloyd Jordan might have called Vermont home for a few years, but he'd never had any interest in learning much about the state. The only newspapers he subscribed to came from New York and Boston, the radio he enjoyed was beamed in via satellite, and he generally avoided contact with the locals, all of whom he'd labeled "woodchucks," in any case.

He was an urban animal, trained to a different pace, and — more important right now — dulled to a rural environment's sense of priorities.

Thus it was that while he knew he should dump the Hummer and figure out how to exploit what he had in Kravitz's daughter, he had both a crook's inborn contempt for law enforcement and a city dweller's inured dismissiveness about street violence.

What he didn't compute, therefore, was that kidnapping children in the middle of a police shootout was a showstopper in Vermont, and that every cop within seventy-five miles of Pownal was aware of him and his eyesore vehicle, not to mention its on-board gadgetry.

Which helped explain why, less than two hours after he'd squealed away from the racetrack, he saw a pair of blue lights flashing in his rearview mirror in Brandon — almost to his goal of Burlington, where he'd been hoping to pause and regroup.

"Shit," he said, almost conversationally.

"What?" his passenger demanded from her seat on the car's far side, as distant from him as if they'd been riding in a mobile home. He had taken the time to duct tape her wrists and ankles, and to fasten her seat belt, but he had left her free to speak after she'd agreed not to scream or yell.

He didn't answer directly. "Well, let's play

devil's advocate — maybe it's not me."

Without touching the brakes, he twisted the wheel as he passed the fire house, and pulled onto something named High Street, where he immediately hit the accelerator to extend the gap between them and the cruiser behind.

The blue strobes followed.

Jordan gave a dour, tight-lipped smile, the situation bringing him back several decades, to when cat-and-mouse car games with the Boston cops had been routine.

"Here we go," he said to no one in particular. Far in her corner, Sally did her best to brace her bound feet against the rubber-matted floorboards, as the oversized vehicle began to leap and shudder over the road's imperfections.

They could hear the wailing of the patrol car tailing them.

High Street ran straight for several hundred feet before crossing Park and becoming Marble, just by the church. The Hummer virtually flew through the intersection as Sally closed her eyes against another car's headlights that seemed close enough to her window to be within reach. An angry, belated horn blast briefly commingled with the siren.

A split in the road came next, where Jordan bore right based solely on the widest option. By now they were pushing eighty miles per hour, on a dark and narrow residential street.

There, inevitably, they ran out of luck. Or so it seemed.

On what would have been a gentle curve on Forest Dale Road, Lloyd caught his left wheels on some gravel, overcompensated to correct the skid, and ended up launching them into a dense growth of trees, which appeared before the broad windshield with the abruptness of a slammed door. Instinctively, they both screamed, Lloyd threw his hands up, and they became enmeshed in an orchestration of slaps, thuds, crashes, bangs, and tearing sounds.

But they stayed upright, and they kept moving. Through it all, Jordan had kept his foot on the gas pedal.

Sally opened her eyes to his suddenly yelling, *"Yeah. Damn. You son of a bitch."* Through what was left of the windshield and thanks to one headlight only, she saw a smooth and undulating gray-green wasteland, rapidly disappearing beneath their wheels as they kept careening forward, although now accompanied not by a siren but by a raucous orchestra of rattles and metallic complaints.

"Where are we?" she asked despite herself.

He was laughing, she thought, almost hysterically. "It's a fucking golf course. Can you believe that? We got that prick cold."

It was a short-lived triumph. Exhilarated by his newfound invulnerability, Lloyd took a low rise before them at full power, throwing them airbound once more, along the edge of a large sand trap, and from there — as if in slow motion — over onto their side.

There was a deep structural groaning like a metal building collapsing, a feeling of weightlessness amid an all-encompassing whooshing sound, and finally — at last — complete and utter silence.

Sally blinked, staring straight ahead, hanging upside down by her seat belt, and waited for something else to happen.

It did. Lloyd Jordan, groaning, crawled out of his shattered side window and disappeared. Several minutes later, accompanied by flashlights and much shouting, the police arrived.

"That rich enough?" Joe asked. "I hate it when cocoa's too thin."

Sally nodded in midsip, her expression appreciative. The two of them were alone in a pleasantly decorated interview room two blocks from Brattleboro's police, usually reserved for recorded conversations with traumatized children. Sally didn't totally qualify, but her involvement in all this was vague enough — and Joe had enough pull locally — to allow for a little leeway.

Still, the camera in the corner and the mic discreetly placed on the low table between them spoke to why they were here, offers of cocoa notwithstanding. This young woman's father was a suspected criminal, and her role in his activities was unknown.

It was by now almost midnight.

"No, it's good," she answered after swallowing. "Thank you."

"Least I can do for someone who's been through what you have," he said.

She smiled wearily. "Yeah."

"Did you know the man who grabbed you?" he asked.

Her voice rose. "I have no clue. One second, I'm heading downstairs for a bull session with the maintenance guy, the next it's people shooting at each other and this crazy man throws me into the car."

"Did you see what actually happened? Who was shooting at who?" Joe asked, keeping his tone offhand.

For a split second, she thought about correcting his grammar, but resisted the urge. Instead, she answered truthfully. "No. I just saw gun flashes all over the place. A bullet whizzed by — I heard that — but that was about it."

So she didn't know that Hauser had died, he thought. "What did the man tell you once you got out of there?"

She thought for a moment. "He just wrapped the duct tape around me and told me to shut up. That was it until the police began chasing us."

"You'd never set eyes on him before?"

"No."

"You ever hear the name Lloyd Jordan?"

"No."

"Your father never spoke of him?"

That stopped her again. No one yet had associated her with her father this evening. It had just been a succession of people handing her off to one another — all the way here. They'd asked her questions about how she was feeling and whether she had suffered any damage or pain. Nothing about Dan.

"No," she said cautiously.

"Do you know where your father is now?"

"No."

"But he was with you at the racetrack."

It came out as a statement. She pondered how to handle it.

"What were the two of you doing there,

Sally?" Joe asked.

His voice made her study him more closely. It was kind — genuinely fatherly, as if he were an interested friend.

But even though she remembered meeting him a year ago she knew better.

"I didn't say he was there," she said.

Gunther smiled, respecting her thoughtfulness. It might stretch things out, getting her to open up, but he suspected that it would make her a more reliable witness once he got her there.

Assuming he succeeded.

"You know Julie Johnson?" he asked, out of the blue.

Sally's mouth half opened in surprise. "From school?"

"Yeah."

"Sure. Why?"

"She was tortured by Jordan in order to find you."

"*What?* Oh my God. Is she all right?"

Joe frowned. "No, she's not. He didn't kill her, if that's what you're asking."

"But why?" Sally demanded, increasingly baffled. "What did *I* do?"

Joe's more pleasant demeanor returned. "Sally, you're a very bright girl. I asked. Everyone says good things about you. You tell me: Is this happening because of what

386

you've done? Or because of who you are?"

He stumped her there, posing the question in an almost classroom manner. She furrowed her brow, trying to sort through the possible answers. Thankfully, she settled for the truth, triggered in part by her curiosity.

"My dad?"

Joe rewarded her with a smile. "That's what I think. You were a pawn — a way to get to him."

"Which is why he grabbed me," she suggested.

"Yup."

"But what does he want with my dad?"

"Come on, Sally. Put it together."

She became quiet and sat back in her chair, her gaze on the floor.

"You ever hear of Willy Kunkle?" Joe asked softly.

"No."

"He's a friend of mine. A colleague. Works for the VBI. He and your old man go back a few years. Dan played a big role on that case involving Nicky King, when you and I first met."

She stared at him, astonished. "Nicky?"

Nicky, now locked up in a psychiatric facility, had been a boyfriend of Sally's when she and her father had lived with

Nicky's mother, over a year ago. An odd arrangement made stranger when it came out that Nicky had also killed a man in a psychotic break with reality.

"Your father helped us figure that out," Joe told her. "He's helped Willy a lot over time. He's a keen judge of character, for all his eccentricities."

She smiled at the reference.

"Unfortunately," Joe continued casually, "those eccentricities got a ball rolling with Jordan that hasn't turned out too well."

Sally made a face. "I guess not."

"And because Jordan got away after you crashed, I'm not so sure what trouble your dad may be in now. Jordan's getting desperate, and he no longer has you as a bargaining chip to keep things civilized."

She was silent at that, mulling it over.

"We need to find Dan so Jordan doesn't kill him, Sally," Joe said softly.

Her eyes moistened. "But I don't *know* where he is. What about that Willy guy? Did you ask him?"

"Yes," he said simply. "He has no clue. You know how Dan is — makes a hermit look like a frat boy."

She knew the truth there. She rubbed her face in frustration, caught between protecting her father and saving him from a menace she now knew personally.

As if reading her mind, Joe then said, "Sally, let's start at the beginning — or at least some kind of beginning — when you and Dan visited Gloria Wrinn, looking for Paul Hauser."

"You *know* about that?"

Joe leaned forward and placed his elbows on his knees. "Tell me what you know, Sally," he suggested kindly.

She scowled in concentration. In the end, however, she followed her instincts, and trusted what she saw in this man's eyes.

"We're here."

Ben Underhill opened his eyes and gazed out the van's side window. It was raining, and the streetlights reflected off the puddles across the parking lot in an almost festive manner.

"Boss? You awake?"

"Heard you," he said softly, stretching his legs and arms.

He knew that riding in a van went against the grain of most guys in his line of work — and it sure as hell embarrassed his bodyguards. They were all supposed to like Caddies, or at least high-end SUVs with tinted windows.

But this was roomy, comfortable, with

captain's chairs and a TV, a full communications setup. Not to mention bulletproof. Plus, for its size, it was all but invisible — just another soccer mom's means of transportation. More than once, he knew he'd coasted by a surveillance team only because they hadn't registered a run-of-the-mill van.

He operated the control by the side of his seat and brought it out of recliner mode — another plus for the rig.

"They ready for us?" he asked his driver.

"Ready when you are," was the answer.

The routine was the same — a perimeter check, a phalanx of armed and armored men, a quick but dignified march from vehicle to previously vetted building. He'd seen the same thing supplied to the president of the United States, which pleased him. Ben Underhill might not have been on that level — and who would want to be? But he had his hard-earned status, and no problem being protected from people wanting him dead.

After all, he'd wanted a few dead himself.

Which now they were.

Enjoying the cool night air, Underhill stepped from the vehicle and crossed into the building beside them — the back of a closed restaurant in Fitchburg, Massachusetts — one of a dozen or more locations across the state that he used for private purposes.

Although tonight's was known only to him. Through a phone number used only by a select few, his people had received a call from a man saying that he knew of a threat to Underhill's financial integrity — an unusual and curiously arresting choice of words.

Not to mention that the trace they'd put on the call had been stopped dead in its tracks. Not the sign of any average snitch or turncoat. Nor — the movies notwithstanding — the obvious handiwork of any underpaid and ill-equipped cop, federal or otherwise.

And it hadn't ended there. The caller had recited a few facts and names from documents he'd claimed to possess that had caused the call to be routed directly to Ben, despite his standing order never to be awakened.

That had been a good move — and the reason for the long drive out here in the middle of the night.

Underhill stopped inside the restaurant's empty, shadowy kitchen, enjoying the quiet as his men fanned out and double-checked what the people already there had gone through before his arrival.

No one took offense. They'd all been caught by surprise in the past, one way or the other. To these folks, life was a transient enjoyment, best protected and never taken for granted.

"We're good," one of them eventually murmured in his ear.

"He here?" Ben asked.

"Has been for half an hour. And he's clean."

Ben went forward alone, through the swinging kitchen doors into the darkened dining room. All the curtains had been drawn, only one table light was on, and, aside from the slender man seated at the same table, no one else was in the large room.

As Ben approached, he noticed that his guest had arranged the lamp, the salt and pepper shakers, and the small sugar-pack container in a meticulously tidy manner. The man himself looked perfect — clean, unwrinkled, precisely postured with his back straight and his palms flat on the tablecloth before him.

He looked up as Ben sat opposite him. Neither man offered to shake hands.

"Pleasant drive here, I hope?" Ben asked.

The man nodded.

"Were you offered anything like coffee or something to eat? I gave orders."

"Yes," the man answered. "They asked. I'm fine."

Ben nodded. "So who are you? You know *my* name."

"Dan," he said.

Ben waited for more, but nothing was offered. Still, he was curious enough to allow for more leeway than was standard.

"How did you find me?"

"I broke your code."

"I kind of guessed that. It couldn't have been easy. You have help?"

"It wasn't that hard."

Ben studied him, slowly realizing the depth of the man. Whoever he was, he was being totally straight. For some reason even he wasn't sure of, Ben knew that much at least to be true.

"Well, let's cut to the chase, then, Dan," he said. "You want to show me what you have?"

Dan pulled several sheets of notepaper from his pocket and slid them across the small table.

Underhill didn't touch them immediately, glancing at them first, controlling his reaction. Merely seeing what was written across the top sheet triggered a complicated adrenaline rush of dread, confirmation, and deep-seated anger.

He slowly reached out and read what Dan had delivered, while the latter sat as still as a statue, waiting.

Ben took his time, translating the arcane coding in his head, while dealing with his emotions. This strange, thin, silent man had just saved him a great deal of potential trouble — trouble he'd feared was lurking just out of sight, but which he'd never been able to prove actually existed.

The document in his hand was a lifesaver for him and his business — and a death sentence for the man who'd written it.

"You going to tell me how you got hold of this?" he asked.

"No."

"You going to swear on your life that this is it, and there aren't any copies?"

"That's a sample only. You know that," Dan told him. "I made no copies and the rest is with the guy I took it from."

"And just so we're on the same page," Underhill said, "let me ask who it is we're talking about. We can't make any mistakes here."

Dan's eyes were unwavering on his. "Lloyd Jordan."

Ben looked at him thoughtfully before saying, "You obviously know the value of this. What are you expecting I'll do with it?"

"You asking me what I want?"

"That, too. But answer the first question."

Dan blinked and glanced at the papers between them. "Those are photocopies of documents that he shouldn't have and that you don't want out of your control. The fact that they exist tells me they were made for insurance — call it blackmail-in-waiting if you want. I wouldn't be too happy with that, in your shoes."

"You think I should deal with him? That's why you're here, isn't it? So I'll take care of your problem?"

"I thought it was our problem."

"Which I'm used to taking care of, and you aren't. Am I right?"

"Maybe."

Now that Ben had confirmation of what he'd long suspected, and was suddenly feeling quite relieved, he decided to stretch this out a little more.

"Will you tell me what Jordan's done to you, to make you hate him so much?"

"No."

Ben crossed his legs and sat back comfortably. "What if I choose not to do anything?" He tapped the papers with his fingertips. "This is ancient stuff."

"We're sitting here, aren't we?" Dan challenged him.

Ben conceded the point. "Still," he said. "Humor me."

"I have a letter to Jordan from Susan Rainier."

Underhill filled in the gap. "Ah, the old girlfriend."

"And the ironclad alibi for the night Jordan's first wife was killed," Dan added, having spent hours reconstructing the case in his white room.

Ben smiled. "True. Don't tell me you've got the smoking gun."

Dan was about to answer when a buzzing went off in his pocket. He pulled out a cell phone and studied its screen, his expression a mixture of confusion and sheer joy.

He looked up at Underhill with his eyes shining. "Only one person has this number."

Ben was amused by now. What the hell else was this crazy man going to pull? A phone call? Here?

"Go ahead," he urged.

Dan opened the phone. "Sweetheart?"

Underhill watched as Dan listened, and saw the man's features transform from the pure tension he'd first witnessed to relief, then concern, finally to tenderness, and at last to something teetering on tearfulness.

A few minutes later, Dan closed the phone and replaced it in his pocket. "Thank you."

"Good news?"

"The best."

"You were telling me about Jordan's alibi."

Dan was still smiling, and became suddenly more eloquent, as if he'd finally been told that he could breathe again. "I didn't know it when I got hold of it, but Rainier's letter makes it clear that the dates don't line up for what she told the police after Jordan's wife was found dead."

"The blackmailer was being blackmailed?"

"So it seems."

"And you'll give that to the cops if I don't do something about him?"

"I will, especially now."

Ben pointed at Dan's pocket. "The phone call."

Dan chose his wording carefully. He was loath to tell Underhill too much about himself, even though he was aware of the man's resources and abilities. As joyful as he was feeling, Dan remained cautious to the core.

"Jordan took something very important from me," he said slowly. "I came here to enlist your help and to make it worth your while. Now, through dumb luck, what was stolen's been returned." He indicated the financial paperwork. "That was supposed to be my buy-in, so to speak — a way to win you over. But I don't have any reason to be here anymore. You're free to do with that stuff whatever you want."

Underhill absorbed that quietly for a few seconds. "But you are still planning to send the letter to the cops?"

Dan frowned. "He's a bad man. I think he did a bad thing."

Ben laughed gently. "He did more than one. Trust me."

He stood up and extended his hand for a shake, which Dan accepted after standing up in turn.

"Let me put it to you this way, Dan — assuming that's really your name: You can do with the letter what you want, but when and if the cops get around to rounding up Lloyd Jordan, I'd be amazed if they find him alive."

With that, he bowed his head, turned on his heel, and walked off whence he'd come, leaving Dan in the darkened dining room as before, alone and with a new set of mixed emotions with which to wrestle.

Chapter Twenty-Three

"What do you think?" Joe asked.

The room was in the basement of the municipal center, its door locked against any accidental intruders, including anyone falling outside this investigation.

They weren't looking for more input. Already there was Joe's entire team, along with Ron Klesczewski, J. P. Tyler, and their boss, Tony Brandt. Between them, they were already baffled enough.

Spread out across several tables under the harsh overhead lighting were the six albums they'd secured from the car that Paul Hauser had stolen and driven to the racetrack and his own death.

"I think they're bogus," Willy said with his usual directness.

"I can't tell," J.P. commented, ever the cautious scientist. "And I've been studying them for over an hour."

"I think they're scary," Sammie said quietly.

"They are that," Brandt agreed. "But are they real? We've already ruled out that they're connected to the Connecticut River Valley murders."

Tyler was back to analyzing them with a powerful, illuminated magnifying glass made especially for scrutinizing photographs. His face was inches from one of the open albums as he recited.

"Six albums; six women. Each book laid out in an almost cinematic style, more or less, starting with general shots and ending with a series of close-ups. They're old photographs, taken with film. None of them are recent, and none of them look doctored, which would be easier to detect with these than with digital images. And each album is accompanied by a hank of cut hair."

"Who cares?" Willy challenged them. "The point is, we don't have any missing women fitting any of this. These are staged. That crazy bastard probably used them to jerk himself off." He waved a hand over the whole array. "What d'you want to bet you'll find every one of these women selling Dunkin Donuts or waiting tables, with five kids each at home?"

He pointed to one picture for emphasis.

"Look at her eyes. She's covered with blood; it's all over her and the picnic table underneath — enough to float the *Titanic*. But her eyes are clear and her pupils are small."

"That wound looks pretty real," Joe said about the same picture. "I'm not saying it couldn't be makeup; maybe a glued-on rubber phony like they use at disaster drills. But with either the focus being off a bit or just the lens being crappy, it's hard to tell."

Tyler straightened and switched the position of two of the albums so that they were side by side. "Could be those two are the same woman."

Sammie approached and stood beside him. "Wearing a wig, you mean?" she asked, pointing.

"The earlobes look different," Ron said.

"Different angle," Tyler told him. "That can alter how things look."

"Okay," Joe announced with finality. "We've been doing this enough. We clearly have nothing right now. We've checked our databases, we've sent all the hair samples and other stuff to the lab for analysis, and despite how old this all seems to be, we'll send out what they return to us to the FBI and whatever other clearinghouses we can think of for open cases and missing persons.

But that's about all we can do for the moment."

"I wouldn't mind getting a plant expert in here to see if we can match these outdoor scenes to some specific region," Tyler mentioned.

"Works for me," Brandt said, covering the logistics of who might pay for it.

"I'm not saying we should just close the book," Joe added. "Now that we have Hauser on ice, we can chase his prints and DNA and see if we can build a history. If he has a criminal record or a decent background report, maybe we can trace where he's lived or traveled and see if we can't narrow our inquiries."

"I wouldn't put a ton of effort into that," Willy counseled.

"I think we got your opinion," Sam told him. "You want to be the father in Albuquerque who never finds out his daughter's dead because some dumb redneck in Vermont got lazy?"

Willy usually received with aplomb what he dished out in insults, but that crack got him red-faced. Sammie had struck home.

"Just saying we shouldn't hold our breath," he said dully. "Not that we shouldn't try."

The room was quiet as everyone absorbed

both what had happened and the evidence that had stimulated it. The sheer mass of the albums and their contents — even if eventually proven fictitious — were enough to make each of them wonder. The perversity behind their creation lingered like a cold draft.

Joe walked to the door and flipped the lock. "We need to get out of here. It's almost o-eight-hundred now. It's been a hell of a night and we all need sleep. If those women are dead, they've been that way a long time, and if Paul Hauser killed them . . . well, that's been taken care of, too. Let's get a little rest and then we can do some homework."

"What about Norm Myers?" Willy asked sharply, still smarting. "You goin' to write him off as one of Hauser's, too?"

Joe stared at him. "As far as anyone knows, Willy, Myers was a fluke — a natural death in unusual circumstances. I even consulted Hillstrom again. It happens."

"Maybe in your world," Willy said, walking out.

As the others began following suit, Sammie asked Joe, "What did you do with the girl?"

"Sally? She's upstairs watching TV. Either that or taking a nap." He rubbed his eyes.

"I hope so, anyhow."

Sam scowled at him maternally. "Meaning you aren't going home right now."

He smiled. "Oh, no. I'll be keeping her company. I just wanted to come down to check this out and see what we'd found. She called her father, and he's heading in."

"You going to arrest him?"

By now, they were alone, the others having left. Joe kissed her cheek and said, "Go home to Emma, Sam. How's it worked out, coming into work now and then?"

"Weird," she admitted. "I thought I'd like it better."

"You're a mom now," he said. "You're in love for the rest of your life, whether you know it or not. Get used to it. Enjoy it." He smiled broadly. "We'll still be here when you're ready."

But her face remained serious. "Will you be?" she asked. "Here?"

He reached out and squeezed her shoulder. "Yeah. This is what I do, and some smart people have been telling me I better stick with it for the time being."

She patted his chest. "Now I'll go home to my daughter."

The insides of Joe's eyelids felt covered with sandpaper as he stood just outside the interview room on the first floor of the municipal building. The VBI didn't have one of these — that remained among the Grand Plans that management was still pondering — so Joe and his crew borrowed the PD's when they needed to apply a little pressure.

Not that there was a demand for the space at the moment. It wasn't quite nine in the morning.

He took a breath, cleared his mind, and opened the door.

"Where's Sally?" Dan Kravitz demanded, sitting with his knees together and his back rigid. He, too, looked utterly drained.

Joe crossed the tiny room to the one available chair, and sat down, trying not to display his exhaustion. "Upstairs, safe and sound," he said.

"I would like to see her," Dan said softly.

"I know you would, Mr. Kravitz," Joe sympathized. "But we're going to have to clear up a few things first. You've been a busy man."

In response, Dan removed a crumpled two sheets of handwritten paper from his pocket and placed them on the scarred tabletop. He didn't actually slide them across to Joe, so the latter restrained himself from reaching for them.

"What's that?" he asked instead.

"My bargaining chip," Dan said.

Joe smiled. "Isn't that like putting money on the table for an item you haven't identified yet?"

Dan stared at him. "We both know what's going on here. A few hours ago, you gunned down a man in Pownal. According to the news, you found another one dead on Hawks Mountain, and we all know about the murder downtown — off the bridge and into the river."

He sat forward anxiously and asked abruptly, as if suddenly reminded, "Did you find the suitcase? With the albums?"

Joe shifted and crossed his legs. This was not the traditional route for an interview, where the cop tries to coax, cajole, or finagle the truth from a suspect. This man was at once smart and distressed, clear-sighted and confused, and in any case eager to be free and clear of the mess he'd taken on.

Joe could only sympathize.

But he wasn't going to show it. They had a good idea of what had gone down. Kravitz was correct about that. But Dan still had a lot of explaining to do, to Joe and the state's attorney. People weren't let off the hook simply because they were good at heart and loved their children.

Still, there seemed to be wiggle room here,

certainly in regard to the question Dan had just asked.

"Tell me about that," Joe answered obliquely.

"I will," he said. "But tell me first: Are they real? I looked and looked and I couldn't find anything. I spent hours on the computer, but I only had a quick look at a couple of the pictures." He added, "They made me sick."

"We don't know," Joe told him. "We're still checking. Now talk to me."

Dan was looking down at the table, carefully arranging the two sheets of notepaper atop each other, tidying the edges and aligning them in turn with the table's edge.

"I found them by mistake."

"Where?"

"You know where."

Joe stretched his neck and cleared his throat. "Okay. This is how we're going to do this. You say you have a bargaining chip. Great. We'll get to that. You know what it is, and it looks like you're pretty sure it'll be a solid-gold, get-out-of-jail card. Let's go with that. I'm totally game. I like you. I like your daughter, and as you said before, we all pretty much know what the big picture is here. So, what you're going to do right now — so that you can present me with that chip

— is take me through your whole adventure, from the time you left a Post-it note on Lisbeth's K-Y jelly bottle, to what you've been up to until the moment you crossed the police department's threshold. Is all of that crystal clear?"

"What about Sally?" was the predictable response. "When do I get to see her?"

"That's *my* bargaining chip," Joe told him. "You have to tell me the truth — straight down the line. You don't know what I know, and that's a shitload by now, so if you lie or screw up or jerk me around, I hope you have a good photograph of Sally, 'cause that's all you're going to see of her in a jail cell." Joe then fed the man's well-known paranoia by throwing in, "You have *got* to be smart enough to know that I can drop the ceiling on you if I want to."

Dan was staring at him glumly. "You'd do that?"

Joe let him stew for a couple of seconds before stating, "You bet your ass. I'm old, I'm tired, and I'm pissed off at the world — more than you'll ever know. I got dead people, missing people, and people who might not've even existed but who need checking out." He took a breath before adding, "And one bird in hand. Start talking."

■ ■ ■ ■

Two hours later, Dan wearily, almost mumbling, pushed Susan Rainier's letter over to Joe and said, "*Now* will you take this? It proves she cooked up his alibi for the night his first wife died."

"It doesn't prove he killed her."

Dan sighed heavily. "That's your job. I just want my daughter back."

Joe touched the letter. "And you think this'll do that? You killed a man, you've admitted to a series of burglaries, you've been running around conducting your own criminal investigation. Once I replay the tape we just made for the state's attorney, we'll be able to charge you with a half-dozen offenses."

Dan placed his forehead in his hand, nearing his limit of social interaction. The man needed solitude like fish need water.

"I was trying to do the right thing. I know being the Tag Man was out of line. I've stopped that. I was between a rock and a hard place. I *had* to investigate on my own. Would you have just said 'thank you' if I'd dropped by and said, 'Oh, hey, when I was in Gloria's house in the middle of the night, I discovered a monster'? You would've busted me for being there in the first place."

Joe couldn't deny it. He knew how things tended to work.

But he also knew that based solely on the tape of Dan wandering around the Jordan house, the prosecutor wouldn't be too thrilled to nail him for the Tag Man rap. Therefore, getting Dan to spill his guts was a must. To Joe's mind, however, that was exactly the problem.

He happened to agree with Dan. He *had* done the right thing — at least from his viewpoint.

Joe stood up, his entire body complaining. "I see you as a man of honor, Dan. You've acted that way with Willy for years; you've done proud by your daughter, who thinks the world of you; and you showed a sense of responsibility and conscience through all of this. I think you're one of the oddest guys I've met in a while, but by itself, that isn't illegal. In fact, it's probably why Willy likes you.

"So, here's the deal: If you swear on Sally's head that you won't skip town and that you'll come in to meet me about this whenever I ask, *and,*" he emphasized, tapping the table with his finger, "that you'll stop this Tag Man bullshit — now and forever — then I'll let you go. You have to tell me

410

where you're living and working at all times, until the dust has officially settled, but other than that, I'm happy to know you're just hanging in the neighborhood while we figure out what to do with you. Now, if the state decides I'm being too soft-hearted, there's nothing I can do about that, but I'll do my best to recommend everything but jail time for you. You understand?"

Dan looked up at him, his eyes dark-rimmed and bloodshot, but grateful. "I do, and I appreciate it."

Joe studied him for a moment, comparing their fates. He, as Joe saw it now, was looking at a life of solitude with his books, his woodworking, and his job. Dan Kravitz — the self-imposed social hermit — might just be spared a life of solitude in a cell, if he was lucky, in exchange for the company of the love of his life.

Funny how things sometimes worked out.

He crossed to the door and opened it. "I'll take you to your daughter."

CHAPTER TWENTY-FOUR

Sammie sensed more than heard someone's presence at the living room door, at the precise moment that Willy's voice gently reassured her, "Just me."

Typical, she thought with a smile. He even enters his own home like a cat burglar, silently and through the least-used entrance. She'd known him to park a block over as well, not for her sake but to throw off the neighbors.

No wonder he kept company with the likes of Dan Kravitz — a man she'd barely heard of until recently.

She turned her head only slightly, so as not to disturb Emma, who was fast asleep in her arms, her eyes firmly shut, her face still, aside from the reflexive churning of her jaw muscles as she massaged the pacifier in her mouth.

Willy floated silently across the room and crouched beside them, murmuring, "Hey, little girl."

Sammie thought she could see a tiny extra relaxation touch the child's face at her father's voice. Not many would believe that Willy Kunkle could have that effect.

"You're home early," Sam said to him, slightly concerned.

"Yeah," he said simply.

"Everything okay?"

"Oh, sure." He was watching Emma intently, but smiling.

"Then what?" Sammie pressed him, knowing his moods well enough by now to read them reliably, at least most of the time.

He tilted his head thoughtfully, before admitting, "It's just goofy. Nothing serious."

She laughed, and her moving chest made Emma smile and hunker down a little more into the crook of her arm.

"You are too much. Spit it out."

Willy kissed her cheek. "I missed you guys."

She flushed with pleasure. "Then you did the right thing."

He rose, stroked Emma's smooth forehead once, as was his habit, and retreated to the doorway, where he stopped to look back at them, mother and child, rocking by the window overlooking the sun-dappled lawn.

He had been missing them. That much

was true. But of course — considering his complicated psyche — the motivation hadn't been purely sentimental. He'd been sensitive to what had almost befallen Dan, when Sally had been grabbed. He'd embraced the man's panic.

It had taken Willy a long time to reach this point in life — a long time, a lot of luck, and an inordinate amount of kindness and patience from people who — had they been remotely reasonable — wouldn't have expended the effort.

And now he had a daughter. Tiny, frail, and utterly dependent.

He'd come home in the middle of the afternoon to be reminded of that, and to bask in the proof of his good fortune.

But he'd also come home to refresh his memory of them. Because he knew — was haunted by the knowledge — that life could change faster than it takes a teardrop to travel a cheek.

That night, late as usual, Joe walked down Main Street from the office, swung right on Elliot, and walked into a bar named Silva's, created and named by his much-missed companion. When Lyn had been alive, it had become a routine for him to drop by during her shifts, just to sit on the last stool, hard against the wall, and watch her work the crowd. He had first done that in Gloucester, Mass., several years ago when he'd gone to the local bar to gather information on a case, before he'd even known her name.

He'd admired her then, and had never stopped.

The place wasn't busy. It was midweek. Maybe twenty people were spread about, chatting, laughing, and enjoying their time off.

As he paused in the doorway, taking in the scene, the woman at the bar, reminiscent of Lyn in fact, if far younger, slapped a can of Coke before his usual place, flashed him a wide grin and a thumbs-up, and went off to tend to a man calling out from the bar's far end.

Joe felt a double pang of pain and relief, walked over to his spot, and settled in before the cold can, admiring how Lyn's daughter Coryn, who'd inherited the business, had so quickly adapted to a life she'd never anticipated.

Like her mother, she had a knack with people.

Later still, long after most of the town had gone to sleep, Dan Kravitz settled down to enjoy the quiet of the night — his favorite time of day. He was feeling more kindly disposed toward the world and its inhabitants, if perhaps only for the moment — a mood no doubt helped, just hours earlier, by his addressing the lingering problem of what to do with Leo Metelica's dark and ominous Colt .45. He'd dropped it into the Connecticut River.

Not surprisingly, he did know himself well enough to realize that his fears and mistrust would eventually take him back. But for now, life could be worse. He wasn't in jail — always a plus; his daughter was safe and sound and back to doing the things that gave her pleasure; Hauser — whoever or whatever he'd been — was no longer a concern; Jordan would be dealt with by the police, assuming Ben Underhill hadn't already acted, which Dan guessed he had; and his dealings with the state's attorney had led to an acceptable arrangement with the state's department of corrections — specifically their parole and probation unit.

He now had a corrections handler with the unlikely first name of Clark, who seemed delighted to be dealing with someone who wasn't a drug dealer, a pervert, or a hardhead disposed to punching people's faces.

They saw each other once a week.

Dan had a new job as a lawn-care and landscape-maintenance assistant, according to the official listing. It put him outside and working alone, often mowing cemeteries or tending to parks and green spaces that lay far off the beaten path. Clark had proven sensitive to Dan's needs.

And he had a new apartment, too, as sparsely furnished as always, and as neat as an operating room. It was quiet and on the top floor, and had a separate entrance, which mattered a great deal to him.

He also still had his secret lair. No one had known about that, after all. Not even Sally. So why give it up?

Compromise was a good thing, after all, now and then. Joe Gunther had shown that, as had the prosecutor.

And as Dan was showing now.

He rose from the armchair he'd been enjoying and crossed over to the couple in the large bed at the far end of the bedroom, pausing to pet the cat that lay stretched out on the Turkish rug.

Dan wasn't going to leave a Post-it note behind, after all, or remove anything from the fridge downstairs.

He'd told Joe that he was done with the Tag Man thing.

And so he was.

ABOUT THE AUTHOR

Archer Mayor is a death investigator, a sheriff's deputy, and a volunteer firefighter and EMT in addition to being a novelist. He lives in Newfane, Vermont.

The employees of Thorndike Press hope you have enjoyed this Large Print book. All our Thorndike, Wheeler, and Kennebec Large Print titles are designed for easy reading, and all our books are made to last. Other Thorndike Press Large Print books are available at your library, through selected bookstores, or directly from us.

For information about titles, please call:
(800) 223-1244

or visit our Web site at:
http://gale.cengage.com/thorndike

To share your comments, please write:
Publisher
Thorndike Press
10 Water St., Suite 310
Waterville, ME 04901